Into the Mill - A Judas to all Men

Book two: The Mill Series

James W. Scott
4/4/2014

Published by: Artisan Publishing Guild, LLC
APGuild@outlook.com

Dedication -

For those who are putting their words out for the world to read or hear. For those that buck the system, and those that get rolled over by it. For the '*Traveler*' in all of us.

To my family there have been days that *we* have been all *we* had. Was there ever anything more we ever needed?

Love and Strength – James W. Scott

Author's Note:

This is a work of fiction, though it is based on events unfolding in the real world today. I have simply carried these events forward to set the story in the future. The events themselves have not been modified; however, the names of the people concerned have all been changed. While you may find yourself giving a real name to certain characters herein, my hope is that you will allow the book to stand as a work of fiction.

There are several historical references such as Shays' rebellion that were real events and, while rarely taught in school, the importance of these events on our history is paramount. One man *can* make a difference! I would suggest the reader take a moment to research items such as this — you may be surprised.

While this is book two of the Mill Series, it is a prequel to *Through the Mill – A Time for Snow*. Perhaps some of the comments and inside jokes that eluded Snow and Jealousy will be answered. The speeches that my lovely bride is not fond of are limited in this installment (The Traveler *will* have his say). If you miss my speech-writing, don't worry — they will return in book three.

In one part of the story, Judas must invent a game, as part of his development. In the end, Un Sukiru (LuckCraft) was developed by my family. Well over a hundred hours were spent developing an actual board game that can be purchased through my publisher, apguild@outlook.com. My admiration goes out to people who can invent games, as that side endeavor took nearly as long as writing the entire novel.

Quotations were used with permission (when required), and credit is given at the end of the book. Thank you. I hope you enjoy the story.

James W. Scott

Chapter 1

I know we are assholes, but if everyone in this world could just do for themselves, we would not have to be. That may be harsh but, for goodness' sake, people, I am a twenty-nine-year-old traitor to everyone who ever loved me; a modern-day Judas—which is my name, Judas, that's all. I gave up the rest of my name when I swore my allegiance to The Shop.

Oddly enough, it was my allegiance where all this started, to family, friends and team. Getting ahead. My given name was Alec Judas Tearson. It was a family name, and every third generation had it. I was a third and happy for it; Francis and Vladimir were the names thrown in there. I did not say I had a sane family tree, but at least I'm the end of it. But I'm skipping ahead again. *Not cool.*

"Alec, get down here and give your Gramma a hug." She pulled me away from Kathryn, my girlfriend of seven years—actually, as surreal as it sounds, she's my fiancée, as I proposed at the beginning of this, our senior year. If Gram was the guiding force who brought me up after my parents died, Kat was the reason I strived for bettering myself to provide a great future for us. Be it as a Football player and his wife or Engineer (my area of study) and his wife. Gram was so full of life for an eighty-one-year-old pool shark, her powder-blue eyes that really do not see all that well, but she always took in everything. As I hugged her, she whispered in my ear, "There is no need to worry about this game; when you are in your first Champ-Bowl, you will look back on this and realize being a starting quarterback on a National Championship team really is not that big of a deal." That was her dream for me, that I would be a quarterback on a PFL team. She spent hours, days, and weeks of her life helping me, in any way she could, to prepare for it.

I pulled back and looked into her eyes, "Gram?"

"Okay, it was a terrible attempt to help your get your head out of your ass."

"Gram!" I said incredulously, and Kat let out a horselaugh.

"What? I am not allowed to curse? I am eighty-one and I know a few words like that," she giggled.

"I love you, Gram. Just tell it to me." I pulled away again, as she put her finger on my forehead.

"This is the brow of brimstone," moving her finger to point at my eye. "This is the eye of life." Now pointing at my nose, "Bubbly ocean." A quick turn of the wrist and she placed her index finger like a mustache, "Pen knife." Pointing again, this time to my chin, "Chin churey." Then to my neck, "Neck-a-nurey." Finally, getting her other hand into the game, "Skurey-worry-worry," she said as she tickled me. You're never too old to get tickled by your grandmother.

"Thanks, Gram, I feel better," I said, kissing her forehead as I stood up, looking down at her diminutive body. Then I turned and gave Kathryn a kiss. I smiled at them both as I started to walk out to the bus that was taking us to the stadium.

"Alec, remember, if you lose, I won't love you anymore," she said, totally deadpan.

"Not cool," I said as I walked backwards.

Gram blew a kiss to me and said, "Give 'em hell, boy."

"Kat you really need to spend less time with her or that potty mouth may rub off." They both stuck out their tongues at me, "I love you – and see you at the stadium." I blew a kiss back and got on the bus.

I sat on the bus staring straight ahead, watching for the stadium, to start the next step of my pre-game routine. When I finally saw it, I cleared my throat and the bus went silent. "This is the beginning of a new day. God has given me this day to use as I will. I can waste it or use it for good, but what I do today is important because I am exchanging a day of my life for it. When tomorrow comes, this day will be gone forever, leaving in its place something that I have traded for it. I want it to be gain, not loss; good, not evil; success, not failure—in order that I shall not regret the price I have paid for it." The rest of the ride was spent in silence. Once arrived, we walked as a quiet imposing mass to the locker room, and I led the way. What a feeling.

"Ladies and gentlemen, welcome to this National Championship game between the always powerful Alabama Crimson Tide and the high-scoring Michigan Tech Huskies, a team which over the previous three years has been undefeated since this amazing quarterback has crushed all who stood in his way. Many thought this team was good enough last year to win it all, but with the way the points stacked up, they did not have enough opponent difficulty points to make it to the dance. This year, they added some serious challenges, taking the two teams that fought for the National Championship last year and crushing them both, eighty-one to twenty-one and seventy-seven to eighteen," Bronston Girst, the national sports commentator, said.

"Sounds more like a lopsided basketball game than a football game," Terry Brandel, the color commentator, mused.

"It came down to the fullback style running and the cannon arm of Alec Tearson," Bronston continued. "This should be a great game, the number one defense Alabama against the number one offense Michigan Tech. As we set up to kick off, Alabama won the coin toss and have elected to receive. Here we go."

The game would later be called the dirtiest game in College Football history, but today the referees let the game play. Both sides managed to get cheap shot after cheap shot in on each other, with no flags. "After Alec scored his second rushing touchdown, the score stands at 'Bama forty-two, Michigan Tech forty-one with twenty-three seconds left. I can't believe this, Bronston; the Huskies are going for the win." Terry said.

"All things considered, that is a gutsy call; I can honestly say I have not seen a coach in a National Championship game have this large a set," Bronston managed to edit himself. "As soon as the Huskies broke their huddle, 'Bama calls a timeout."

I remember the coach talking; he was questioning whether it was the right call, or something. I looked behind the bench and there was Gram, beaming. Next to her was my Kat, making hand gestures to get her mind off the insanity that was happening. I headed back in as she got to *penknife*... I looked over my team as they stood in the huddle. This group was more than the sum of its pieces, and each individual could not duplicate the effort they have done today. It was the soul of the team that pushed us, and my soul was a melding of those two ladies... Brow of brimstone... Head out of ass... I simply said, "We got this." We broke the huddle.

"The Huskies are approaching the line. The Crimson Tide is lined up for a run. It looks like Tearson is calling an audible at the line," Bronson continued his commentary.

"Dog Sled. Dog Sled." I pointed at the tight end to go out. This bullshit audible is costing time, "Electric slide, boys." The fullback went in motion... Yes! They are buying this shit.

"There is the snap, Tearson drops back, the blitz from the left side looks like it broke through. He dodges one, two, three tackles... runs over a fourth and jumps over his center, getting crushed as he holds the ball across the goal line in midair... he lands and the entire 'Bama team is taking it out on him," Bronson said.

"The referee signals the conversion is good. Someone had better get in and pull that pile off him," Terry was raising his voice.

I remember the cheering; I remember thinking that I had made it, then the tearing feeling, wham and then darkness.

The crowd, upon seeing the replay, let out a collective gasp, "Oh, dear God, he has got to be hurt; he's on the bottom of that pile face up, one of his legs is up to his chin while the other is bent at a weird angle to the side." Just then, the scoreboard shows the replay from another angle. "While each leg was out of the way, a 'Bama player took the opportunity to lead helmet-first into the unprotected groin. Every man and boy in America just crossed their legs. Somebody clear that damn pile," Bronson said in a desperate tone.

"Oh, for goodness' sake, get the camera off him." Later I was told the scoreboard showed the 'Bama player backing away from my unconscious body as blood spread across my groin area. "This is bad, Bronson. That boy is hurt bad. We may have seen the last of this amazing player on a football field," Terry continued, completely taking over for a numb-plus Bronson.

Bronson finally snapped out of his stupor as the camera panned the 'Bama sideline and where the defensive players were high-fiving each other, "Are you fucking kidding me you cheating pieces of shit!" The producers did not get one word bleeped out. "I want a remote Microphone. I am going down there." Bronson had been an amazing linebacker for several years until a cheap shot took him out. "And get me the number of the cheap-shot artists that did this."

"Bronson, let the College League figure this out. You do not need to go hurt someone," Terry said. "The ambulance is driving right out on the field. We can see that someone has covered Alec with a blanket. Thank goodness—that is not something that anyone needs to see. We have to remember there are still fifteen seconds on the clock and Michigan Tech still needs to kick off to 'Bama, giving them a chance to win this game still." Suddenly, there is a commotion on the Alabama side line. "The head coach has two defensive players by their face masks, screaming at them. Based on the numbers of the players, they are defensive players. Two starters are being sent to the locker room," Terry continued.

"Now there is a commotion behind the Husky bench. A girl is screaming for help in the front row of the stands. It could be almost anything. Let's cut to commercial." Bronson, having regained his mic presence, was completely in control again.

Chapter 2

I remember them telling me that I was going to be all right. I remember them telling me that my grandmother — she hated that phrasing — had died from a heart attack. I remember Kat being at my bedside every time I woke up. Mostly, I remember two specific looks Kat had: the first, that of shock on her face when they told me that the damage was irreversible, that there was a chance that I would be able to use my unit normally but that there was no chance of having children — "We attempted, however, to preserve some of your sperm in the hope that it could be frozen for a future chance at having children should you have wanted them." And then I remember turning to her and saying the most hateful thing I had said in my entire life.

"Gee, and you just killed my baby last summer — bet you're glad you had that abortion, aren't ya?" I turned away. The doctor and his staff left the room.

She touched my arm. "Alec." I pulled away.

"Just get away from me. I don't ever want to see you again." She left the room crying, and killed herself that night with a bottle of my Gram's sleeping pills. I remember a lot of things, like I said: the second look, that of horror on her face when I confronted her in front of people about the abortion, my first act as a traitor. The funerals came and went and there I lay in my hospital bed. *Not cool.*

When the police came by, they said there were two notes that Kat had left. The first was sealed with wax and addressed to me. The second note was addressed 'To Whom It May Concern.' "The crime lab looked at both but determined no reason to not deliver them to you." Then he handed me two notes and the ring that I had given her when I asked her to marry me. He simply said, "I am sorry for your loss." I realized I was not crying, and that I thought I should be. I looked at the wax seal and then at the ring she had sealed under the wax. I guess she did not think the cops would read the note. Of course they would; they have a job to do.

I finally decided enough was enough after being stuck in bed while my entire team stood around the bed telling me all about the parades and the trophy presentation. I told them to get out, to just leave me alone. My second act as a traitor. I was their captain, their leader; I had an obligation to listen. Screw it.

"Doctor, I need to leave this place. I am falling into a state of depression," I pleaded with him the next morning.

"Alec, the reason you are in here still is the risk of infection is so very high. If you do get an infection, the results will be something that will cause issues the rest of your life." He removed the x-ray from my chart. "Let me show you..."

"I do not care," I interrupted. "My life is completely fucked and I am fighting to stay sane and simply keep from..."

"Young *ma'un*," an older man interrupted as he appeared behind the doctor.

"Excuse me, sir, but who are you?" The doctor said, turning.

"Doctor, I need you to leave," the man said as he showed the doctor his wallet then returned it to his breast pocket. The doctor looked visibly shaken and gathered his items, walking out quickly. "Thank you kindly, doctor." He waited until we were alone. "Sounds to me like you were about to say something that would preclude us from ever having our conversation."

"First, what are you talking about? Second, who the heck are you? And third, what is in your wallet?" I asked.

"When I was out there," he pointed at the hallway, "and I was waiting my turn to..."

"First, what are you talking about?" I interrupted, "Second, who the heck are you? And third..."

"What's in my wallet? I know. I heard you. I am ducking your questions. Obviously. Let's just say I am here to help." *He had a strong southern accent, but my spellcheck keeps fixing it, so apparently he is now a Yankee.*

"Look, sir, I do not know you and I have never been great at just accepting someone who says they are here to help," I said.

"Very well. Your name is Alec Judas Tearson. Your grandmother, Marianna Yvette Tearsonolich, migrated to this country to have your father. Your father, Gregorovich Francis Tearson, and your mother, Sylvia Lynn Tearson, née Steward, were killed in a car accident, leaving you to be raised by your grandmother. Marianna later became Mary and she worked daily at becoming an American. Most immigrants after forty years still have a trace of an accent; Mary did not. She worked her way up to becoming president of a major banking company, retiring at the age of sixty-eight. She helped you become every bit the man you are and you would die to defend her name. How am I doing so far?" the old man mused.

"You know a lot about me. That is interesting. First, what the heck are you talking about? Second, who…" I did not get as far this time, as the old man started dancing around like a boxer…

"I call it a rope-a-dope… he keeps throwing them, I keep ducking," the old man said as he bobbed and weaved. "Boy, this old man is trained in avoidance of questions." He threw a few punches that let me know he actually knew what he was doing. "But I will tell you this much: my name is Joshua."

"Fine. What can I do for you, Joshua?" I asked.

"No matter what happens to you, do not ever tell *anyone* you are considering Kat's method. You are not ready to open your eyes to the other side yet," Joshua said after he stopped messing around. Looking at me with surprisingly deep and soulful eyes he said, "You have more to give." As he reached out, I knew he really did come to help. His hand was pointing. "I want you to open that letter and read it while I am here." He pointed at Kat's letter. I picked it up and then lay back and read.

I walked into the room that we slept in, and saw the empty bed, involuntarily touching my stomach, the conception of my demise. The choice to end both lives, the easiest and hardest one to make, but as the future is dead without both alive, was there really another choice? The birds I had loved so much are singing outside. I wish my mind would allow me to simply remember lying in your arms and listening to them like so many times before. Today it does not matter because I am not able to listen to them over the sound of my soul screaming. It won't matter now; I cannot get back to that place.

I am the one who needs to make the choice now, as I made it alone before. I wanted to stand with you and let the ocean's tide pull the sand over our feet and face it all together. I cast those sands of love into the desert to mix with all the lost dreams I saw in your eyes. I can't look into them and see hate, not again. You used to look at me with the eyes of a child and I killed that child too. I wish I could teach you to smile again, but if I were here you would always know what I took from you.

Take comfort in the future. You have always been the one to pull everyone up to where they need to be. This time you will pull yourself up. You are the best man I have ever known, and you can survive all this, Alec.

I will always love you, please know that, and know that I am
sorry.
Kat

I folded the paper. Joshua held out his hand, "I will keep it safe for you." Confused, I handed him the letter.

"Now get some sleep. You will be starting a new life tomorrow." I lay back and let the sleep wash over me, knowing I had to start all over. *Not cool.*

When I woke a few mornings later, there were clothes laid out, dress clothes, along with shoes I had never seen before. Taped to the clothes was a note that read, '*A month in this place is enough. Get up, get dressed, and meet me outside. –Joshua*' I looked down and saw that the IVs had been removed from my arm and my leg. That barrier having been eliminated, I got out of bed, removing the gown and looked down. *Not cool.* I grabbed the clothes and got dressed, all but the tie—I am not a tie guy. All in all, someone had taken a lot of care to make these clothes fit perfectly. I looked in the mirror. My military-trimmed blonde hair had grown out a bit and my chin and cheeks had a lot of stubble. Those small changes aside, I didn't think even Gram would recognize me when I put on the glasses that were in the pocket, clear glass lenses. I caved and put the tie on. My transformation was complete. *Not cool.*

I walked out of the room and down the hall. No one even questioned me. I got on the elevator. As it started to go down, the doctors who got on would not make eye contact with me; they simply pushed the button for their floor and faced the door. I apparently cut quite an imposing figure— must be the tie. When we got to the lobby, the elevator doors opened and a boy of about twelve years old rushed into the elevator.

After the boy crashed into me, his mother said, "Ronald Snow, what are you thinking? I am so sorry, he is really nervous about his father." She looked at me. "My husband, his father, has never been in a hospital."

"Sorry, mister," Ronald said. "Hope I didn't hurt you."

"It's fine. You should think about taking care of your mother; she will need you until your father gets out," I said.

"Thank you," his mother mouthed.

As the doors closed, I saw the boy take the woman's hand and I heard him say, "He's right, Mom, I am sorry."

I turned and started to walk toward the front revolving door. The security guard at the desk hailed me over. "You are going to need to sign out," Robert (according to his badge) said.

"I did not sign in," I said.

"Then I need some ID," Robert continued. I reached into the inside pocket. Sure enough there was something. I pulled it out. I could not believe it; the ID picture was me in these clothes. The name said simply 'Judas' on the other side, a platinum box with a black 'S' inside it—The Shop. I held it open to the security guard who about soiled himself and turned grey. "I am sorry, sir. Have a good day, sir."

I walked out the front door, where a black Suburban pulled up. The back door opened. I got in. "So you have accepted my job offer?" Joshua asked without looking away from his paper.

"What job offer?" I said, confused.

"Well you did flash that ID, and impersonating a Shop agent carries a death sentence," Joshua said in his grandfather-like southern drawl.

"Did you just threaten my life in the most nonthreatening manner in recorded history?" I mused.

"Young ma'un, I never threaten. I just gave you the opportunity to believe this was a choice. I think I pulled it off like a champ. Well, until you asked that rather stupid-ass question." He finally looked away from the paper. "I would rather have this quaint repartee in the car—please get in; we have a doctor for you to see." Joshua turned back to the paper.

"Joshua…" I started.

"We will be somewhere that we can talk, very soon. For now sit back and answer a couple questions," Joshua said, still reading that paper.

"Okay."

"Kat—your first love?" Joshua started.

"Yes."

"Best friend?"

"Yes," I said.

"No—who was your best childhood friend?" Joshua continued.

"Steve Davirens was—until tenth grade, when he passed away in a game of stupidity," I said, taking a deep breath and blowing it away.

"Expound upon that." He looked up briefly, I noticed out of the corner of my eye.

"Every day we drove down this road, racing and playing at being stuntmen. We thought we were invincible. The shit we did, I am surprised he was the only one of us to die." I was there again, living the stupidity.

"How did he die?" Joshua asked.

"The day that he died I wasn't actually there. I was told it was during a mobile Chinese fire drill... on a pickup truck. We had all done it dozens of times, but that time when Steve was walking on the running board on the driver's side he slipped and the truck managed to run over his head." I finished the story.

"How did this affect you?" Although showing no emotion still, Joshua had at least put his paper down.

"I guess I tried not to listen and take advice from fools. I changed; I started lifting weights and running every day. It felt like the right thing to do for me. I ended up getting close with Kat and she became my best friend." I noticed that Joshua was intensely staring as I finished.

"Do you feel *anything*?" Joshua whispered.

"I love a lot of music. I guess all the words to everything someone wants to say are already out there. I do not need to recite them so someone else feels better. You can listen to the music yourself." I looked around the area we were in and continued, "I am and I feel, but as an engineer, I am very compartmentalized."

"I will let it go at that for right now," Joshua said. "It may have been a chance to let out some pain before the real questioner gets a hold of you."

"So what is going on?" I asked

"To start with, we're going to get you looked at, try to find out when you can be ready for your training. Before the physical portion, we have a group of questioners who will be breaking you down into little tiny pieces and seeing if you can put the puzzle together. And then determine what makes you tick, smash the clock, and see if you can play the horologist," Joshua explained.

"Okay." I really could not think of anything to say, mainly because I had no idea what a horologist was. So I sat back in the seat and watched the road. Joshua let me be. After about an hour, I looked over at him. He held up five fingers. I started looking for a big grand building, but we were in the middle of nowhere. The vehicle stopped. We were at what appeared to be a construction site that seemed to have a tent built over the entire thing. I stepped out and waited for Joshua to shoot me. When he got out of the Suburban he shut the door and then he knocked on it twice. The driver took off. "Joshua..." I started.

"Almost, not yet," the old man cut me off, again; he was quite good at that. He led me to a construction elevator, which only had one direction—down. I pulled the interlocking doors closed and he hit a button. The elevator began its descent into the darkness of the hole. I remember thinking it was like casting a die deep underground, and I hoped this was not symbolic. "These are the best doctors in the world; they will probably hurt the shit out of you." That grandfatherly southern voice could make anything sound good.

"Not cool," I said.

Chapter 3

When the elevator finally stopped, it seemed like we were getting off two floors above hell. Getting off the elevator, I asked, "What floor is this?"

"It's negative twenty-one. Medical floor. It needs to be down here, so the doctors are close to the lower floors, but below is above your pay grade, as it were." After about five steps outside the elevator, nurses appeared and sat me into a wheelchair. They began fussing at Joshua for allowing me to walk. "Well, I was not exactly going to carry him. He's a bit big for that," Joshua fussed right back.

As the nurses wheeled me away, I remember hearing Joshua saying something like "good luck and talk to ya soon." Everything started getting farther away. I must have been sedated by one of the mother hens as they were undressing me and getting me into the proper gown for a hospital. They wheeled me into a room where a team in surgical scrubs took possession of me. I was feeling really good by now, and the conversations faded into 'Glory, Glory, Glory,' a hymn that I remembered from going to church with Gram. She was in the choir and sang lead soprano. What a beautiful voice she had. She always tried to get me to sing with her; I never would. "Alec, you have such a lovely voice," she would say, but all I wanted to do was listen to her. I did not tell her that enough. I remember thinking *damn you, Joshua*. Or maybe I said it—who really cares. All finally went black.

"Young *ma'un*." I awoke in a dimly lit room. Joshua's blurry figure stood at the end of the bed. "I heard you were cursing me out," Joshua said, "I have that reaction from most people," he chuckled to himself. "Did I kick up some emotions that you forgot about?"

"Maybe, sir," I replied, more to myself than him.

"Not 'sir'... Never 'sir'... Joshua," he interrupted.

"Okay, Joshua, but Gram always said if I didn't show proper respect to my elders, they would never trust that I understood they had knowledge I had not yet been..."

"Privy to..." he finished the sentence. "Smart woman, your Gram. But for you and me, I am Joshua," he pointed to himself, "and you are Young *Ma'un*," pointing to me. The morphine clicked and I went skipping away into a cloud.

This time it was a group of doctors standing around me as I awoke. "Here he comes," a woman's voice said. "Okay, Judas, is your head spinning or are you okay?"

"I am spinning a little," Click. The world came into focus. "Okay. That was weird. Okay, I am here now, and I am fine," I said, fully awake.

"Judas, we are Drs. Strandtov," she indicated the old man, "and Khera," indicating herself. "We will be working on your case. It is not weird; that is your tax dollars at work," she said.

"Are you going to tell me I have new bion..." I censored myself.

"Ah, good, he has his *huuuumar*," the older man had a Scandinavian voice.

"No, Judas, not bionic, but you do have some fairly advanced testicles. They will regulate your testosterone levels automatically. First you need to understand, testosterone production is under the control of the luteinizing hormone, or LH, whereas sperm production is under the control of the follicle-stimulating hormone, or FSH. In your case, we do not care about the latter, so let's focus on the former, the LH — well, technically, both of these are controlled by the pituitary gland. Testosterone and oestradiol, which is produced by aromatization of testosterone, act at both pituitary and hypothalamic sites and are the principal regulators of LH secretion. Basically, we are interfacing into this natural control loop," Dr. Khera said.

"Ooh, the pituitary is where all of this really happens. We make your new smart testicles talk to the pituitary, this pea-sized master gland, which controls so much cool stuff in your body. Size is a matter not." This Dr. Strandtov is really into this shit. "And through this, through this we also allow for an adrenaline increase when needed, and also even pain-blocking." He took a moment to breathe. He looked to be about a few days older than Noah was when he built the ark.

"Thank you, Doctor Strandtov. Judas, I am not sure how much you understand about endorphins," the first doctor interjected.

"I know that when I lift I release them," I said.

"That is correct. Endorphins work by attaching themselves to receptors that are designed to decrease the feeling of pain. As a result, once the chemicals are released, people can perform activities that may once have been impossible because of body pain. In your case, we also added the ability to call beta-endorphins, classified as a peptide neurotransmitter. These substances are found around both the central nervous system and the peripheral nervous system. These are the trauma endorphins, and need to not be called on unless it is an emergency, mainly because you can physically damage your body, tear muscles, et cetera, but you will simply experience a dull pain." She completed her lesson and my head was oddly focused.

"So I am an experiment?" *Not cool.*

"Of a sort. See, you would be taking shots for the rest of your life, and the problem with the shots is you need to start high and allow it to fade over the course of time. This is a loop- driven system even better than before." I love this Doctor Strandtov guy.

"Did I cost six million dollars?" I joked.

"If we had put in a quarter of one testicle, you would have been a little more than twice that," the Scandinavian voice quipped back.

"So my privates are worth a hundred million dollars?" I said, astonished.

"That's enough talk about how much they cost. Tell us how you *feel*," the woman doctor interjected.

"Actually, I *feel* like a million bucks." The aches and pains from the surgery and sitting in bed were all gone. I felt like I could run a marathon.

"Good, that is very good. But what Dr. Khera left out is that you are not actually as good as you feel. It will allow you to push through pain and even extreme agony, but you need to realize that you need rest," Dr. Strandtov said, taking the lead. This is an odd group. I had no idea who was the leader.

"It is part of the all new you, all chemically enhanced with natural chemicals. You can cause yourself to have an increase in focus simply by flexing your testicles like a double mouse-click. This flexing is referred to as a Kegel exercise," Dr. Khera explained. "Adrenaline can be increased via two long Kegels; emergency need is a long-short-long; a standard endorphin is a short-long-short. It will take practice, but this will prevent any accidental release. But those chemicals come with a price and a limited supply. As for the limited supply, you have a port that allows a recharge of the specific chemicals you have depleted," Dr. Khera finished. This was getting confusing.

"The refill containers look like a standard high-end ink pen and will even write." I could see this third doctor was smiling, even with his mask in place.

"I'm double-O…"

"Young *ma'un*, copyright laws are still in place you know…" Joshua cut me off. He surprised the doctors by his presence, as they all jerked their heads to him. "What? I already knew all this stuff and I scrubbed." They all looked back to me.

"Well, not really; you are a Shop agent in training," Dr. Khera continued. "You are not, however, released for physical training yet. Your classroom work starts tomorrow so get some rest. Let me emphasize to you that the cost of using the chemicals will be a need to recover. Your body will burn out if you do not allow for sleep after you use them, so do not overdo it." They all walked out leaving Joshua behind.

"Well, ain't that the fiddle playin' the cat," Joshua said.

"Um… I guess," I said, confused.

"Those doctors, they did not actually give you anything you did not have before — you know that, right?" Joshua asked.

"You know, I actually did think I was getting more…" I started.

"No. They can't give you more. They can only try to get close to what you had before. I do not care what it cost or if there are potential side benefits. What was taken away from you cannot be duplicated. They don't see it that way. Bottom line, there is a difference between a human being and being human. They just do not understand that. They are just human beings. Simply being what they are is good enough," Joshua said. "But being human means understanding the fears that people have or feeling compassion for something they lost. Yes, it's a neat gadget, but until this is right," he poked me in the head, "you do not need gadgets; you need simply to understand and be understood."

"Thanks, Joshua," I said, contemplating what the old man had said. I had a feeling he would have a lot of things like that over the course of our time together.

"Now, that's enough schooling for today. Get some rest," he said, sitting in the chair next to the bed.

"What are you going to do?" I asked

"Sit here and make sure them idjits let you sleep," he said as he got comfy.

"Sir, I can't..." I started.

"I told you not to call me 'sir.' Next time I will kick you in those shiny new tiddlywinks of yours and we will see if they tied in the 'ouch' factor," he scolded.

"Joshua, I am not going to be able to sleep. Tell me why The Shop is important. I mean, I know all the history they teach about it, but what really happened? Why is it important?" I asked, while I considered whether they actually did add the 'ouch' factor in, with a slight shudder.

"For a second I thought you were going to ask for a bedtime story. This is a good old-fashioned scary tale that could be told around a campfire... bound to give a nightmare or two," Joshua started

"Sweet. Let me get the marshmallows." I got into a position where my incision did not itch, as he started.

"Well, it really starts with a simple statement that was not fully thought through, a threat really, when President Dhoulou told Syria the use of chemical weapons would cross a red line. This statement was barely out of the president's lips when the US Embassy in Benghazi was attacked and four Americans were killed. This action was addressed by the president through an apology for an American making a movie. No action was ever taken. A simple question: if any person with diplomatic immunity living within the United States, such as an ambassador, were killed, would we rest until the guilty were caught? Not to mention that the country where that person was from would be burning our flag, calling for blood, or worse. We, as a nation, turned our backs on the victims—and worse:

part of our congress got up and walked out when the families tried to talk to them about it. Then Syria used chemical weapons to no response. This set the course: America was a dog with no teeth and a bark that did not even carry. Basically, we were cowed by Russia and China.

"This lack of action allowed several things to fall all at once: Iran finished their nuclear armament; North Korea invaded South Korea making Kim Dong Deal think he was even more important than he already thought he was. The next course of actions lent itself to everyone in the world as if this was all a well-scripted conspiracy.

"Syria used its chemical weapons on Israel. When Israel invaded and crushed Syria, the now unified Korea declared war on Israel, and President Dhoulou backed Korea, which caught the entire country off guard. Before we had an opportunity to fix the blunder and get to the United Nations for a clearing of the air, Israel declared war on the unified opposition front, Korea and the USA. Israel simply stated, "It is an obvious effort to destroy the sovereign country of Israel when Syria is allowed to attack an ally and be backed for it. You were right, Mr. President; their use of chemical weapons was a game changer. It allowed you to attack us without actually pushing a button." I remember the news organizations ran wild with all the posturing of, 'How will the president react to this?' Before anyone could react, the next day, Israel put one hundred airport hubs in the United States out of commission without a single Israeli dying or being caught.

"I remember being at the office Monday morning; I had gotten in late, which never happens. As I was walking to my corner office, there was a commotion from all around; people were rushing to the break room. I walked in and remember the TV being turned up very loud and the frantic news anchorman saying, "... they simply walked into the airport right up to the TSA agent checking IDs, and apparently they left a large bomb." Holding his finger to his ear he paused. "Wait, reports are flooding in from across the country: the same reported attack that occurred here, have occurred in several airports. This is apparently a coordinated attack on the United States." This was of course true. Israel had pulled off, in twenty-four hours, an attack against the United States that shook us to the core. When all the reports were in, within a span of an hour, over seventy-five thousand people were dead and another fifty thousand were injured. There was no airport security in our major hubs and the gates were basically back where they were in the 1980s.

"The Israelis proved they were more than up to the task of going on the offensive. As a follow-up to the bombing in America, the self-proclaimed god in Korea was killed twenty-four hours later, after Israel told him they were coming for him. This time, the team that performed the attack was caught, but they did not speak a single word from the moment they were caught through their tortures and deaths, proving that these agents were made of serious iron, and the world was put on notice.

"When in September of 2015, President Dhoulou declared a State of War against Israel, he ended up cancelling the elections that year and the next four, allowing his presidency to continue for twelve years, setting himself in a situation where he was above a lame duck, and at the same time he had no concerns about reelection, which allowed him to work his true agenda. Additionally, as we were at war, he could force certain things through the system that no Congress would have passed. We were stranded watching such things as National Electric Solution Hydroelectric Turbine, National Education Restructuring Acts and our favorite, the National Preservation Act, pass, which in the end allowed The Shop to form.

"The decision was made that spending a large amount of money on a new hydroelectric turbine would reduce the cost of electricity to zero, thus reducing the cost of goods and services and pulling America's economy out of the tailspin it was in. Then the four-hundred-billion-dollar deepwater hydroelectric turbine indexed into its position and the capacitor bank they installed blew out, costing an additional hundred billion, bringing the insurance company that had been forced to insure the monument to stupidity to go into bankruptcy. And even while the new capacitor bank was being built, it was determined that the drag from the deep water impeller had caused a slowing of the mid-Atlantic current, which scientists calculated had slowed the earth's revolution. The turbine could therefore actually create a true global warming and could not be used. It would sit with a full-time crew of scientists, on the government's dole.

"After a strong outcry from the people of the United States about the education of her children, President Dhoulou pushed the National Education Restructuring Acts or NERAs through both committee and counsel. The goal was to make it clear that the nation's children needed a village. They rolled out a new academic curriculum and forced it down every school, not allowing the schools to waver under fear of losing their federal and state money, and not giving the parents a chance to review the new books or curriculum; the schools simply flipped the switch.

"As the children were getting ready to graduate from high school and were applying to their colleges, the parents found that the colleges would not allow their children to enter without signing up for a newly certified pre-C curriculum. This made college become five years and added twenty-five percent to the cost—so all the parents who had put their money into college accounts for their children were now faced with this additional cost as an upfront cost before they could get into the *schools*. The banks would not grant loans on this new pre-college and many parents could not the find the money. As I am sure you recall there were an astronomical number of suicides.

It also threw many high school graduates into a job market that had no room for them. The unemployment numbers did not reflect this new entrance, because until you have a job you cannot collect unemployment. So even though they could not find jobs, unemployment numbers gave a false lowered number.

"In January of 2020, Congress voted unanimously to end the war and to remove the president and Vice President, putting Hillary Blythe in as President instead of the Secretary of State. In a surprise move, Madam President nominated Michelle Dhoulou as Vice President and plunged the country into two additional years of turmoil, during which time the Congress took action on several old items such as immigration, forcing the old NAFTA legislation to be reworked, explaining that the root of the problem with immigration was that the job market in Mexico was so weak that allowing more work to funnel there would allow our border issues to become irrelevant. This, of course, did not work—just as the original NAFTA had sucked jobs away from the US. Companies that used mom-and-pop shops to make parts decided to farm their business to Mexico, forcing all the small business owners to close their doors.

"I believe that issues like that forced the special elections, which resulted in President Zale, as a staunch conservative, being elected in November of 2022. Before January rolled around, The NSA and Homeland Security, utilizing the National Preservation Act, decided the country was too far gone; they combined their power into the Specialized Homeland and Overseas Protectorate—The Shop was born. They removed the president and Vice President, with a plan of bringing in their chosen leader;

they first offered it to Zale. He, as you know, turned them down, opting to be a high-ranking official within The Shop.

"In 2024, there was a second coup: The Shop gathered the House and the senate and told them they each had a choice—vacate their offices or go to jail. Charges ranged from a general one of defrauding the American people, to specific cases of illegal trading and in some cases campaign fraud. The Shop additionally seized their assets. When the Speaker of the House asked for the justification for The Shop's action, data was produced and handed out, showing that eighty-five percent of those within Congress had invested in companies based upon their advanced knowledge on approvals or disapprovals of products. This is called insider trading. If any person outside of Congress did this, they would face similar actions. Additionally, The Shop brought forward the campaign documentation showing the fraudulent transactions. The cry of 'Nothing illegal was conducted' came as a defense. I remember the reply: 'Just because you write the laws, adding provisions that allow you to skirt the legal consequences that every other person has to be cognizant of, or hide the proof of your action in the basement of a nondescript building doesn't mean you are innocent—it makes you the lowest form of cowards. Get out of this building. Do not go to your government-furnished living quarters, they have been sealed and anything inside belongs to The Shop now.' I laughed myself silly at that; it is by far my favorite memory since becoming a Shop agent.

"When the next election year came around, The Shop thought they had a plan laid out. The goal was to allow the people to continue to have their say so they allowed for three candidates to be selected to represent the states. The Shop addressed campaign finance by making Political Action Committees illegal. As the elections drew close, it became clear that the PACs were in play again, The Shop took action, terrible action, the first of the executions. They wanted it known that 'Every American needs to understand; by defrauding the people who they worked for, these people committed treason. We will not be tolerating such actions any longer. The rest of the world needs to grasp that we are no longer going to be your whipping boy; we have borrowed money from groups to give it to other groups and loaned money to fraudulent companies to better our own retirements—but no longer.' In a matter of months, we retook the world power role, this time with teeth. In the end, Congress was given up on. Today, agents of The Shop fulfill those roles. Mayors and governors, however, are still elected by the people, utilizing the 'Rule of Three' and government-funded elections.

"The draft was reinstituted, up to forty-five years old. The IRS and their tax codes were reinvented and in its place a Nationalized Sales tax. This was how The Shop ultimately stopped the immigration issue: making the 'illegals' pay their fair share made them have to ask for more money. At that point, we actually started enforcing the laws that were already there, taking out busloads. The first reform The Shop did was to allow illegal aliens the right to fight for American citizenship. With the draft having been reinstituted, the cry of bigotry was dead. The simple answer was this was how previous generations had become Americans.

"The Shop stood tall against all upstarts who thought they could bring back the 'good ole days,' but the majority of the people really hated what those days stood for. Especially when it was let out how much the House and the senate actually cost the country," Joshua said.

"Wait—how much did it cost?" I interjected.

"It cost over thirty million dollars a day to have them there.

"Why?"

"Because they had advisors, and the advisors had staff, and when it came down to it... *none* of them knew what the hell they were voting for. They were pretty faces who could speak well and remember things... But we were having them make decisions and set policy for the country based on things they knew nothing about. When The Shop kicked them out, they made it a civic duty to serve. There is still some debate over the Pigeonhole Conspiracy, which in part focused on permitting the right people to make the decisions. Allowing the policies of the government to focus on what really mattered to the country and not the foolishness of the elitist jackasses who were in power before. As an example, if you have an environmental issue, call in environmental engineers," Joshua said.

"But who makes up The Shop? How do they not cost us thirty million dollars a day?" I asked.

"Each member of The Shop is recruited by a few trusted individuals, typically from the observation and surveillance of the American people. Our cost will never be as much as Congress because we are paid the same as civil servants, like the military. We are assigned to various duties, depending on our ranking. We each serve on different roles within the full spectrum of needs."

"Umm?" I was not following.

"Look at it this way: our pay structure changes depending on what post we are holding at the moment. There are five who sit on the Supreme Court; they will be there a year."

"A year? What about the continuity and consistency of rulings?" I asked.

"Seriously? You think because a person sits in a position for a long time they are consistent? That is a great debate, perhaps for another time. When that assignment is done, they may be on governor watch, sitting in the capital and filling a role of lieutenant governor. After that they may be acting as a lawmaker. Each of those assignments has a pay band, and to get those jobs you have to show competency. This is not at all like the old Congress, where you simply had to smile and speak well."

"Okay, so how do I test for competency?" I continued to interrupt, and he showed great restraint.

"You can see that during the real training classes," Joshua explained.

"So what stops those who are seated as the acting lawmakers from doing what the old group did — screwing around and not showing up for votes, et cetera?" I thought it was a good question.

He laughed. "It's their job."

"As it was back when it was not The Shop," I retorted.

"No. It was their livelihood; they did not owe anything to anyone, except their bank. They were better than those they served; they got free room and board, gym memberships, people to write speeches, and all the things normal people just did not understand. Hell, the majority of them could not turn on a damn computer let alone rule on laws governing computer software."

"Mr. Joshua," Dr. Khera said as she poked her head into the room, "I would like my patient to actually sleep. He has some rather rigorous mental challenges tomorrow and if he is not rested, all of this will have been for nothing." Her eyes were caring; it surprised me.

"Thank you, Dr. Khera. I was just leaving." He winked at me and stood up. "Well, I hope the good doctor did not ruin any surprises for you — tomorrow will be a bit of a challenge."

"What's going to happen?" I asked.

"I told you, compartmentalized or not, when they break you down, those walls will fall, and most likely they will burst into flames. So perhaps the sleep may help you, perhaps some prayer would be nice – are you a religious man?"

"I wasn't raised in the church, but I believe in God and that everyone has a soul. I think that the soul pulls inspiration and virtue from outside the church. I guess I believe that the true spiritual leadership that people need today can only come from the community and family," I answered. He waited until I finished then started for the door.

"Well, look to whomever you need to, because someone is going to need to pull you out of the hell you will face. As long as they can lead you back to the place where you should be, at the right time, because that time may be sooner than you think." He finished his comment and walked out of the room, pulling the door shut. I sat there for a moment considering if my tiddlywinks had an off switch. I dozed off thinking about an old cartoon character that was a human Swiss Army knife, only it was my head on the inspector.

Chapter 4

"The room is dark because it needs to be." The words pounded in my head, each word bringing a different voice, man to woman, low pitch to higher, to a smoker's voice. "I do not want you to move. Do not fight against the restraints; they are there for a reason as well." The room didn't feel right. I waited, trying to gather all that I could. I was not in my hospital bed; I was in a chair. The sound was coming from headphones that were over my ears, not in them. This allowed me to hear the room around me while the person was not talking. The ambient sound led me to believe I was in a large room. I also realized I had a shield of a sort, maybe a welding mask, covering my face. Understanding these things, my heart slowed and I controlled my breathing. "Judas, I want you to say the Russian alphabet," the same strange voice said.

"I do not know it," I said.

"You were raised by a Soviet-era genius spy; you are a deeply trained sleeper cell. Nobody cares so much about changing their history. As a spy, Marianna was married to a Kremlin espionage trainer." The visor on my helmet changed; it went from darkness to Gram's house, and she sat at her piano. Then it changed. We were not in her house; Gram was younger, the piano that she sat at was the same one, but in a different house. There was a man with her. He looked a lot like my dad. "She lived in a large suite in the most exclusive part of Moscow. She had everything, and no one just leaves that." The voice pisses me off; I look deep into the eyes of the woman. It was Gram; it was my Mary Tearson.

"I suppose you are right; no one would leave all that. Not to face the challenges that a single mother would face in a country of strangers whose language you did not even speak — oh, except Mary Tearson, my Gram," I spoke for the first time. My voice was distant.

"You are so young, so foolish." The voice went into a deeper tone, which gave me a slight twinge, "Watch and learn, boy." The woman who said this was Gram. She was once again in the house in Moscow, but this time she was old. "He is one step closer," she said, speaking Russian. How the heck did I understand her? "He knows nothing of what he really is." I watched everything unveil very closely. When I saw the older man sitting at the piano facing away from Gram, it was the piano I noticed. That is the same piano. I don't really think she moved it across the ocean, nope. Blow it away, brow of brimstone... I got this... It's all fake. Just watch the show.

The world went black again. I waited for the next phase to start. When it did, Kat and I were sitting on a beach; it was the night I proposed. "Alec, you and I should just go with Gram and sign up for the Combine; we do not need to go back for this season." I remember this so well. "Gram would be good with it; you only have three credits and your senior project—you will have time to finish it before you start." She was pleading with me.

"I promised," I said. She looked away from the 'me' in the play-back and looked into my eyes. "I promised that I would see it through. The school asked me before they went after the schedule."

"But you are going to hold me to my decisions," she walked right up to me, leaving the memory me sitting on the beach. "You made decisions, too, Alec—oh, I'm sorry— Judas." The venom was palpable, "You want me to live half a life, the precious little girlfriend, and how embarrassed you were when your friend wanted to get married in a church when they were pregnant—no, sorry they were 'PG.'" I could feel the truth in the words. "Here, let's look how life would be if you had listened." She took my shoulders and gently shook. "Alec, it's time." I looked over at her and her face had the look of someone who was in a controlled pain, no makeup on but her hair was brushed and pulled back. "Alec, honey, you need to wake up. We need to go to the hospital." I followed her hands down to her stomach as her breath came out in a gasp. "Three minutes apart, Alec. There's no time for your thirty-minute wake-up routine," Kat said.

"Oh, God, how? Really? Why didn't you wake me earlier?" I stammered all the questions into a non-comprehensible flow.

"There he is. Okay, handsome, it's time to go meet your child." She led me out of bed. She of course had her bags packed.

"Look at you, all dressed and ready to go." I took her hands. "You are so beautiful. God, you would not believe the dream I just had."

"Babe, this is not a great time, unless you want to deliver this baby in our bed. I called Gram; she is taking a cab and is going to meet us there — and if she beats us there, you're probably going to get some brow of brimstone upside your little tushy!" she laughed.

"Gram is alive?" I asked.

"Alec, sweetie, you really are out of it. *Oh...*" she squeezed my hand.

"Okay, I'm here now. Sorry. Let's get you out to the car." We walked out of the room. I grabbed the bag on the way, looking at the handle. It did not look right. Keep moving, she needs you, I thought. The car was already in the driveway and running. "Gee, were you worried I would drive through the garage door? Again?" I chuckled.

"Just because your line makes holes big enough you can drive through does not mean you should drive through that poor garage door every chance you get," she said.

"Oh, you always give them all the credit," I poked.

"Well, you always do too," she said, not giving an inch.

"But, if I did not they would let those rabid Cro-Magnon monsters hurt little me," I said.

"*Oh…* that was pretty quick," she said as she panted like a dog.

"Remember that breathing is not until you push. Slow breaths for now, and try to stay calm." I tried to reassure her. The drive was spent with her asking questions about training camp. I knew it helped her to keep her mind off the pain.

"So are you going to lose the starting spot because you're with me?" She got serious all of a sudden.

"What?" I was shocked at the question.

"This time you're taking off—is it going to hurt your chances?" She was crying.

"Kat, first, we are still in camp, I have a place on the team, and the team has a Star-Bowl quarterback; I am not going to start this year, regardless. You are not hurting anything; this is exactly the way everything is supposed to be." The words did not feel right; I pulled into the hospital and tried to shake the feeling of how wrong everything was.

"Gram!" Kat yelled as the diminutive woman rushed toward the car with a wheelchair she had hijacked.

"Did he drive ten miles per hour? Mr. Cautious!" Gram poked as she helped Kat into the wheelchair. "You, big boy, wheel her in, I will park this POS." She loved to make fun of my beautiful 1969 fastback.

"Careful, remember that clutch is…" the sound of peeling rubber cut me off, followed by her laughing herself silly, "…is touchy." I said.

Kat was also laughing. "That old woman is going to see you into the grave with her antics." She continued her laughing right up until the next contraction took her breath. We wheeled up to the desk where the nurse was already waiting with a clipboard.

"Your grandmother already filled out all the forms," the nurse said.

"Do not let her hear you say that; she hates that term, makes her feel old," Kat said. "Hates that term..."

"Well, she makes me feel old, bouncing around here like that," the nurse laughed.

"*Oh!...*" the nurse took the wheelchair from me and rolled Kat down the hall. I followed, looking around trying to take everything in. The hospital had several pieces of art that Gram had in her house. *Wait – the furniture did not look like...* "Alec—*Oh!...* Boy, this is crazy—my husband is looking at furniture while I am about to pop." I snapped out of it and jogged to catch up; Kat took my hand as the nurse pushed her into the elevator.

"Is your doctor on her way?" the nurse asked.

"I called her," Kat said between puffing out her cute little cheeks.

"I hope she is in the parking lot, because this baby is going to be here any time now," the nurse said, looking at her watch. "These contractions are less than two minutes apart. Oh and there's the water, right on cue," she said as Kat's water broke.

"But, she, we, I..." I started babbling, wishing the elevator was quicker.

"Does this always happen?" Kat said, pointing at me.

"Every first-time dad is a babbling ball of cuteness," the nurse said, pinching my cheek.

"I figured. He is usually... *Oh...*" we wheeled off the elevator and into the private room. The room was very familiar. I turned and faced the door. The doctor was standing in the doorway. There was little possibility I missed someone behind in the hall a second ago.

"Where did you come from?" I asked the doctor.

"Surgery," she said, ignoring me and going to Kat. "Well, dear, the nurse says contractions are coming back to back, let's get your feet in these stirrups and see what we have." The doctor put on her gloves and looked under the hospital gown. *I did not remember the gown. When did she get into the...* "Coach, she is looking for you." The doctor interrupted my thoughts.

"You're doing great, Kat," Gram said from the doorway. She got my attention, pointing at Kat like I was shirking my responsibility.

"Hey, gorgeous, I'm here," I said, taking her hand.

"You need to stop checking out babe... I need you, *Oh...*" A dagger to the heart.

"Breathe — who-who-heeeee... You're doing great." She squeezed my hand.

"Okay now dear, it's time to push, just like they told you in class. Coach, when the contraction hits..." *Class? I do not remember the class.*

"He was at training camp, doctorrrrrrrrr," Kat exclaimed as she went into a contraction.

"Okay, push to the count of ten. One, two, three, four, five, six, seven, eight, nine, ten, breathe..." I said.

"Okay, Kat, stop pushing; wait on the next contraction, okay? Or just keep pushing..." the doctor said as Kat continued to push.

"I got this," Kat said as she bore down.

I looked at the doctor; she made a rolling motion with her hand, "One, two, three, four, five, six, seven, eight, nine, ten, breathe..." This time she did take a quick breath and started pushing again.

"Okay. There's the head. You need to stop pushing so I can guide the shoulders. There we go. Okay, dear, one more should do it," the doctor said.

"Push?" Kat said, looking at me.

"Yes, gorgeous, one more, just a little bit's enough," I said as she looked at me with a tear.

"Okay," she said as a tear ran down her cheek. I leaned down, taking the tear on my finger, and kissed it.

"I love you, Kat. Just a bit more and you'll be there." I felt her body start pushing again, then I heard a glorious sound.

"Wahaa." The baby's cry filled my eyes with tears as I looked into the eyes of my one and only soul mate.

"It's a girl," the doctor said.

"Babe, it's your girl," Kat said.

"Well, Daddy, do you want to cut this cord?" The doctor held out a pair of scissors and I cut the cord, surprised at how tough it was to cut. The doctor took her back and they got her cleaned up real quick. I sat up by Kat's head and held her hand. "Well, Mommy, here is your six-pound baby girl. Did you have a name picked out?"

"Aubrey Broschell Tearson," Kat said. I kissed Kat on the top of her head as the doctor put Aubrey next to her, this little thing with huge eyes staring at us, all shiny where they had put the ointment on them; she was blinking over and over and her tongue kept poking in and out of her lips. She looked quite a bit like a wrinkly old man, until I held my finger out to dab a bit of drool off her chin and her skinny little fingers wrapped around it and the cold little fingers held tight and I looked into those shiny, blinky eyes. I started to cry and kissed Kat again.

"Gram, are you seeing this? I can't believe it is real." Somewhere in my brain the battle was lost; I looked into those eyes and I could not admit I knew none of this was real. I was done in and did not care. When Gram came in, she was crying.

"You know the truth, Judas. You need to focus on it." She looked at me and I shook my head. "I tell you what;

you can come back if you need to but right now, it's time to pull it together and give 'em hell, boy."

I saw Gram saying that before the game. I kissed Aubrey, then Kat, and I took back my mind. I looked out into a pitch-black nothing. I heard the sounds of people in the room; they were walking toward me. "Ursula, disengage." The helmet came off and I saw Dr. Khera, and of course Joshua stood there. "The important part of all this is that we have no idea what you saw, and we do not want to know. Ursula does not make a report; she simply knows you now. Everyone who has gone into her world has had their own experience and it need never be discussed. Ursula will tell us if you passed and she will tell us how often you must come back," the doctor finished.

I turned to Joshua. "Young *ma'un*, are you okay?" he simply asked. "Compartments intact?"

"Yes, Joshua, I am and they are." I closed my eyes and I could see everything that had happened. It was insane. "What is Ursula?"

"Joshua, if I may," the doctor said as she stepped around him. "We have originated this training, URSULA, or Universal Renaissance Sapience Unlimited Life Adaptation, as the next step in virtual reality and cognitive computer intelligence. She actually can read your mind and reconstruct your desires and fears. She is also the first artificial intelligence that has reached self-awareness. This allows her to actually teeter on the edge of violating the three laws of robotics." She paused to allow that to stick.

"Self-awareness? Isn't that like free will for a robot? That is truly unreal," I said.

"Yes, it is. Judas, this technology, if spoken of, will be an immediate death sentence," she said.

"I would assume if I talk to anyone about anything I learn as a member of The Shop will be met with the same rules," I said.

"That is a very intelligent observation young *ma'un*," Joshua said. "I would not even discuss the lunch menu outside of people who you know are Shop agents. It's just safer that way." He did not smile. No surprise there.

"Today's session was a pass," Dr. Khera said. "You may go to the first classroom training." With that, she walked out.

"I will take you," Joshua said. "Like I said, the human condition does not make sense to some of these doctor types."

"This is a very odd place, Joshua," I said

"That it is, young *ma'un*. That it is," Joshua said between chuckles. We walked out of the room and down the hall; the doors were all smart ID, meaning they knew us before we passed through—no FOB or keycard, just the door saying, "Hello, Judas."

"You know I'm not having as hard a time with my name as I thought I would," I commented.

"Why would you? It is your name; some people get a completely new name, but as you never actually wrote it on anything, just 'J.,' there was no reason to change it," Joshua replied.

"Perhaps, but until now I have never been referred to by that name. Yet I respond to it rather easy," I said.

"Must be your new tiddlywinks," he said.

"Dude, get off my tiddlywinks," I managed to say, straight-faced.

"Nope." He led us right up to a door that did not open. "You should use them now—see if the door will open."

"Bastard," I said, crossing my arms.

"Actually, no, I'm legit. Did you read my file? Or was I part of your Ursula scenario?" *Boy, this old man was quite a character.*

"It was rather erotic. I don't think we should talk about it," I continued.

"Good plan," Joshua said as the door opened. The man in the doorway made me feel small, even though he was only around five foot seven. He had a long blonde ponytail and what looked like a week's worth of growth on his chin—it may have been his five o'clock shadow, a week for me—and he had muscles on his muscles. "Hello, Andelos, this is Judas. He will be starting in your class today." He reached out his hand; I was surprised that it was not bigger than mine, although I did have huge hands. "I will leave him with you. Do I need to come back and get him or…?"

"I'll get him to his room," Andelos said, interrupting. "Sit anywhere." A man of few words—this will be different. I found a seat. The room had thirteen other people in it. "All right, everyone is here." I could not place the accent as it sounded a bit Russian, but not all the time. "We have a whole lot of information that needs to be covered." He was definitely Russian. Boy, he has really worked on losing his dialect. "The first part will be on your computer." Several laptops opened up. "You there, Judas— here," he tossed a laptop computer to me from across the room; I caught it. There was a port on the desk that was obviously for docking. "Good catch." The class all laughed. "Better than some others did." The class looked at the two right in the front. I set the computer on the desk, plugged it into the port and waited. "Everyone ready? Let's go." He clicked his remote and everyone's computers fired up.

"Welcome, students, I am your instructor for this part of the class. I am Ursula. We have already met, though not been introduced." There was an obvious shifting from many in the class. "I need you to clear your heads of our previous meeting, and I will give you a moment to do that." The computer started talking again after a delay. "We will be discussing the elements that led to the fall of the Electoral College. We will be starting with the issues that were called out by the press as mistakes by President George W. Bracken that caused people to start losing faith in the presidency: the tragedy that occurred in New Orleans with hurricane Katrina and the governmental inability to respond in a way that was acceptable. Let's first look at the nomination of the government's leader of FEMA, Michael Spades, who resigned in disgrace. Several comments came up in the aftermath challenging his qualifications, even though he was confirmed by the senate, and the confirmation under a democratic majority senate no less.

"Spades' requested resignation allowed the shadow of doubt to fall on the president's ability to select adequate leaders. When the reality of the entire situation is laid out, the failure of the city to provide assistance in the evacuation of the poor, the sick and the elderly forced the conditions in the Superdome. Supplies were delivered by FEMA, but they grossly miscalculated the required supplies due to the inability of the local government to evacuate these people farther from the city. This doubt was further cast on the Republicans in later elections.

"The next area considered a failure in the Bracken administration, which contributed to the weakened confidence in the Electoral College and the election process itself. When the second stimulus package went into effect in 2003, it contained tax reductions on investment income, from capital gains and dividends. It was later stated that this was a large contribution to the increase in the deficit. While Washington was attempting to stimulate an economy that was crashing, they conveniently overlooked the option of downsizing of government. These were the types of cuts that successfully stimulated the economy when President Reagan did it during his two terms.

"Additionally, had some old laws such as the Community Reinvestment Act, which addressed the governmental encouragement to lending institutions to loan money by reducing discriminatory credit practices, been reviewed and revised, the crash in the economy could have been slowed. This piece of legislation contributed to the loaning of money on new and refinanced mortgages, at a higher proportion to income. This resulted in many families being encouraged by bankers and realtors to purchase houses they could not actually afford.

"In the elections of 2008, future President Dhoulou made several comments attacking the financial situation and the country being led into this decline by the housing market. Additional attacks were made about Bracken's administration and its inability to handle the disaster in New Orleans. Through these attacks, the respect of the office of the president was more greatly diminished than any single previous election.

"Why is this important to The Shop? Andelos, please discuss with the group in an open forum. I will wait, and begin again when I feel your discussions have met diminishing returns," Ursula finished.

"Thank you, Ursula. Why are we starting your Shop orientation discussing the shortcomings of a specific president? Who would like to start?" The room filled with conversation mainly around the way the president reacted and the fact that things were or were not his fault. I raised my hand.

"I think The Shop wants us to know this because they want us to understand how this department came to be and how these mistakes forced their hand. While I am sure there are many additional reasons that will solidify the opinion that things had to change, the fact that things needed to change had to start somewhere. When the president, in 2008 during the elections did not defend the actions of his administration and offer continuing opportunity to show that they did everything the best they could and that they actually *did* have results with what they did, it allowed the people to start embracing the need for change. Actually, I believe it was the main theme of the Dhoulou election, Vote for Change," I finished.

"Thank you, Judas. That was the first response that actually addressed the question that was asked. We are not looking to solve or debate the problems that they faced in 2008. We asked why this was important to The Shop. Andelos added on, asking why we were telling you this information," Ursula scolded the class. "You are here to learn. You do not learn by assuming, and by not listening."

"Does anyone else have a comment?" Andelos said. When no one did, he continued, "Very well. I think you scared them, Ursula."

"Good. Judas's answer was for the most part correct, and had he not chosen to add the piece of trivia at the end, it would have been exactly right. To understand the beginning will allow us to continue to move forward without repeating mistakes of the past.

"As I said before, I did hear a couple of small comments on dirty campaigning, and politics were a dirty game. The difference in the case of the Dhoulou attacks was that the Bracken administration did not dispute the attacks; typically, there would be more pushback. In this case, it worked out as a positive for us.

"Then we will move forward to the Dhoulou administration and how it put the final nail in the coffin of the structure of the United States Government. Tonight I want you to study the first term of the Barrack Dhoulou administration." Ursula signed off.

"For the rest of the day we will tour the portion of the facility that you have access to." He stood up and waited as we all closed our computers. Picking them up, we fell in line. He walked through the corridors and showed us the medical facilities (I of course was familiar with that area). Then we walked to the training area. It was amazing; they had things I had never seen—and I spent a lot of time in gyms. Then to the shooting area. I had not said anything because it never came up, but I had never shot a gun in my life. All the other people in the class started looking at the guns and commenting. "Okay, you will have your time on the range soon enough; start thinking about what type of weapon you are going to be selecting *and* why. I do not give a man a firearm until he can justify the choice." *Not cool.*

"Excuse me, Andelos?" a girl in the back of the class said.

"Meglar wasn't it?" he said

"Yes, sir." She stood up straighter. "Will we be able to fire multiple types of guns prior to making that selection? The military was the first time I had fired and they only used…"

"I know what they use. That is a fine weapon, but if you elect to go away from that, yes; you can qualify on every type of gun in here prior to making a selection. Anyone else?" Andelos asked.

"Sir?" the boy who had been sitting in the very front of the class, with the butterfingers, raised his hand.

"Billings, I believe."

"Yes, sir," again with the standing straighter. "Are you also our range instructor?"

"Excellent question." He started pacing in front of the group. "The truth is I am your instructor for everything while you are Level Ones. Each class has a special director instructor, Ursula, and has subsets for each area, but I am your primary human instructor." As if on cue, the overhead monitors lowered from the ceiling.

"Ursula targeting systems online." Andelos walked up to the table, taking the helmet and putting it on. The group let out a collective gasp. What he was seeing was being displayed on the screen overhead. He looked down at the table and grasped the pistol that rested there. The target currently showed two dots, a blue dot and a red one. As he moved the gun in various ways, the dots would get farther apart or come closer together.

"Ursula audio commands to public," Andelos said.

"Alter pistol grip clockwise two minutes." As she said this, the two dots came together and he fired. The bullet struck where the two dots had come together. "Alter pistol grip to seven degrees forward four minutes counterclockwise." This time he held the shot, the two dots came together and there was an audible tone. He fired. Again the bullet struck right where the dots were.

"Cancel audio commands. Play back the last two shots." The shots that we had watched were repeated. "Can anyone say what I did wrong based upon the playback?" Several people raised their hands. "Meglar."

"It appears you fought the recoil," she said.

"Yes. Anyone else?" No one raised their hands. "Replay previous playback," Andelos said. I noticed that immediately after the shot there was no blue dot on the screen. A moment later it showed up. There was a delay while Ursula calculated. It was a fraction of a second. "Anyone?"

"You held your eyes closed?" I said.

"I'm sorry—I thought I heard something," Andelos said.

I raised my hand. He indicated to me. "I said you closed your eyes, held them closed after the shot."

"What made you think that?" he said—actually, the class as a whole was muttering that.

"Sir, the blue dot on the target was gone for a fraction of a second after the shot; when it came back, it took…" I started.

"I am sorry—what exactly did you say?" Andelos asked after interrupting me.

"About the holding your eyes closed?"

"After."

"The blue dot was not on the target," I said.

"Judas, right?" Andelos asked. "Come with me." He took me, leaving the rest of the class. As we walked past another agent, he indicated for him to continue the tour with the group. We continued to walk through the halls and then we ended up back at my room. Joshua walked into the room with a confused look on his face.

"What?" Joshua asked.

"Who is this boy?" Andelos was very intense.

"This is Judas," Joshua answered.

"You understand what I am asking you, Joshua; this boy was not in any of the pre-studies, none of the counsel discussions. The others up there have been selected for years. This one just showed up in my class." He did not take a breath until he finished. Two of the doctors walked into the room along with five others dressed like agents and one who looked like a movie star—obviously Sensenmann. I saw Joshua's posture change when he saw this man walk in to the room.

"Andelos, I am confused. What has caused this?" Joshua said. He swept his hand across the room; he kept his composure very well.

"Andelos, I am also confused; Ursula said you called a Twenty-One Gun Salute," the movie star said.

"You did what?" Joshua stared, completely disgusted. The group at large looked to Andelos to explain.

"Tell this group what you told me," Andelos said, looking at me.

"You asked the class what you did wrong," I said.

"And you said?" Andelos said.

"That you were keeping your eyes closed after the shot," I continued.

"How did you know?" He was getting very irritated.

"I said that the blue dot left the target for a brief period of time," I finished, and looked around the room. They were also visibly shaken, even Joshua, though he had the best poker face. "If you could explain to me what the grand hoopla is?"

"Young man," Sensenmann, our fearless leader, started, "how far was the target from where you stood?"

"I would say he was shooting twenty-five yards; I was ten yards behind him." He looked over to Andelos for confirmation. He nodded his head.

"So at thirty-five yards you not only saw a dot that is no larger than the head of a pin—not only that, but you saw that it was blue, and that it was gone for a microsecond, and finally determined that when it returned, Ursula then started her calculation for correction," Mr. Movie Star stated.

"Well, she could not really determine the correction, if her targeting laser was not in place," I said. This brought a smile to his face.

"Blue laser at this rating is not visible to the naked eye. How did you know this information?" he said, staring into my eyes deeply. I suddenly understood why he had been selected to lead The Shop: his depth of knowledge and his ability to bring a person to a point of questioning themselves with just a look. His squared jaw and piercing grey eyes gave him his handsome look, his salt-and-pepper hair gave an air of confidence, while his muscular frame would carry his confidence into the middle of a fray without the bodyguards even being needed.

"I can see it. I saw the red and the blue and when they come together they turn green. I did not know that before I saw it," I stated.

"I have never heard of such a thing. Doctor, I want a full complement of eye exams, and I want it now." The movie star walked out of the room. It definitely sparked a large amount of action. The majority of the people left the room in Sensenmann's wake, leaving Joshua, myself and the two doctors.

"Well, doctors, you heard the man—how can you prove what Judas is saying?" Joshua said.

"We can't do it with a simple eye exam," Dr. Khera said.

"You could use the same type of test they use for hearing tests: 'Judas, push this button when you see a blue light,' then do the test again with green and then red," I offered.

"That sounds like a reasonable test," Joshua added.

"Well, it isn't like I can just pull that type of test together in a day or two, let alone right now, Dr. Kadodadeh, can you do anything with what was requested?" Dr. Khera asked, obviously upset.

"No," the other doctor said.

"If you need help I can do it for you. Give me an old hearing-test station, and about two hours, and I can give you what you need," I offered.

"I really think that would be a bad idea," Dr. Kadodadeh said. "But I don't have any thoughts; I wish Dr. Strandtov were here today."

"So I will get the unit and some tools," Doctor Khera said. She was back in a few minutes. I knew there was not much to these units; I took it apart and determined exactly how it worked and modified the input to also produce an output to turn on the laser. There was nothing difficult about it. I showed them how they had to connect it up for the test.

"Okay, let's head out to the range," Joshua said, and led us out of the room. Andelos met us there. "We're ready. When this is done, you and I are going to have words."

"Whatever. I will be conducting the testing," Andelos said as Dr. Khera handed him the activating panel. "Take your spot." I did. "Press your button when you see the indicated color. The test will be starting with the blue first." As I watched, colored lasers flashed on the target— green, green, green, blue (I pushed the button), red, blue (pushed), blue (pushed), red, green, blue (pushed), green, green (pushed—shit), blue (pushed). "Push on red." Red (pushed), red (pushed), blue, blue, green, green, red (pushed), blue. "Okay. Green now." Red, red, red, blue, blue, blue, red, red, green (pushed). "Okay. That is unreal. I am sorry," Andelos simply said. "I looked every single time and I even thought I saw one. You did not miss even one, aside from the accidental push, for a color." The doctors disconnected the cables and they headed back to their areas as quickly as they could.

"So do you have anything to say, Judas?" Joshua said.

I let it out in a rush of air, "I have never shot a gun." The two men's jaws dropped open and they stopped and stared at me. "I am serious; Gram hated guns," I said.

"You know that is actually really a great thing," Andelos said.

"Um, why exactly is that?" Joshua was still in shock. Turning to me, he asked, "Not even a BB gun?"

"Nope," I said.

"That's not a bad thing. We have someone who does not have any preconceived notion of how to shoot. This will give Ursula a chance to have a complete beginner. I am so stoked. When will you be able to start shooting?" Andelos was almost jumping up and down now.

"Doctors have not said yet," I said.

"Actually, he really needs to call it a day. This has been more walking around than he was supposed to be doing," Joshua said as he started to guide me back to the hospital wing. I had to say he was right. I was spent; as I got back to my room and my head hit the pillow, that was it. And while I remember my dreams that night very vividly, I will keep them to myself.

We all met in the cafeteria. I was absolutely thrilled that I could finally eat real food. I felt as if I had lost half my size in the last six weeks. "Can I get a dozen egg whites scrambled with a half cup of Chi seeds and a quarter cup low-fat sharp cheddar cheese? Please." The woman, who really had not looked at me, jerked her head up to see if I was playing a joke. Her eyes were green with a yellow ring at the center; her face was soft, lacking the crisp lines that the rest of The Shop personnel, including myself, had. It was not that she was overweight; it was simply a face that was molded, not chiseled. Her face was kissed by the sun, as Gram used say about people with freckles. All in all, her face was that of a beautiful mother who could be counted on to do what was right.

"Really, a dozen eggs?" she asked.

"Egg whites, yes ma'am. I am not real hungry today," I said.

"Not—er, eh... *not* hungry?" she looked like her head was going to pop off.

"I usually have about a half-pound of turkey in it and a half cup of peppers," I said.

"Well, okay, I guess I am going to be increasing the amount of eggs and meat I have at breakfast if you are going to be here for a while," she said with a smile. "Do you eat a side of beef at lunch?"

"Well, if it wasn't illegal, I might eat beef, but I do like turkey and broccoli a lot," I said.

"About how much turkey is a lot? And do you like steamed broccoli?" she asked

"Well, I eat about five pounds of turkey breast and two heads of steamed broccoli at lunch and dinner, when I am back into full training mode," I answered.

"Is there a hidden camera somewhere? Do I need to triple my milk order as well?" she said, shaking her head.

"I drink about a half-gallon of milk and two gallons of cranberry juice everyday as well," I said with an apologetic look on my face.

"Unbelievable. I have never met someone who eats that much food. What is your snack food, or do you not eat any junk food?"

"Well, if I am in a class that has heavy writing, then I eat *a lot* of licorice—it is writer food, after all. But, typically, I go through about a bag of unsalted almonds a day."

"Well, as I am your only supply of food, I guess I will start buying almonds and writer food in bulk as well," she smiled.

"I am Judas, by the way," I held out my hand.

"I'm Molly; most of your group call me Miss Molly," she said, shaking my hand.

"Pleased to meet you, Molly," I said.

"And you, Judas. Now go sit; I will bring you your trough in a moment," she laughed and went to work.

As I walked over, Meglar called out, "Judas." I waved back and went and sat by her and a couple others from our class. "Welcome," she held out her hand.

"Thank you," I said, shaking her hand, and then all the others' as well.

"So, what the heck happened after we were taken back to our rooms?" Meglar asked.

"They had the doctors give me an eye test and then they took me back to the range and had me duplicate what I said I did," I answered.

"What exactly happened at the range? Nobody really understood what you had said or the reaction of Andelos," she asked.

"I saw the laser-targeting dots," I said

"All the way out at the targets?" a different girl asked.

"Yes. Apparently that is not possible," I said. Right then Molly brought my plate. She also brought salt, pepper and hot sauce. "I love hot sauce on my eggs — thanks."

"You are welcome. All you big blokes like hot sauce. So that was you with the crazy eyes?" Molly asked.

"You heard about that?" I asked.

"Young *ma'un*, Molly knows everything," Joshua said he as walked up. "Shovel that food into your gullet; we have to meet some people."

"I just made that for him; he is not shoveling that anywhere," Molly interjected.

"Even if eating slowly is keeping Sensenmann waiting?" Joshua said as he looked over his shoulder at her.

"Um — shovel away; do not keep him waiting," Molly stammered. "Especially on your first meeting."

"I met him last night. Well, he was there during the craziness that occurred," I said as I finished a couple bites of my breakfast and had to leave it. "Meglar, can you make sure that Andelos knows where I am? Thanks." I stood up and followed Joshua to an elevator that we had been clearly told just yesterday was never to be used. When the doors opened, there were two of the largest men I had ever seen — and that is saying a lot considering I spent so much of my life playing a game of large men.

"Joshua, is this Judas?" the older of the two men asked. He appeared to be of Indonesian descent. He wore glasses that were very thick, and although he was obviously in his forties, he appeared that he did not need to shave. While he was a large man, he did not look like a healthy, well-fed large man, but rather like a huge sick kid with bad eyes. The two men were dressed exactly the same, but were set apart from all the other members in The Shop by the red ties that they wore, and the tie tacks that had four rubies in the corners of the square.

"Yes, Sampar. Judas has not been here long enough to finalize his ID in the system," Joshua said as he got on the elevator.

"I realize that he is simply tier Level One; you do not need to say anything except 'yes' when addressed," the man called Sampar said. What an ass.

"Yes," Joshua said. This made the man grind his teeth together. "Sampar, you look like a one-armed man folding a road map."

"Please enter the elevator, Judas," the unnamed giant said to me. He was both younger than the man called Sampar and physically superior to the older man. He was dark-haired and had the skin of a Latin American, and in contrast to his partner he had a five o'clock shadow, even though it was only eight a.m.

"Thank you." I got on and offered my hand. "I am Judas." The unnamed giant looked at his partner who turned his lips down as if to say *do what you want.*

"I am Guerra," he said, shaking my hand with a strong shake, but not like that of some of the assholes who squeeze with all their might. He gestured to his partner. "This is Sampar." I reached out hand; he of course shook it with all his strength. I did not wince. "We are two of The Four."

"I appreciate what you do. I studied your position in my government class," I said.

"Thank you for saying so." Sampar's voice and demeanor seemed to mean what he said. Their jobs really were that of complete servitude to The Shop; The Four were the bodyguards of the head of The Shop, Sensenmann. They were within twenty feet of him, twenty-four hours a day, rotating their sleep schedules, so that two of his guards could watch over Sensenmann while he slept, every night.

"Yes, that is a surprising comment from a Level One," Guerra said, slowly nodding his head. "We are here — please allow us to the front and back." I had a feeling this explanation was more than they gave most people. We walked out of the elevator in a line that said we knew that we were in our proper place.

"Joshua, Judas, please join me." Sensenmann waved us to the table he sat at. I looked at Sampar, he gave a slight head movement in that direction. I followed Joshua. "Tell me," he started as we sat, "have you eaten yet?" He had two plates of fruit on the table.

"Yes, sir, we have," Joshua said quickly, probably so I did not take his food.

"Oh, well, I guess that means more for me," he chuckled. "Do you know why we asked you up here, Judas?"

"I have a strange gift of eyesight," I said.

"Well, that starts it; I am assuming that is part of what made you the MVP in that National Championship game." He saw the surprise on my face. "Well, come on, I am the head of The Shop. I do get to know a bit about the Level Ones." He once again showed that disarming actor smile. "I actually have you here as 'currently not released for duty.' That is fine. I would like to get you out in the field with Joshua quickly. There are some interviews I would like to get you involved in. Not anything like targeted selection, but I need you to have your weapons proficiency and classroom studies to Level Two before you are allowed to go in the field." He took the napkin from under his silverware. I felt the big men take a step forward; the meeting was over. Joshua stood up just as I started to. There was a flicker of light and Sensenmann shot out of his chair and ran over to his desk. "Interesting," he said and indicated for us to join him around the other side of the desk. While we were looking at his computer, Sensenmann promptly began launching all his computer protection programs — Worm-Runner, The Spy that Hacked Me, and of course Trap Scan. As we watched, none of the programs alerted, but there we were on a Web portal and the site was 'We Are Traveler.Gov.' The site seemed to be a personal freedom site. Sensenmann's picture with a little mustache added to it was in the middle of the screen with the caption, *'What can I take away from them next,'* and the words *'We Are Traveler — We Are Many.'*

"So what exactly are we looking at?" Joshua asked, coming straight down to business.

"Someone hacked through our firewalls and managed to put a virus on this terminal that allows them to change my computer's home page and launches my computer into the Internet," Sensenmann said.

"If I may?" I started.

"Please," Sensenmann said.

"I would be surprised if they actually changed anything in your computer. Most likely they changed the pointer on the home page, which is a far easier hack than to a direct computer."

"Makes sense, and then all they would need to do is hack the UPS to do a diagnostic on your specific office — again easier than a single computer," Joshua added.

"Let me tell you this: if I find this guy, I am going to give him a job." Sensenmann was dead serious. "Anyway, I am sorry you had eaten already. Pleasure to meet you." He smiled as he walked back to the table; I noticed the smile did not reach his eyes.

"And you as well, sir," I said as I left with the escorts.

"Oh, and Joshua," Sensenmann said as we reached the door. "Make certain Andelos understands what we talked about first. And one more thing—Article Eighty-Seven on this, *all* of this." He went back to his fruit platters. "Just as what you have learned about Ursula is."

When we got in the elevator, Sampar said quietly, "Not bad, kid; Article Eighty-Seven means you are going up in the ranks right quick."

"Now, don't you get on with that. Keep your head in the game. All you need to know is Article Eighty-Seven means *no* talking about this verbally and most definitely no writing, email, or any form of communication," Joshua said.

"About what?" I asked.

"Exactly," Sampar said, "Look how quick he is catching on." Rather than turning it into a comedy skit, I just gave him the thumbs up. The doors opened. I felt a big hand on my shoulder. "Hey, kid—good luck." I turned and saw Guerra giving me a closed fist; I nodded my head and walked off the elevator.

After the doors closed, Joshua said, "I can honestly say I have never seen that lot warm up to a Level One like they did with you. Your Gram raised a good 'un." He patted me on the back as we walked. "Article Eighty-Seven means that you're dead if you share anything about what happened up there, or anything that follows on this assignment. I think that makes it as clear as I can."

"Yes, that makes it clear." I almost said 'sir' again; I could see his foot twitching. "Joshua, how are you going to make Andelos understand without breaking that order?"

"You'll see," he said, smiling. We got to the class. I opened the door and went to my desk. "Andelos," Joshua said, and then he started making quick hand gestures. Heck, I knew what he was saying and I could not follow, but apparently Andelos did, as he nodded his head in agreement. As Joshua left the room, he looked at me, making a pistol with his fingers and giving me a big grin.

"Class, forgive the brief interruption. Ursula, we are ready to start now," Andelos said as he chuckled to himself. "Pew pew."

"We broke last time after discussing the administration of George W. Bracken, and his contributing to the disenfranchising of the US Government, which led to The Shop. He and his group did not, of course, cause nearly as much damage to the reputation of the office of the president as the following administration did to not only the executive branch, but also the legislative and judicial branches of government." A video screen lowered at the front of the class with a timeline on it. "I will be superimposing some critical information for you." The number '400 Billion' appeared, with a line starting at 2007 and going back in time. "Prior to the 2008 Elections, welfare spending had averaged around 400 billion for the previous five years." The number '500 Billion' appeared above 2008 and '600 Billion' above 2009 and '800 Billion' above 2010. "The first term of the Dhoulou Administration saw a significant rise in welfare spending, doubling the spending in three years of office. These increases could be attributed to programs such as providing people with cell phones, coupled with not only the provision of lessons on how to apply for, but encouragement, through advertising, to apply for food stamps—and this did not even count the hospital overruns. Significant financial losses in public hospitals were due to new policies forced upon them by the administration. The policy involved the requesting of identification from any person who may be of Latin descent. While this established a profiling-based policy, it was allowed due to the betterment for the racial group. This allowed for several people to have the same exam, if a doctor prescribed it—for example, ultrasounds for pregnant women.

"Several additional events occurred that lent themselves to the disillusionment of the common man, when a group of illegal aliens held a march, holding banners, illegal and proud. The common man, when interviewed, stated, 'I would have just loaded them all on a bus and sent them home.' When the government does not utilize the laws that are on the books to uphold the laws, all three branches of government are called out on the shortcoming. One such shortcoming was the integration bill named the 'Secure Fence Act of 2006' that was passed, securing one point two billion dollars to build a fence and add new technology to secure the border. The fence was never built.

"We step away from the welfare issues and step back into the 2008 election, the housing debacle that was continually brought up, as well as the unemployment rates. President Dhoulou continued to sacrifice the office of the president for the next two years, utilizing his oratory skills, making comments denigrating his predecessor even further, such as he did not know how bad the economic state of the country was, and when a bus is headed down a cliff you can't stop it in midair. The truth of the matter is that the common man knew how bad the housing issue was, and the unemployment issues that were laid open for the people to see did not even include the students who got out of college with their huge debts. Nor the kids who did not get to go to college, who just wanted jobs but could not find them.

"A large issue in the job market was the elderly, who were retiring and taking grocery-bagger jobs. Employers were giving them the jobs over younger people because they did not require insurance. Other jobs such as landscaping were being handled by illegal aliens, and excuses such as 'Americans do not want these jobs' were thrown up as justifications. When interviews were conducted, several of the employers questioned gave answers such as, due to the cost of having an employee, FICA, state, and federal matching along with unemployment, and workmen's compensation insurances, the small business owners were willing to risk hiring illegal aliens under the table. As the migrant workers did not need to pay taxes out of their income they could take a lower wage, roughly equal to or greater than what a legal worker would get after taxes.

"While bi-partisanship had been discussed in many previous administrations, in these cases the data lends itself to the parties within the House and the senate creating the party-line partisanship. In the first months of the Dhoulou administration the president specifically omitted the Republican leadership in the forming of a stimulus package, as he had the votes to push it through. Being written by a group of nine Democrats, the stimulus package was called a success by the National Bureau of Economic Research, stating that the recession ended in June of 2009, just three months after the stimulus package was rolled out. The problem with this? The recession never really ended; the median household income continued to drop at an equal rate as it had during the recession. Also, the poverty rate increased and the unemployment rate continued to hang at dangerous levels for years to come.

"The two final situations that occurred within the first term of the Dhoulou Administration, when Syria entered into a revolutionary war, with government trying to make the American people understand about the issues in Syria and why we were supporting the side we were, defining the situation that was started in 1967 when Syria lost the Golan Heights to Israel after the Arab defeat in the Six-Day War. This hate for the Israeli State caused Bashar Hafez al-Assad to be the most intransigent opponent to peace with Israel; however, with a great deal of rhetoric and chest banging, Syria never raised a finger to Israel. In fact, the border of Syria and Israel was exceedingly safe. While there was a group, including the US, Turkey, the Gulf States, France, and Britain, that recognized the National Coalition of the Syrian Revolution as the "sole legitimate representative of the Syrian people," the civil war was not so simple, as several other nations, including Russia, supported the Assad government. But was the lack of support for the Assad government simply that loss of Syria as an ally? And the concern to lose this nation to Russia?" Andelos waited. Billings raised his hand as well as Sebastian. I waited and thought it was too simple an answer. "Billings."

"I see the loss of the Syrian nation as our ally as one of the largest failures of Dhoulou's administration, but the Imperialist regime could not put down the rebellion and this caused two concerns for Dhoulou; first, the opposition to the Assad government was the Muslim Brotherhood, remembering that Dhoulou had committed to work with the Muslims to accept them into and with his presidency — even though the Muslim Brotherhood actually supported the Nazis, and the world still holds Hitler as one of the most evil people of all time," Billings said.

"And the second?" Andelos queried.

"The hatred that he himself apparently had for Israel," Billings said.

"So what do these two points add up to?" Ursula asked.

"Together, they equate to the reason why Dhoulou didn't commit, or what he did in a lackadaisical approach which in the end allowed for the attack on Israel and the invasion of Syria by Israel," Billings added.

"That is a good observation," Ursula said. "This concern and hesitation that Dhoulou had for crossing swords with the Muslim Brotherhood was duplicated in the lack of outcry from the Whitehouse following the attack on the Embassy in Benghazi."

"He and his administrative staff did everything in their power to blame the incident on an independent film. When that failed, the true nature of his leadership was shown through the evolution of this debacle. His disjointed team continued to contradict each other day after day, and in an attempt to silence it Dhoulou addressed the nation stating that the endless parade of made-up scandals and posturing for political gain from distractions had to stop. On the surface he had done this hoping to get the American people on his side by showing that his political opposition was needlessly picking on him. The real reason was to distract the American people from actually looking at each float in the parade and noticing they were real," Andelos said, interjecting into the middle of Ursula's speech.

Regaining her thread, Ursula continued, "Even in terms of doing something great, the country was split down the middle to the point that some thought Dhoulou's handling of Hurricane Sandy gave him the election. The true data shows that in the states that were affected by the hurricane, he actually lost votes from 2008 to 2012, nearly eight hundred thousand. What is it that this tells you? Discuss."

"Well, I think Ursula did not believe you were paying attention. That toss to me was the first time she has done that," Andelos said. I raised my hand. "Judas — you have something to offer up?"

"I believe it tells me that the country may have been led by significantly biased reporting and photo ops that allowed the president to look on top of his game going into an election." I finished and waited for the ubiquitous comments, but none came.

"So, Judas, are you saying the press misled the people about how good or bad President Dhoulou actually did during the National Disaster?" Ursula asked.

"Yes, that is what I am saying," I answered.

"Does anyone else wish to weigh in on this?" Andelos asked.

"Hold that question, Andelos," Ursula interrupted him. "Judas, if the press treated this information as you say, would this have been illegal?"

"There was nothing illegal about this," I said.

"Judas, are you implying that when Dhoulou eventually made freedom of the press only apply to those with the National Press Certification, NPC, it was not actually needed because the *real* press was always there to protect his backside?" Ursula asked.

"There are several reasons that this law was put in place, but there were few true justifications for Dhoulou imposing it on the country. Had he imposed instead the Internet Tax earlier, the majority of the bloggers would have fizzled out. He simply wanted to force further control, or, conversely, take away more freedoms," I said.

"Very good, Judas. Thank you. Okay, Andelos, go ahead and continue your question," Ursula said.

"Wow, Ursula, you are a bit moody today. As I said, anybody else want to weigh in on this?" Andelos said.

"I am very much of the same impression as Judas. If the president had done such a great job, why would the voters in the areas that were hit by Sandy not have gone out and voted for him? But were there not any news organizations that showed the truth?" Meglar said.

"Ursula, you want this one?" Andelos asked.

"The records of the time show there were several news organizations that did in fact show the president coming in and out in a very short order. Additionally, and more importantly, the people in the area were not interviewed by any news organization except the Fox Network, which the majority of the country classified as an arm of the Republican Party, and this information was discounted. Why is this important to The Shop?" Ursula went still.

"Well, we will start with this question: what is the difference between why The Shop wants you to understand Bracken's mistakes and Dhoulou's mistakes?"

Many hands went up. I sat for a moment trying to understand the question, and formulating my answer, while the others in the class were trying to be the first to answer. Andelos called on Sebastian, a smaller boy who I had heard was a computer nerd. He spoke with the confidence of a person who was always the smartest in his class — and he may have been, for that matter; he may be the smartest in this class as well. But he, like the people who answered yesterday, fell into Ursula's trap. Giving an answer much like that which I had given yesterday. We need to understand the beginning.

"Andelos had given you a hint. Judas, you are holding back. Raise your hand." Ursula said.

I did as instructed: I raised my hand. Andelos indicated to me in a flourish. "It seems the Bracken Administration made mistakes that were less contributory of blatant disregard. Reviewing the Katrina situation, the actual screw-up came when the governor did not call for help. The Federal Government is not in charge of declaring an emergency or forcing their help; it is supposed to be done at a state level. Also, when the cities called for the evacuation but did not dispatch buses to assist the elderly, sick, and poor, this again was not a federal-level mistake. Yet, President Bracken was vilified by the press — and in the same light, President Dhoulou was canonized for his handling of Sandy. Whether it was all a photo op or not is not even the issue. It really came down to the press not asking questions in order to understand what really happened. Instead, they followed the original thought process of blatant disregard, lying, covering up and back-peddling, allowing the world's view of us as well as the country's view of the presidency to suffer. The proof would come in the 2012 election when Dhoulou lost a substantial amount of the vote in New Jersey, the state hit hardest by Sandy. Had he done all the press — and the governor said he did — wouldn't he have gained votes?" I finished.

"Judas, that was quite succinct and spot on again," Andelos said.

"Last question for the day, class. Given the previous answers to the questions that were posed to the class, is the small amount of censorship of the press and news agencies that is currently being carried out warranted? Or even the NPC — should it continue?" Ursula asked, once again catching Andelos off his game.

There were a few answers that made valid points. I was impressed with Sebastian's answer. I did not want to jump in; they were in a very well-articulated debate, with Meglar on the side of censorship and Sebastian on the side of human rights and repealing the NPC. During this conversation, I watched Andelos, and when certain buzzwords were stated, he gave an involuntary flinch. *Not cool.* "Judas, share with the class the observation that you just made," Ursula said, interrupting the debate.

"Excuse me?" I said.

"What was not cool?" Ursula asked.

This time I had thought my answer as opposed to saying it aloud. "Seriously?"

"Yes, seriously," she said in two voices inside my head.

"What I was noticing was that whenever Sebastian said certain words, Andelos would slightly flinch."

"I do not," Andelos said incredulously.

"Actually, he is right—you do, but it is very slight," Ursula said. "The reason for that is we have a negative reinforcement policy. In this case, I allowed the discussion to go on for far too long without providing any. To such an extent that Andelos's micro-expression became perceptible. This was not the reason I allowed it to go on; it is, however, a serendipitous outcome," Ursula said. "As for the debate, please continue."

"When I was recruited here, I did not say that I embraced all the ideals of The Shop. I did, however, agree with ninety-five percent, and I thought this would be enough. But on the topic of censure, I am opposed to The Shop. The freedom of speech..." his body twitched and he stopped talking abruptly. He appeared to be in a great deal of discomfort, but not pain. I looked at Andelos, and his eyes were affixed on Sebastian, "allows us to speak our minds and ..." he twitched again and stopped talking, but this time he looked as if the discomfort actually hurt.

"So we know that there are two sides to every argument and there are few discussions   in here that will end up in such treatment. This will occur should you trip on one," Ursula said.

"Why is it that we are not told in advance which areas will excite this reaction?" Sebastian asked, obviously still trying to shake off the previous experience.

"That is an interesting question. Does anyone have an answer?" Ursula asked.

"If I said right now 'do not think about your first love,' the majority of this room would shortly be thinking about their first love. It's a psychological imperative," I said.

"Interesting. I would not call it an imperative, but I understand your meaning. Tell me, how many thought of their first love? By show of hands—and remember, I can read your mind," Ursula said. All except one raised their hands, that being me. "Very good. Point made."

"The next class will continue tomorrow, at which time we will discuss the Dhoulou years. Thank you," Ursula said. The screen pulled up and we were done.

"Judas, stay after for a moment," Andelos said as he waited for the rest of the class to empty out. As the last person filtered out, Joshua came into the room. "So, Joshua, what exactly is going on? I have never in my time with The Shop witnessed Ursula get sideways like that."

"I was not in fact sideways," Ursula interjected.

"I apologize — it's an old saying," Andelos explained.

"I understand; it means to become distracted from one's course of action," Ursula said, "You feel I was distracted in class today?"

"As I have heard this lecture at least fifty times, I would say I noticed a large distraction, yes. Perhaps it was that you were rushing?" Andelos finished with a question.

"That is what I was trying to do — exactly. I did not have time for the incorrect answers; I needed to guide them to the answer quicker than typical," she answered.

"Then I come back to you, Joshua — what the hell is going on?" Andelos said, turning on Joshua.

"There has been an order from on high, to get Judas Level-Two-certified in ridiculous time," Joshua said and he removed a piece of paper from his pocket.

"Shooting?" Andelos sounded like a kid going to the zoo to see his favorite animal for the first time. Joshua handed him the paper, he read it and handed it back and then looked at me and his face cracked into a million pieces as it smiled for the first time in what might have been his entire life. "Come on, li'l one." He reached up-to pat me on the shoulder. "We got some fun ahead of us." He guided me out of the room. Joshua did not follow.

"Li'l one'?" Ursula was repeating as we left the room. Joshua was telling her to play back class discussion as I lost sight of him.

"We have one thousand rounds today, and then you have to get evaluated by the medical team," Andelos said, his little legs actually pulling me along.

"One thousand rounds—won't that take all day?" I asked.

"Well today it will take a while because we need to try various guns with you," Andelos said, the smile stuck on his face like an idiot. We got to the range and he bent down to the cabinet, entered a code and then it scanned him. He opened the door and then handed me a briefcase and then another. Then he came out with two more. We walked up to the shooter's box and lined the briefcases up. He opened them all up. "The first thing we need to do is find a gun that feels right in those giant mitts of yours."

"The proper fit allows you to release the safety without having to shift your grip," Ursula added.

"Safety?" I thought I understood but let's make certain we understand.

"I am sorry; I am not used to having a student that has never been certified on a hand gun in my class. There are several things you must understand before we start." Andelos fell into his teaching mode. "I am going to give you four tenants of gun safety that you will need to take to heart."

"Yes sir." I said.

"First; assume all guns are loaded. Treat them with the respect they are due. The most important part of that tenant, never let a gun *be* empty, an unloaded gun is nothing more than a nut cracker. Second; never put your finger on the trigger until you have made the decision to engage your target. At that point engage them do not talk or debate any longer, do you understand?"

"I do."

"Third; consider the muzzle of your gun as the scythe of death, if you allow it cross something you are willing to allow that something to be destroyed. That goes for yourself also, mind it well. The fourth and final tenants always understand what is behind your target, remembering you may miss or your bullet may go through your target therefore you need to know what else you may hit." Andelos finished.

"Judas please repeat the four rules, or tenants as Andelos called them." Ursula said. I did.

"Today we will simply get you to feel the gun; tomorrow we will give you the basics of gun construction." He handed me gun after gun and they were all very small.

"Judas," the voice came from behind. Two huge men were walking up to us. The speaker was Guerra, and the other was even bigger—he must have been the third of The Four. "Try this one." He removed the bullet magazine from the gun and handed me the empty gun. It was a perfect fit. "I thought your hand was about the same as mine. That is an STI 2011, custom. We gotta run but go ahead and use that to practice; I am headed back to my quarters. I have another—well, five others." He smiled and handed Andelos the magazine.

"Thanks, Guerra," I said.

"Judas, this is Deces, he is three of The Four," Guerra said.

"Thank you for what you do," I said simply. He reached out and shook my hand. His hands were smaller than Guerra's. He stood about seven foot. It surprised me to be looking up at these guys.

"I shoot a Kimber 1911 custom, pretty much the same modular frame," he said in a French dialect.

"Thank you both for the information." I watched them leave.

"Well how does that one feel in your hand?" Andelos asked.

"I hate to say it feels natural, because I do not know what natural is. It feels like it is not foreign. Does that make sense?" I asked.

"Well, yes and no. Can you reach the release for the magazine?" he touched the little lever, and I moved my thumb and operated the lever. "Can you release the safety?" he indicated the button by the trigger. I pressed it without moving my grip. "Perfect. Now you are going to shoot." I was actually shaking. Nerves? *Not cool.*

"Hold it—what do I do?" I asked.

"First put this magazine in, rather than the one Guerra released." It was longer. "That is a double magazine. It holds twenty-four. So if you start with one in the chamber, you get twenty-five shots. These first twenty-five shots will be just you, no guidance from anyone." He handed me the magazine; I slid it back into the same slot the smaller magazine had come out of. "Now, pull the top back." I did. "Now eject the magazine again." He indicated the smaller lever on the grip. *Not cool*, I actually was already reaching for it. He handed me a bullet to reload the single round that was chambered. I set the gun down on the table, loaded the single round into the magazine and then picking up the gun I put the magazine back in place. "Put on your earphones, release the safety, aim at the targets and then do what comes natural," Andelos said, putting his earphone in place.

"You mean drop the gun and pray to my Gram for forgiveness?" I said, smiling, not waiting for an answer. I fixed my earphone in place and released the safety, trying to feel the gun's weight as I extended it. I drew in a breath and *bang*, the gun kicked and I thought it was going to fly out of my hand. "Am I supposed to hold the gun loose or tight?" I asked, while I looked at the target—I had hit it, which surprised me.

"I would say a hair tighter than you were but not a lot," Andelos said. "I want you to do that again—but this time shoot five without stopping."

"I can do that," I said as I felt the gun in my hand, rotating it nine o'clock to three o'clock on the rotation and then felt forward fifteen degrees and then back fifteen degrees. Having felt that, I sighted in on the target and once again tried to add five degrees forward and back, as well as clockwise and counter. Then, moving my elbow closer into my body, which I noticed caused my wrist to go into a clockwise direction, I pulled the gun to my hip, gun fighter style then drawing on my target, to what felt like forward two degrees and counter clockwise 5 minutes. I pulled my elbow in and under enough to make up the five minutes to the perfect twelve o'clock position. Bringing the gun down to my hip again, and then drawing it again, this time clockwise zero, backwards one degree, I fired. I felt the recoil took me to two minutes counter clockwise, and eight degrees back, I brought it to what my hand thought was zero and negative once again, firing again. This time I ended up at one minute counter clockwise and negative eight degrees. Again, adjusting to zero and negative one degree—*bang*, repeat *bang*, repeat *bang*. Engaging the safety, setting the gun down, I turned to Andelos. "That kicks more than I could have imagined."

"Tell me what you were doing before you shot the gun," Andelos said.

"I was trying to feel where my hand ended up," I said.

"So why only one hand?" Andelos asked.

"I didn't really think I needed it; the gun was light, but when I shot it and that recoil kicked up after the second shot," I answered, "by then I was already in the process of firing. Should I have used my left hand to stabilize my right?" I asked.

"You need to determine that yourself. I would offer a small piece of advice, if you are going to shoot one handed you may want to rotate the gun counter clockwise making your zero at approximately 10:30 or forty-five degrees. It does not take away from your accuracy but it does give you a more physiologically stable base. Which has an important affect; it allows for a faster follow up, as you are not fighting your own musculature. And with you it's a lot of musculature. Mind you, not like the fools in the movies that take it too far shooting their 'gats' at 9:00 or ninety degrees.

"So if I tell you to fire again, will you use the stabilization hand?" Andelos asked.

"No, I think if there is ever a time I need a second gun, I want to be ready for that," I said.

"That's how I also see it." Andelos smiled at me. "Let's get your score." He reached up and wheeled in the target. The first shot was pretty low. "This guy sleep with someone you know?" he joked, as he put the finger through the bullet hole in the silhouette's groin. "For the first shot you ever took, that is low, but center line," he looked up at me with his head cocked in such a way that he looked like a bull dog. "Now, those other five shots, I rate those as expert. Any shooter who can cluster five shots within the area of a fist takes significant practice — but for a person who has shot one shot to do this is crazy," he took down the target and put up a new one. "We are going to do this again." As he was saying this, he was letting the target ride out. "So this time, we are going to do it at fifty yards."

"I am fine with that. I'm ready," I said.

"Think the same way you did last time: ten shots then safety on," he said as he started to walk away.

"Ten shots — got it." When he was out of the shooter's box, I picked up the gun. It was warm which was surprising as I had not noticed it being warm. I released the safety and took the gun down to my side, took a breath and quickly raised the gun—zero minutes and negative one degree—*bang*, feel and redirect the recoil back to zero minutes and negative one degree, rinse, repeat. I reveled in the exhilaration. *Not cool.* Safety set and gun down.

"Judas, step back here," Andelos said as the gun touched the table. I turned and walked back to him. "Did you have a chance to look at the target after you shot?" I actually started to turn. He reached out and physically stopped me, surprising me with how strong he was. "No, no, no. How do you think your shooting was?"

"I believe your comment from before holds true. I felt the shots were repeatable and clustered as you said before," I said.

"What would you say if I told you the shots were not like your last grouping?" he asked.

"I would say then they are better," I said and watched him allow a grin to touch his lips.

"Judas, the word 'natural' does not begin to touch on it." He turned me around. "You hit this target center mass." As the target was wheeled in, it became clear that the cluster was smaller than if I were to punch the target. "The result of this—ten for ten kill shots. It took me months of shooting to do that at fifty yards." We spent another nine-hundred eighty-four shots proving that it was not a fluke, and then we went to see the doctors.

"Judas, we are going to examine you for the strain of the physical activity that you just went through. My guess is you will be fine," the Scandinavian doctor whose name I can't recall said. He was joined by the doctor from the hearing test. He was obviously a military man, based upon his demeanor. He had one arm, which during my previous encounter with him I had missed, and what was left of his other was a short stump tied to him. My guess was that it was too nerve-damaged to attach a prosthetic to. "We will be hooking you up to the same machine you were hooked up to before. The initial connection will perhaps give a twinge of pain. So let's do this." The doctor said as I changed into my hospital gown and climbed on the examination table. The doctors all gathered around the monitors while the technician came up to me.

"Judas, this is going to twinge," the technician said, smiling, though she did not have a confident smile. It looked more like a "I have no idea how this is going to go."

"Go ahead," I said trying to determine exactly what a twinge felt like. Apparently a twinge was the equivalent of the pins and needles of a body part waking up after a long sleep, except this feeling spread from the center of my thighs all the way up to my armpits.

"The initial hookup is done. That was not so bad, was it?" the technician said, standing back up.

"I love being a guinea pig," I said. "If you ever do this to someone again, you can describe it as..." I told her and made useless conversation until the doctors gave her the thumbs up and she disconnected them.

"Now we are going to do your first refill," Dr. Khera said as she approached me with the stylish fountain pen.

"May I do it myself?" I inquired, "As I will most likely have to do it in the field without assistance."

"That is a great idea," the one-armed doctor said from the terminal. "This is the type of self-medication that could in fact save your life." I noticed Dr. Strandtov standing behind him nodding his head.

"Thank you for your input, Dr. Kadodadeh, but this is still in the experimental stage and..."

I reached up and took the pen out of her hand. "I think I have had enough people trying to learn from me today. Just tell me what you think is supposed to happen." I did not say it with anger, or even malice, but she really looked freaked out.

"Mr. Judas, the item you are holding in your hand is worth approximately…" Dr. Khera started.

"Doctor, you were the one who told me to stop worrying about the cost, so just tell me how it is supposed to work," I said, cutting to the point.

"Remove the base of the pen as if you were putting a new ink cartridge in it." I did. "Those three pins are to line up with the sockets that are in the port." She indicated the same port the technician had just hooked up to. I started to feel the port with my finger, two close barbs then a gap, then one barb. Then, looking at the pen to determine which way it went, I moved the pen into place as she once again began speaking. "When it finds its home, the needles will extend; this will be more pain than the last test." As it was already happening, the warning came too late. *Not cool.* It hurt real good. "From the look in your eyes, it found home. When it finishes filling, it will automatically release." Right on cue, the cartridge released. "Good, it is finished. Can you describe the sensations?" Dr. Khera asked.

"I would say the initial connection was that of a bee sting on steroids, I guess three bee stings on steroids. Followed by, well, have you ever basted a turkey—you know, with the plastic tube and rubber ball? You squeeze the ball and then put it in the liquid; when you let go of the ball it fills up the tube. I think that is what I felt like," I answered.

"I can deal with that answer," Kadodadeh said with a smile. I noticed that Dr. Khera was showing a bit of resentment in the way she glared at him, but it was quickly replaced by a more neutral expression. I wondered if I had just witnessed a changing of the guard, as it were: Dr. Kadodadeh was now my head doctor, and Dr. Khera resented it immensely. "Well, Judas, the reports show you used very little additional resources. The testosterone usage was a bit higher than we had predicted so you will need to refill every five days instead of seven; however, since you have done no actual physical exercise like running or lifting weights, that number may end up closer to three days. The base unit will have enough for one hundred full charges. If you use the unit every other day, you will most likely get two hundred charges before you will need to charge the base."

"Is there an expiration date on the chemicals?" I asked.

"*Oh*, excellent question," Dr. Strandtov said. This guy was awesome. "The chemicals will last around five years if they are kept below one hundred fifty degrees; however, at one hundred fifty they will become useless," he explained.

"If I was in one hundred fifty degrees, the chemicals inside me will be useless also?" I asked.

"Yes, but most likely you would be dead if your insides saw that temperature. So it's okay," Strandtov answered.

"Oh yeah, I was not really thinking," I smiled and started to sit up.

"There is one last thing I..." Dr. Khera paused, "we need to test."

"Okay — what is that?"

"Blood, lots of blood. So lie back, go on, lie down." Strandtov had such a manner that I was fine giving up lots of blood. By the time they finished, it ended up being two full pints and twenty vials of various sizes, and I was glad I had lain back. *Not cool.*

"Well, young *ma'un*, are you ready to move into the real world?" Joshua stood over me. I must have fallen asleep. "For they say you are ready to start your new life."

"What about my classroom stuff?" I asked.

"Tomorrow they are covering stuff we have talked about and I can instruct you on other stuff if you miss much, but Ursula is ready to let you leave. Her opinion is the class will struggle more without you than the other way round, and that is good," Joshua said.

"All right then, let's kick this pig," I said with a smile.

"Um, you do not plan on speaking like that in public do you?" he said, looking at me.

"Hell, I am not the one who throws out that good old southern charm. Even a blind squirrel gets a nut once in a while. *He-yuck*," I shot back.

"You know, I make most people as nervous as a cat in a room full of rocking chairs, but you *he-yuck* me..." He shook his head and chuckled to himself.

"I guess that makes us even; most people treat my size and intimidating physique as though I would be stupid, yet you speak to me as if I possess an intellect," I said.

"Wait—how does that make us even? I treat you with the respect that you are due and you knock me down a rung or two," Joshua said, looking at me. "Never mind, I think I got it myself."

"And?" I prodded.

"We both need a partner who can treat us like that," he stated.

"That is how I see it too," I said.

"So I am supposed to get an expert on micro-expressions to meet us on our mission? They will test and train you. What is that about?" he asked, changing the subject.

"Well, Ursula noticed my reading of Andelos," I answered.

"You read an agent?" he asked perplexed. "Seriously?"

"Nope—it's all a lie, including them telling you to find someone to train me further." I pounced on his stupid question.

"Good. Saves me some effort." Joshua was good at deadpan.

Chapter 5

When we got to the plane, I asked Joshua about the clothes. "I have this suit and that's it. I do not even have a change of underwear."

"So, tell me, young *ma'un*, do I look like the type of person who wants to smell your stinky dirty clothes for the entire trip?" Joshua said, looking at me.

"Okay, so what are we going to do, stop at a men's clothing store?" I asked.

"I got it covered, from the socks and shoes to the suits, ties and even your bizarrely sized dress shirts. I'll be darned if the woman thought me a dang fool — twenty-inch neck, thirty-eight-inch sleeve. Heck, I even got you toiletries," Joshua said with a twinkle in his eye. "I have a little something for you. This was my first shoulder holster." He handed it to me. "I want you to have it."

"Joshua, that is very generous of you," I said looking at it.

"Not really. I ordered you a new one and when I went to wrap it, I realized it could not possibly fit your redwood-sized chest," he said, laughing. "If you do ever want to get rid of it, let me know please."

"Deal," I said.

"Hello from the flight deck, this is your pilot Captain Roy Orbison, and no I am not related. We will be traveling today at twenty-one thousand feet and the trip should take four hours. Please buckle up; we will be departing soon."

"I have never flown on a private plane before — anything I should know?" I asked.

"Well, for the most part it's like a regular airplane," Joshua said, looking out the window.

"No jokes?" I asked looking at him.

"I hate flying, and I do not joke about it," he said, staring out the window. "So to pass the time, we are going to discuss the assignment, and for us to do that you need to understand The Shop's philosophy of government structure."

"Should I take notes?" I said, reaching for my briefcase. When the hell did I get a briefcase? I wondered what was in it.

"No, you do not need to," Joshua said.

"Darn it," I said, mainly because I wanted to look in the briefcase.

"You like to take notes?" Joshua asked.

"No, never mind; my mind was somewhere else," I said.

"Ah, you want to open that briefcase, don't you?" He watched me. I tried to look coy, and failed miserably. "Well, go ahead—I can wait." I reached down and grabbed it. It was just like the one Joshua carried, which made sense; it had a name-tag with The Shop logo, and there was a combination lock with four numbers. I tried my social security number then realized there was no such thing since The Shop did away with that department. Hmm, what to choose… then I just tried the '0000' that it was set to and it opened. "Good guess," Joshua said. The briefcase had a small case that had ten of my recharge cartridges, a couple notebooks, a leather folder that had The Shop logo and my name inside, three files with papers in them that said "Confidential," and two expensive fountain pens. Upon opening them I found one was real and the other was my injector, and a diaper. *Not cool.* "Oh, that was my suggestion," Joshua said, pointing at the diaper. "We do not usually put them in, if you wondered, but you are so new you're not even to training pants yet," he chuckled to himself.

"I thought you just put your Depends in the wrong case." I regretted saying it instantly.

"Okay, that one hurt a bit," Joshua said, smiling. "Good one."

"So this name inside of the notebook, Judas III, there were two other agents with that name?" I asked.

"No, that is your level. You are officially Level Three," Joshua said.

"Um, how did that happen?" I was confused.

"To be honest, I do not know. But I got the notification this morning straight from Sensenmann. So you can trust that it's true, by the way; there can only be one agent that ever has the name you have, so forever you are the only Judas. If someone punches your name in a computer it will pull up Betrayer of Christ, and a song by some flash-in-the-pan pop artist and potentially a heavy-metal band," Joshua said.

"That is interesting," I said.

"So let's get started on your next training." I put away the briefcase and got comfortable. "When The Shop initially took over, they had not really decided how they were going to govern; they simply had to get the country out of the dangerous situation it had caused."

"What situation is that?" I asked

"By allowing everyone to vote for the president, the country was forcing itself into bankruptcy. The world could not continue to falter the way it was and we were leading the way. We were being bankrolled by the world—they simply were making fake money and loaning it to us. Dhoulou forced the issue when he took the ceiling up without allowing the Congress or senate to vote. The world questioned why other countries were going bankrupt but not us. The answer in reality was the petrodollar: back in the mid-1970s we negotiated a deal that forced all the oil to be traded in US currency, therein giving value to the dollar. This explains a lot of deaths through the rest of the old government's tenure. When other countries pushed back on this, Iraq trying to trade in euros, we pushed back with embargos. That is a lesson for another day.

"The Shop took over the Electoral College first, naming a president. They then began great discussions on how the rest of the government needed to be set up. At the two-year mark they allowed the states to submit three names for each elected position. Bottom line, the political action committees..."

"PACs," I said.

"Correct—the PACs were still running the show. They forced their way into the election through whatever means possible. So did the political families that have actually had their fingers on the pulse of the government for decades upon decades—as did the all-powerful Federal Reserve which. Again, is a topic for a different day. Basically the people were not really electing the best person for the job; they were electing the person who the enfranchised said was able to run for office. This group needed to be neutered." He paused and stood up. "Would you like a beverage?" Joshua asked as he walked across the plane.

"A cranberry juice would be great, if there is any," I said.

"Molly is in charge of stocking the plane; she got you some cranberry juice," Joshua said.

"Excellent. Is there food too?" I asked as I walked to where he was.

"Seriously?" he said as he opened the door to a large refrigerator. Labels on everything: Judas, Judas, Judas, Joshua. "Look at this—you got three to my one. Like you really eat that much," he looked me up and down. "Okay, maybe it's right," he smiled. I grabbed a 'Judas Breakfast' and two cranberry juices and went back to my seat. "You going to eat with your hands, caveman?" he shouted. I looked back just in time to catch a silverware packet aimed at my head. "Good catch!" He let out a belly laugh.

He sat back down and ate his little meal and started to talk again. "The neutering came in the form of three executions. This was followed by The Shop taking away the rights of the citizens to nominate three candidates. This was of course the first attempt to form an alliance against The Shop. The old families pulled their money out of banks and attempted to convert it to other forms of currency — gold, diamonds, platinum and, in some cases, soy beans. Feeling this was coming, Sensenmann sent twenty thousand Shop agents, pretty much all that he had, to the homes of these individuals, and arrested them, seizing their assets, which were all liquid, citing Crimes against The Shop. He only kept them in jail for a year, which was the most he had the right to do based upon the laws The Shop had established. When they got out, all their wealth was gone. Their homes were converted into Shop offices. At the same time, the country was put back on the Gold Standard, having secured enough gold to carry the country." Joshua looked down at his hands and his brow furrowed.

"Joshua, are you all right?" I asked.

"I was in charge of the group responsible for seizing the wealth of the most prominent families in America — but worse than that, I was there when they got out of jail a year later, and I was in charge of their integration team." He again looked down at his hands, "Men and women, boys and girls who had everything, now they had nothing, not even clothes."

"They were left destitute?" I asked.

"No, they all had something somewhere, but they were given an option: they gave us their loyalty and we gave them access to their hidden funds. Or we simply let them leave the country. If that was their choice, they would not ever be allowed back. Some took that option, and we flew them to where their money was — well, where it was supposed to be. That in itself was not our problem — we gave them a change of clothes and a plane ticket," Joshua said quietly.

"What did they really find?" I asked

"Let's put it this way: the asshats told me that if you distributed the wealth of the world evenly, in five years the same people would have it all back. You know, that made it easier. That is what they found: for each member of the family, they received one eight-billionth of the world's wealth, or about twenty-five thousand each." He shook his head, "It's many years past that now and I do not see that occurring." There was no happiness in him when he said that, just contempt.

"So now all three branches of the Federal Government were controlled by The Shop?"

"No, at that point the Judicial branch was left alone. The Shop still needed to figure out how the state and local governments could fit in the mix. As many states were applying to secede, they all had enough signatures, but what were they going to do? Not many of the states could be a sovereign nation; they do not have enough exportable goods to sustain themselves. So Sensenmann went on air— the only on-air coast-to-coast speech he has ever given.

"'Good evening, I am addressing you tonight as a fellow American, not as the leader of The Shop. Over the past years, the changes that have been forced down upon us as a country have been very hard to take without rising up. The fact is, we as a whole have stopped being 'We' a long time ago. The last time I felt proud to be an American was when I was a teenager and Ronald Reagan said, 'Mr. Gorbachev, tear down this wall.' Several other actions took place in America that made me proud, but Ronald Reagan just had something about him that made me feel good about the state that our country was being led from.

"'Leading is something that has fallen off; the people who have been in Washington have not been leading, they have been taking up a call to be reelected, and that is all they care about. From the day they arrive in Washington as a freshman with all their ideals a-blazing, through the day they decide they have to follow the group while they get acclimated, until the day they realize they cannot buck the establishment and still get reelected. So they started voting for laws that would shape the country, making them look like they had hearts, that they cared about their constituents. When—and *if*—they were leaders, if they cared they would enforce tough laws, tougher school expectations, and tougher welfare reform not because it was easy but because it was right for the country. Our kids keep getting dumber—but, hey, none of them got left behind. Our people are taken care of when they fall on hard times, but who ever thought someone would worsen their hard times so they could continue to be taken care of? Aren't you tired of someone telling you what morality is? Aren't you tired of paying for campaign ads which bash the other guy? Of course you are. How about this; are you tired of everyone not paying their fair share? I mean *everyone*.

"'Now I am addressing you as the leader of The Shop. Here is what I am doing about it: I am changing it, all of it. The states will need to follow so that we can make this work. This is what I want the states to do: accept the restructuring The Shop is bringing. I will put into the restructuring that if this country is not at a balanced budget in three years, then we will repeal The Shop.

"'How will I balance the budget? First, I am doing away with the income tax system. It does not work. There are too many loopholes. I am replacing it with a forty percent sales tax. Everyone buys stuff, whether you are an individual or a business. People who are legally in the country or not—everyone purchases food, clothes, cars, et cetera. The states will no longer collect taxes, not income, not property taxes, none.

"'Big Business, understand this: you will be paying your fair share. If you want to move out of my country, go ahead, but I will not allow your products to be sold here. *Period*. I will personally burn your patents and turn your plants over to the highest bidder. Do not think you are taking your equipment with you. You will leave this country with the money in your bank accounts and that's it. Or you can stay here, understanding you are not special and you do not get exemptions to make your bank accounts fatter. You will pay taxes on your raw materials, and supplies.

"'Next, the governments for the states and local areas will be revamped. The primary positions, those of the governors and the mayors, will be elected positions. They will, however, not be elected in the old manner. There will be no campaign costs; therefore, there will be no allowable contributions from any sources. In order to get a stipend for the election, candidates will need a certain number of signatures. If a person is caught trying to defraud this government by placing a candidate or buying a candidate, I will personally kill that person. Take that to heart. This is going to be the true people's government, not old money's government. Not the people who are demanding the free stuff's government. No one is getting free stuff anymore. You need a hand? Fine, I will give you a hand, but you are going to work for it. It's time that you realize every action has an equal opposing reaction, and nothing is free.

"'The business of the state government is to evaluate all the needs of your state. Those needs will be laid out by your local governments. The needs are then forwarded to the Federal Government. The Federal Government will then evaluate the needs and pay what can be covered. Not all needs will be met—we are a business, not a charity, and this country was great when people tried to do their best. We invented things that made the world look at us in awe; now we act, we preach, we eat, and we get fat. It is time for America to figure it out. We are not going to go down, not without swinging and definitely not due to our own stupidity.'

"That speech closed the deal. The American right pulled together and led the change to shut down the discussions about seceding. The people were tired of those not pulling their weight. The people who did not pull their weight quickly learned how they could. The military reinstituted the draft, for every able-bodied man up to forty-five and woman up to the age of twenty-five. The people who were in college could exempt out while in college, but they would serve their time after. The draft worked in a reverse randomization, allowing more of the older people to be drafted first. He then opened the recruitment to illegal aliens, allowing them to become Americans if they enlisted and spent eight years in the military. The initial reinstated draft did manage to crush the protesting for equal rights.

"The big surprise came when the military was opened to civilian senior citizens, the mess halls, the laundries, the mail rooms; every part of the base that did not require you to have security clearance was opened to the elderly who wanted a job.

"The adaptation of the old government styles to the new was a cumbersome process. At the local levels it went relatively well, there was not a major problem, The Shop made appearances in several cities during the elections and even the larger cities like Detroit, New York and Chicago really did not deviate from the requested plan. The states had some concerns, but after sending the agents in, there was not much of an issue." Joshua took a break and looked at me. "Young *ma'un*, are you understanding all of this?"

"I think so. The basic setup of the governments at the state and local levels is the same: there is one elected position that is the head. But how is it that The Shop can keep an eye on them?" I asked.

"Good, you were paying attention. The Shop has a first lieutenant in each office of the mayor and a deputy in each governor's office. All decisions must go through them. When the governor needs to get advice from the outside, consultants are requested. The request goes to this Shop officer. This keeps the front-line briberies from taking place. By removing the middleman, the consultants present their opinions straight to the leaders. This has allowed the legislative branch to be reduced to practically nothing."

"But wasn't that legislative branch needed?" I asked.

"Their job was to make laws and to approve presidential appointments, declare war and 'substantial investigative powers.'"

"Yes, it seems like a big job to me," I said.

"I would say, yes. This job sits as one of the most important jobs that have ever been established in the country. The Shop continues this tradition, and we do it without allowing stupid assholes to perform 'pork barreling' or riders into bills. The same group that would not allow a single-line veto, even though forty-three of the fifty states allowed single-line vetoes," Joshua said, with a significant amount of contempt in his voice.

"Okay, so how is The Shop handling this differently?" I asked.

"When the government under Blythe allowed the line-item veto, this was overturned by the Supreme Court, contending that the action of striking a single-line gave too much power to the president, allowing violation of the Presentment Clause held within the Constitution. It stood that way while contested on a federal level. Many legal authorities challenged this ruling. It was the 'pork barreling' and 'riders' that should have been challenged. Single-line vetoes would not be needed if bills didn't pull riders with them, and that is how The Shop is handling it, dealing with the problem the law is to cover and not the unnecessary baggage," Joshua said.

"So why didn't that get addressed by the courts, to allow line-item vetoes for items not part of the intent of the law? Better yet, allow the courts to strike items that violate the intent," I asked.

"Perhaps when things are rushing forward, no one stopped and looked and said, 'Hey, guys, let's stop and review how we got here, and see if we can fix what isn't working correctly.' I can't know that—as a child I once knew would have said," Joshua commented, thinking back emotionally.

"While that all makes sense on the federal level, how is this supposed to work on the local level?" I wondered aloud.

"There is no real difference, Judas. The Shop handles both state and federal in the same manner: when a law needs to be reviewed, we pair the laws with other matters that need to be reviewed by like groups. We determine what advice is needed to assist the group of Shop agents and other members of The Shop to make the decision that best answers the concern at hand. The challenge really comes in when the governors are in their role for so long that they understand where the holes are," Joshua said.

"Why don't we simply put in term limits?" I asked.

"To me, that would be an excellent answer, but the leadership in The Shop does not really wish to continue to have new faces within the leadership of local and state governments."

"What is it that we are heading out to specifically do?" I asked.

"Sensenmann has reached a conclusion that this freshman group of leaders has a need to be visited; however, we are going to visit *all* governors, primarily due to the concern that there have been some underlying sounds of rebellion. So it is possible that some element managed to get in and they did this with the assistance of other rebels who were already in power.

"Let me tell you a quick story. In 1786, Daniel Shays led a group of farmers with the overall goal of closing down the courts that were seizing their farms — this after seeking justice and being forced to sell all their personal possessions just to make ends meet. The interesting part of their issues stemmed from a lack of federal power, and the reaction of the state's leadership, including the collection of funds from the businessmen to implement a militia army. Instead of simply listening to farmers who basically did not have money to pay debts, largely due to the fact that the money they had been paid for fighting in the Revolutionary War was worthless. In a letter to George Washington, Henry Knox wrote, 'What is to give us security against the violence of lawless men? Our government must be braced, changed, or altered to protect our lives and property.' This brought Washington out of retirement, and led to his attending the Constitutional Convention. Washington's leadership was paramount in establishing our Constitution, determining the type of government the United States of America would have. None of this would have been brought about without Shays and his rebellion.

"Now, take a step back to today and understand that one man can change everything that has been put in place," Joshua said. "Now, as you were found out to have exceptional eyes and the ability to see these micro-expressions, you are going to be my lie detector," Joshua finished.

"Oh, am I?" I commented more than asked.

"And the stupidest part, I think you can do it," Joshua started. "At our first stop there is a Shop instructor joining us. She will be explaining in more detail about how this works."

"Sounds like fun," I said.

"You know, if you try to lie to her like that, she will know right away," Joshua joked with me.

"What do you think of this?" I asked.

"There has been a lot of research in this field; it has several practical applications for those who understand all the nuances. The problem comes in when people take a piece of a science and try to apply it," Joshua said.

"So I am probably going to cause more of a problem than good?" I asked.

"You are not going to do anything except watch— what problem could that possibly cause? You will simply take notes on each facial change, and each body movement. Later, when we review the interview, you will discuss what you saw," Joshua explained.

"Sounds easy enough," I said.

"Perhaps. That remains to be seen," Joshua said. My face obviously was showing an 'um what...' look. "Okay, you are standing in the corner and this sleazeball is obviously lying— how easy is it going to be to simply sit back and shut up?"

"If that is my assignment," I stated.

"I promise you. Those words will be tested in the next few months," he said.

"I will do my very best to stand true to them," I said.

"Great answer." Joshua smiled and got up to stretch his legs. "Can I ask you a personal question?"

"Sure, Joshua—I am an open book," I said.

"Ursula said you are ready, and you had not showed me any reason that I should question that you are ready for this..." he started.

"'*Had* not?' That implies that something's changed your opinion," I said.

"When you addressed the class about thinking of their first love, as an example of why The Shop should not tell the agents-in-training what the taboo mindsets are," Joshua said.

"Yes?" I inquired.

"How is it that you actually did not think of Kat? Judas, it's okay to have thoughts about your past. I have been in this business for several hundred years, and I still think about things that I have lost that brought me here," he said.

"I am not a person who can allow those things in. While I currently need my walls they will not always be there; I am able to think about my parents. But as far as Gram and Kat, I am just not ready to think about it. I do appreciate your concern, and if it helps you to know I am not a sociopath, we can talk about it. But I do not need to have the compartment opened to allow me to function," I said.

"Okay, that is understandable," he said. "Thank you for helping me understand you a bit."

"As I said, I am an open book."

"And an interesting book it is, my boy," Joshua said.

"Well, under that guise, that of trying to read a book, how about your book?" I started. "What is it that you think of when you, as you said, 'think of things I lost that brought me here?'"

"I opened myself up to that one, eh?" Joshua asked.

"I would have to say yes," I answered

"Well, let's start by me saying I was born into a very rich family. I studied incessantly—history and literature were my favorites, but I was very musically gifted," Joshua said. "I actually had a scholarship to Juilliard."

"Holy cow that is impressive," I said.

"I appreciate you saying that. I never made it through," he said.

"What happened?" I asked

"I had fallen in love, and she was a very strong woman, but not a skilled one in anything musical, so she was obviously not going to Juilliard. So I decided I would pursue a career in politics as I felt that, of my other two major assets, literature and history, history was the most important subject for a successful political person — the second being literature, the ability to speak with conviction and sound educated. Some say my southern drawl is in direct contrast with my intellect; however, when put together, they allow me to present a great acumen in political decision-making."

"Acumen? Now that is a word you do not hear often," I poked.

"So you know the meaning of such a pugnacious word?" Joshua asked.

"The ability to perceive, judge, or choose with accuracy," I said, sticking out my tongue, "Although I would not say it is a *pugnacious* word."

"Maybe not, as it is really quarrelsome on the surface," Joshua said.

"No — but you sure are a pugnacious and acuminous man."

"I think that settles it; I am in the right field then," Joshua said as he smiled.

"Well, now that the obvious is discovered, what happened to the girl you fell in love with?"

"Her name was Sarah, but when I told my parents that I was not going to Juilliard, they were very angry. They had supported me in my dreams and as they seemed to come true, I abandoned them. Anyway, my parents died before I graduated and they never forgave me for this betrayal. Sarah and I completed school together, first and second in our class; while we both finished with one hundred percent average, I had more points in total valuation to the class and I took first place."

"Nice," I said.

"Well, not really. It actually caused a lot of strife in our relationship," he said, in deep contemplation. "Although we stayed together for five years, I played the part of a campaign manager through two elections. She won both and, young *ma'un*, it did have a lot to do with me and the work I did in the background. While she was making strides to move into real political arenas, the work that I had done in making a complete unknown candidate come to a victory in two elections against incumbents had gotten me some national recognition. The people who came to see me simply said, 'We have seen that you dedicate yourself to the goals that you establish and we have witnessed firsthand your ability to lead people, and that they would walk through hell for you.' They presented me with a card — in this profession it was the equivalent of a golden ticket. She heard and saw the brief conversation, and when we were alone that night she simply said, 'I know that those men were from the national Republican campaign committee. Why are you staying here?' When the only answer I had for her was 'because of us,' things were destined to fail thereafter," Joshua said.

"She ended your relationship because you put it ahead of your personal achievement?" I asked.

"It was the eighties, you need to understand; women were getting past the *wanting* to feel they were empowered, and actually taking the reins. The thought that she was not doing it alone was, well, more than she could handle." He sat back and rubbed his eyes, and then he stared deep into my eyes. "Who pushes someone away because they would rather put their life together ahead of their personal agenda?" He waited long enough to make me think he was not asking a rhetorical question.

"As I was not part of that culture or time period I can't possibly offer you an answer that could ..." I started.

"Sorry — of course not. And it did not really matter; I left for Washington and things were going very well for me. Four years later, I got a phone call from my Sarah saying she needed me. I put in for a leave of absence to assist, to help her pull her campaign out of the toilet. There was no one who had an issue with it; I had everything lined up for my candidates to simply walk into their elections without an issue." He paused to reflect. "The fact that she had called meant there was no chance that she could pull this out. I pulled all the information I could about her district, the issues that were smacking her in the face, and the wins she'd had over the last term. By the time I got there I had a plan. I remember the reunion; it's what I always remember when I am down or nostalgic. We met at the restaurant where we had our last dinner together. It was like the four years apart had never happened. We talked, we laughed and we discussed the problems of her election campaign and how I planned to fix it, and then we walked back to her place — there was the proverbial washing the palette clean," Joshua said.

"Very interesting. So you got back together?" I asked.

"That was not meant to be. The next day I was called — my primary candidate was in a bit of a scandal. I told Sarah I would walk her campaign manager through the plan, but that was not going to work; she had fired her manager when I told her I was coming. It was time again to choose between my future and hers. I chose, again, hers; I called and told them what to do to fix the problem but that I had given my word. This time they were not happy. They told me to come back or I was done. I told them I was bowed up like a banty rooster. I gave my word and if they could not understand that, then they could take their job and place it where their credibility already was." Joshua's eyes were squinted and the anger was showing. "I stayed on and she won the election. I have to say, it was my best work. She returned to her office with an entirely different agenda: she changed out some advisors and asked me to take a position, as her lieutenant. I was honored, but I knew I was not the one who should be in front of the camera."

"So you obviously did not stay to help. What happened?" I asked.

"I was asked to come to Washington to discuss the issue that had occurred. I agreed and gave Sarah the number that I could be reached at. I remember kissing her and walking out to my plane. When I was seated, I looked out my window at the back of the plane and she was standing right there holding a sign, 'I love you. I owe you more than I can ever say. I'm sorry I ever let the world get in the way.' Even back in the eighties, letting someone on the tarmac was insane — I remember thinking she should not be there, but I just waved and blew her a kiss. Then the explosion hit. The plane simply blew up. Twenty-eight people died, twenty-four who were on the plane and four around the plane. Sarah was one of those four; I was the only one on the plane who survived. I wish I could explain it, the feeling when I woke up a month later and heard what had happened."

"You do not need to try and come up with words; I can sympathize with your feelings," I said, not in any way trying to diminish the feelings he was having then or now.

"I tend to think most people can't — but you, I know you can." We flew for a while in silence. "We truly are an odd couple, peas in a pod: me, like a million years; you, like a hundred days… lol…" — yes, he said "LOL."

"I am thankful someone saw the fit; I do not think I could have gotten through everything without your help, my friend," I said sincerely.

"Okay, enough of this folderol; we have a job to prep for."

"Ready when you are," I said.

"Here is the list of questions I will be asking. When I ask them, you note anything that happens." I nodded my head. "You must not at any time show any emotion or say anything." I nodded again. "I know you said you can do that, but I cannot stress it enough: the challenge may not come from where you expect," Joshua said.

"Wait—what?" I stammered.

"What if the aides start jumping in and saying stuff?" Joshua continued.

"What aides?" I asked, extremely confused.

"Exactly—that is what I mean. The rules seem to be changing and no one is saying anything, but right now it is not your job to be surprised or say anything. We may walk in and there may be four lawyers with the governor, all on the taxpayers' dollar, and what do you say to that?" Joshua asked.

"Nothing. I say nothing," I said.

"Good. And do not be surprised if I do not comment on it either. I will simply ask my questions, you will take down the answers, and we will leave. All observations will not be written on my sheets. As they are the official transcript of the questioning, your notes go straight to Sensenmann," Joshua concluded. "We will be at our first destination in about twenty minutes, get a drink, use the restroom—whatever you need. I need to have privacy for a quick call." And with that he got up and walked to a small room at the back of the plane. I watched him for a minute and then decided using the boys' room probably would be good. When I got out he had returned to his seat. "No changes in our approach. I just had to see if anything had shaken free since we left. This is going to be interesting," Joshua said, then got up and used the rest room as the captain said to take our seats; we would be landing in about three minutes.

"Timed that just right," I said as Joshua sat back down.

"It's all in the wrist," he laughed and sat down.

"That's messed up," I laughed. We landed and taxied to the private portion of the airport.

"Well, let's do this." Joshua stood up and I followed him off the plane to the waiting car. "Agent," Joshua said to the man standing at the car.

"Agent," he replied. Joshua and I got in the car. The other agent followed. Okay, this was weird; we drove for twenty minutes and no one said a word. "This is the office. There are a few others inside. The governor is expecting you."

"Thank you," Joshua said as the car stopped. The agent got out and we followed. We continued to follow him to the elevator. No one approached us, and actually no one even acknowledged us. While we were in the elevator, the agent looked at his own reflection in the polished doors. Then they opened and he led us out. We walked up to the desk where a girl about twenty-one sat.

"Christine, these are The Shop agents we discussed earlier." She simply nodded her head and pushed a button. The doors opened into a large office. "Thank you," the agent said as we walked past her. I did note that she was sweating on her upper lip and her hand was trembling as she pulled it away from the buzzer. We walked in the room and the doors closed immediately behind us. I saw the governor pulling his hand away from the side of his desk; he had obviously closed the door.

"Governor, I have six questions. To each I want a simple 'yes' or 'no.' Do you understand?"

"Yes," the governor answered.

"Are you currently plotting against The Shop?" Joshua asked.

"No," the governor replied.

"Do you know of anyone who is plotting against The Shop?" Joshua asked.

"No," the governor answered.

"Are you *willingly* ignoring any laws The Shop has established?" Joshua said emphasizing the word 'willingly' very strongly.

"No," the governor answered after a momentary pause.

"Do you wish to stay in the position that you currently hold, as an elected position within the government?" Joshua asked immediately upon the answer of the previous question.

"Yes," the governor answered.

"Is there anything that we, as Shop agents reporting to Sensenmann, and only Sensenmann, should know?" Joshua asked his last question and waited.

"No," the answer came after several seconds of delay.

"Now I want you to leave the room," Joshua said, looking at the other Shop agent. After a quarter-second of thought, he walked to the door. "Please open the door, governor." The door opened and closed again. "Sir, I am going to ask you six questions. To each I want a simple 'yes' or 'no.' Do you understand?"

"Yes," the governor answered.

"Are you currently plotting against The Shop?" Joshua asked again.

"No," the governor replied.

"Do you know of anyone who is plotting against The Shop?" Joshua asked.

"No," the governor said again.

"Are you *willingly* ignoring any laws The Shop has established?" Joshua asked once again emphasizing the same word.

"No," the governor answered, this time without a pause.

"Do you wish to stay in the position that you currently hold, as an elected position within the government?" Joshua asked with the same expedience.

"Yes," the governor answered again, no pause.

"Is there anything that we, as Shop agents reporting to Sensenmann, and only Sensenmann, should know?" Joshua asked.

"No," the governor answered.

"Thank you, sir. That was all we needed from you. Please open the door." The door opened, and the agent looked in. Joshua indicated for him to return to his post. After he entered the room, the door closed behind him. "This is considered Article Eighty-Seven. No conversations outside of this room regarding what just happened here. Are you one hundred percent clear on this?" they both acknowledged Joshua's question. We headed for the door, pausing to wait for it to open, which it did, and we walked out. As we headed out to the car, the other agent was seriously butt-hurt, his posture like that of a child who had to sit out of a game at school. When we got to the car, he opened the door and gave a slight, passive-aggressive head bow to Joshua as he got in the car. Without a word, we drove to the airport. Upon arriving outside our ramp, Joshua and I exited the car. We then got on the plane, leaving the other agent with his lips pursed standing next to his limo.

As soon as we sat in our seats on the plane, Joshua burst out laughing, "Oh, young *ma'un I a'um* such a jerk..." he managed to squeak out between large snorts of laughter. "I just decided to do that when I saw that bellicose face on that asshat."

"I did not feel that he did anything lending toward being a traitor," I said.

"No, he was just an easily excitable jerk," Joshua said, calming down.

"My dear Joshua, you have not changed a bit." The woman's voice came from the direction of the soundproof room in the back of the plane. "You are such an honest person. People like you are so few and far between. I had forgotten how much I appreciate you." We both stood to face her. "Ah, you must be the new prodigy?"

"My dear, this is Judas—"prodigy" remains to be seen," Joshua said.

"Ma'am," I said, reaching out my hand to shake.

"Judas, this is Jinau. Oh, how cute—we are team triple-J."

"Pleased to meet you, Judas," Jinau said, shaking my hand more firmly than I thought she could. "And 'my dear' is sexual harassment," she said, turning her head to Joshua.

"How about 'sweet tits?'" Joshua asked.

"Now that is fine," Jinau said giggling, I noticed, as she said it. "But you are not setting a good example for your young *ma'un*."

"True," he said and then turned to me. "Do not talk to the fairer sex like that." This time she hit him. "What?"

"FFS, you can't call me the fairer sex," Jinau said.

"True," Joshua said, in the midst of Jinau hitting him again. "Judas, your best bet is to call her by her name; I think you will be safer that way," he said, rubbing his arm where she had punched it. "Although you did say FFS instead of for fuck's sake," Joshua poked, as she acted like she was going to hit him again.

"I think I like that plan—plus Gram would not let me call her those other names," I said.

"Er?" The face Jinau made was that of someone told they were a virgin after having three kids.

"No, he is serious. I read the file. That woman may come back if he disrespects a woman," Joshua added.

"You mean it's possible I am meeting a man who has respect for his elders *and* for women? You may rate prodigy for that reason alone." As Jinau stopped bouncing around, I finally got a look at her. She stood maybe four-eleven, her hair had gone completely white yet she could not have been more than forty years old, with her huge, light-gray eyes and her young face with its dark freckles across the bridge of her nose and cheeks, she looked like a drawing of a half-elf I would have drawn.

"He has a lot of positive attributes. But he does not usually stare like that. Smack your head, boy, your eyes seem to be stuck," Joshua said disapprovingly.

"I got this," she popped me with an open palm right on my forehead. "Better?" Jinau asked.

"Sure," I said, completely caught off guard.

"Okay, so did you tape the conversations?" Jinau asked, switching into business mode, snap.

"Of course," Joshua said as I was starting to shake my head no, and quickly changed it to a nod of yes while I turned my head to him. He was taking off his glasses as he said this. He set them on a projector. On the wall next to us, the governor's office came into focus — the replay of what had happened. Jinau hit the pause button.

"Judas, I want you to review the things you noted during the conversation," Jinau said and she threw the remote to me.

"When Joshua started the explanation, the governor was not breathing." On the screen we could hear Joshua talking, "'*Governor, I have six questions. To each I want a simple 'yes' or 'no.' Do you understand?*'" "The governor finally breathes after he answers."

"*Yes,*" the governor said.

"*Are you currently plotting against The Shop?*" Joshua on the screen asked.

"No," the governor replied. "The corner of his mouth slightly rises," I commented

"*Do you know of anyone who is plotting against The Shop?*" Joshua asked.

"No." "Again the corner of his mouth slightly rises," I said.

"*Are you willingly ignoring any laws The Shop has established?*"

"No," the Governor said. "His mouth opened slightly and his eyebrows rise slightly," again I commented.

"*Do you wish to stay in the position that you currently hold, as an elected position within the government?*" "His eyes both opened a little wider when Joshua asked this," I said, wondering if Jinau was even listening to me.

"*Yes.*"

"*Is there anything that we as Shop agents reporting to Sensenmann, and only Sensenmann, should know?*"

"No." "His eyes looked up and away and then seemed to unfocus for a few seconds."

"*Okay, now I want you to leave the room.*" The video showed The Shop agent leave the room. "I continued to watch the governor—I figured it was more important," I continued my commentary. "While Joshua was telling the agent to leave, the governor was looking at the floor and panting." "*Please open the door, governor.*" Joshua instructed the governor. "After the door closes, his eyebrows pull together," I pointed at the screen. "*Sir, I am going to ask you six questions. To each I want a simple 'yes' or 'no.' Do you understand?*"

"*Yes.*" "He had a partial smile," I said disapprovingly.

"*Are you currently plotting against The Shop?*" Joshua had asked again.

"No." "Blank faced."

"*Do you know of anyone who is plotting against The Shop?*"

"No." "Again blank faced."

"*Are you willingly ignoring any laws The Shop has established?*" "He pulls up the corner of his mouth slightly."

"No."

"*Do you wish to stay in the position that you currently hold, as an elected position within the Government?*"

"Yes." "He pulls up his nose." I said and turned to look at Jinau. She was transfixed by the screen.

"*Is there anything that we, as Shop agents reporting to Sensenmann, and only Sensenmann, should know?*"

"No." "This time he gives a more obvious nose pull-up." The tape stopped and I looked over at Jinau and waited.

"Judas, do you know what any of the observations mean?" Jinau asked.

"I think so. Maybe some of them, but they're just guesses," I answered.

"When he pulled up the corner of his mouth, what did you think that was?" Jinau asked.

"I saw it as contempt," I said.

"Very good. How about when his eyebrows go up and his mouth drops open?" she asked.

"He legitimately looked surprised to me. He did not expect that question," I said.

"Again, correct. How about the eyes getting larger, or when his eyebrows came together?"

"I did not see that combination," I said.

"Correct—you did not. What is your take of each?" Jinau asked.

"I did not really get that one, but based on the conversation I would suppose concern or fear, or both?" I answered a question with one.

"One thing I would say: do not suppose; do not even listen to words except as markers of time," she said. "But yes, in this case you are correct: it was fear. How about when our boy pulls up his nose?"

"Disgust. That one I knew," I said.

"That was very impressive. You got the majority of the facial expressions. Tell me, when his eyes were looking up and away, do you know which way he was looking?" Jinau asked.

"Well."

"Stop. Do you know what you just did?" Jinau asked.

"No," I said

"You did the same as the governor. You looked away and to the right. This is what is known as a 'visual memory recollect,'" she started. "The eyes are a huge part of this. I was glad you had indicated the eye movement in that case, as it was the most obvious. But let's watch the tape again and specifically focus on the eyes." She started the tape and on each question she showed me the eye position of the governor. "Basically, left is lie; right is righteous — that is if the eyes are straight or up; down left is to recall a feeling, smell or taste. Level to the right is the remembering of what someone said; up and to the right is remembering something visual; and lastly, down and to the right would be correlated to a person talking to himself." Jinau paused as the pilot told us we were landing at our second stop.

"How many stops do we have?" I asked.

"Well, we had twenty when we started. Now we have nineteen," Joshua said.

"Okay, Judas, you will be doing exactly what you did last time. I will be here to review your findings. I want you to try to catch the eyes more this time," Jinau instructed.

"I can do that." I went and sat down and thought, *when the hell did we take off?*

"Did you back-up the first visit?" Jinau asked.

"Yes, I did that as soon as I docked it. I love these contraptions that allow playback and backup at once," Joshua said, as he got buckled into his chair and turned to me. "Nothing is going to be any different with this visit from the last. Just remember that you need to say—not a word."

"You got it, chief," I said.

Chapter 6

The car that met the plane was the same car as the first stop. The agent was a duplicate of the agent from the first stop and Joshua and I, well, we were still us. We got in and rode to the governor's office. "Agent, have you had any communication about our visit to the other offices?" Joshua asked. A change—yeah, that made me feel better.

"No, the only communication was from Washington telling me that you would be here today and that I was to escort you and follow whatever orders you gave." The agent showed no emotion, although I did notice his eyes looked to the right and stayed level—an auditory memory. Hey, maybe I got some of this. Gram would call me a charlatan. I smiled. The rest of the ride was as before, silent.

We pulled into a garage that had an elevator in the rear with another guard for The Shop at the door. "IDs please." We showed them and the door opened. I watched as the other agent entered a code into the elevator panel and we headed down.

"Why are we headed down?" Joshua asked.

"The conference room is in the basement," Joshua reached in his jacket and removed his gun.

"Push the override," Joshua said. The agent did. "Take us back to the garage." The codes were entered, the elevator rose, and shortly the door opened. "We will wait here for you to instruct the governor to return to his office as he was instructed." When the guard at the door saw Joshua had his gun out, I noticed a change in his body posture and I immediately pulled my gun on him and gave him a no-no finger. He brought his hands in front of him.

"What exactly is going on?" the guard asked.

"Well, your senior officer on this site has elected to completely ignore a direct order and left himself open to a firing squad," Joshua said with his gun trained on the agent.

"I did what?" the agent asked

"You violated the orders; you were given specific instructions and you do not change orders that come straight from Sensenmann." Joshua was holding his temper—in fact I did not feel any anger from him, yet the agent had a range of fear expressions dancing all over his face. "Now *fix it!*" Joshua raised his voice slightly but, damn, it said a lot.

"I will. I will be right back with you." As he stepped back in the elevator, Joshua lowered his gun, and I followed his lead. About ten minutes later the elevator door opened, and the agent held it for us. "We are set to conduct the meeting as originally laid out." We got on the elevator and took it up to the top floor. The man at the desk was around thirty years old, and he stood and released the doors. We walked in and waited for the doors to shut. As the doors sealed, the governor stood up from behind his desk.

"Who do you th…" Joshua cut him off with a raised finger.

"That will do." Joshua reached into his pocket and removed the list of questions. "Governor, I have six questions. To each I want a simple 'yes' or 'no.' Do you understand?"

"I never meet…" Joshua again held his raised finger to the governor who again fell silent.

"Governor, I have six questions. To each I want a simple 'yes' or 'no.' Do you understand?" Joshua asked again.

"Yes," the governor answered between gritted teeth.

"Are you currently plotting against The Shop?" Joshua asked

"No," the governor replied.

"Do you know of anyone who is plotting against The Shop?" Joshua asked, almost quietly.

"No," the governor answered, still through gritted teeth.

"Are you willingly… ignoring any laws The Shop has established?" Joshua said emphasizing the word 'willingly' this time by pausing after rather than getting louder.

"No," the governor answered.

"Do you wish to stay in the position that you currently hold, as an elected position within the government?" Joshua asked immediately upon the answer of the previous question.

"Yes." This was said almost like a growl.

"Is there anything that we, as Shop agents reporting to Sensenmann, and only Sensenmann, should know?" Joshua asked his last question.

"No," the governor answered.

"Okay, now I want you to leave the room," Joshua said, looking at the other Shop agent. He left and the questions were repeated. As Joshua repeated them, the governor sat at his desk again. He answered the questions. As he answered the last question, the governor stood up from behind the desk.

"Now, you will answer *my* questions…" the governor said, rising from his seat.

"No, sir, I will not—and do not begin to raise your voice to me. I do not think you will like the outcome. Good day," Joshua said in an exasperated voice, and he turned to a door that was still closed, taking three steps toward the door. But when it did not swing open, Joshua turned with his gun in his hand. "Three, two…" Buzz, click, the door opened. "I would suggest you start packing your personal effects." He turned and started to walk out. As I started to follow, a glint caught my eye; a stainless-steel orb encased in an acrylic cube was sailing at Joshua's head. I jumped out, reaching my arm out and tipped the projectile enough to allow it to miss Joshua. The lieutenant governor was not as lucky; the agent who was assigned to this office took the deflected force of the governor's fury across his cheek and nose. *Not cool.* Blood came out instantly, like a tomato being smashed, from his nose. Joshua reached to catch the agent as he fell. I turned and saw the governor had grabbed something out of his desk and was raising it with both hands. I reacted, reaching down to my waist, drawing and firing my gun twice. The governor fell back into his chair and it toppled over. It was then I realized that, when I had jumped to block the orb, I had also spun one hundred eighty degrees and the door was on my right side.

"Oh, my god!" the assistant said, running to the governor. I watched him and did not try to stop him, I looked instead at Joshua. He was bent over, holding his handkerchief over the agent's face. He was mouthing something I could not quite make out. I saw a flash and felt heat as I turned to the assistant who was holding the governor's gun on me. I noticed that the gun was smoking. He was yelling. "You murderer! You killed him!" before I could think, my gun had fired two more times and the assistant was joining the governor on the ground. I put my gun in my holster and fastened it into place.

"Are you okay?" I asked as walked over to Joshua.

"Yes," Joshua said smacking the agent's face to attempt to revive him. It worked; he snapped out of his unconscious state. "Agent, we have had a shooting. You need to establish protocol 'Active Shooter.'" He stood up and walked over to me. "And get a medic up here."

"I'm fine," the agent said, standing up. Then he looked across the room at the two dead bodies. "Holy shit."

"Not for you, or for them—the medic is for my partner. He was shot," Joshua said. I looked at him, wondering which of the dead guys his partner was. "Judas, I need you to double click." Ah, the joy of high-tech testicles. I gained focus. "Good. Now take off your jacket and let's get a look at this."

"Glad it wasn't my throwing arm," I said, forgetting I was not really going to be throwing anymore. It made me sad thinking about Gram, Kat and me throwing in the backyard, and then my mind went to the night on the beach when I proposed to Kat, and I remembered for the first time her saying that she could not wait to spend the rest of her life with me and that I was the only one who would always be there to protect her. I took control again; the medicines in my system were causing me to focus deeply on whatever thought popped into my head. "Joshua," I said as I took my new jacket off. The pain shot through me. I gave my pain suppression a test, two long pulls. "We need to tell Strandtov that his focus medicine has an odd side effect."

"I will add it to the report. The bullet is in there pretty good. Glad you remembered the pain suppression," he said as he smiled at my apparently stoned face. "Shirt off too, young *ma'un*." Joshua had his 'everything is going to be all right' voice on.

"Joshua, this one did not go at all like the last one," I said.

"No, it did not." As he said that, I pulled my shirt off my left hand and he grabbed both shirt and hand. "Christ, Judas, what happened here?" I looked down at my hand, seeing the skin laid open.

"That is pretty gross. Must have been that cube he threw at you," I said. "The one that hit him." I started to point my left hand but Joshua was holding it.

"This is also going to need attention." Joshua looked around for the agent, who held up two fingers and tapped his watch. "So let's see if this secretary has …"

"Assistant," the agent said.

"Really, I do not think he minds being called what he really is now. Anyway, let's see if he has a first-aid kit in his desk." I followed Joshua out to the entry area. I saw the cube and walked to it, and then remembered that it was evidence. "Do not touch…"

"I understand it's evidence," I snapped, then realized I'd snapped. "I am so sorry. I didn't mean to give you lip."

"I think I can let it go this time." Joshua was smiling. "Come over here and sit down. He did have a first-aid kit in his desk." I walked over. "The kit has a sealable biohazard bag." He walked over, and with his hands in the rubber gloves he got from the first-aid kit, he carefully grabbed the corners and placed the cube in the bag and sealed it. "Well, we are certain that this is safe now," he mostly said to himself as he walked back to me. "All right, you need to stop moving around. I need to get this bleeding under control since the medical group seems to be taking forever, and I really do not want to deal with losing my partner or any of his limbs so soon," Joshua said as he flattened my hand palm-side up on a pile of paper towels.

"That is very touching; you're going to have to tone it down or I am going to cry," I said, while Joshua sat down next to me and started cleaning the cut on my hand. He was much more concerned about my hand. *Not cool.* My shoulder had been shot, but he had no concern about it. Man, my hand must be… "Ouch—what the hell are you doing?" I screamed.

"Cleaning this up. You need to take two long pulls and shut up," Joshua said. I did, and I lost the pain.

"That is…" I started.

"'Shut up' was the second part of that," Joshua chided.

"Oh. I remember that." I was feeling a tad loopy.

"I do not even know if they are going to be able to stitch this, it's pretty bad," Joshua said with concern. "Where are those damn medics?"

"They are in the elevator," the agent said from the other room.

"Thanks," Joshua said back to him. "Judas, you can't say anything about the high-tech testicles—do you understand?"

"You got it, sir, er, Joshua," I said.

"Good. Just say I gave you an injection, if they ask." Just then, the elevator opened. "Over here."

"Sir, we need to see to the governor," the medic said.

"He is dead. The patient is in here," Joshua said, pointing at me.

"No, sir, we need to investigate this," the second medic said.

"Well, as both of them are dead, and I do not want my partner to lose his hand, let's take a look at his hand." Joshua was trying to keep his composure.

"We do not treat murderers," the first medic said. Wrong thing to say.

"You are right about that. He killed the shit out of that asshole." He slowly drew his gun and slid the action back to verify there was a bullet in the chamber. Then he aimed the gun, flipping on the laser, which put a dot on the hand of the medic. "Do you need that hand?"

"Put that gun down." The other agent had his gun trained on Joshua—big mistake; didn't he realize I had just killed two men for that same thing? Double-click, focus, and my gun came out.

"Do you want to be number three? I will count it for you if you'd like. One, two," the gun went down. "Drop it and kick it over." He did. The blood was now pouring down out of my hand.

"Judas, I want you to show them your badge." As I pulled it out of my pocket, I felt my sight starting to blur. Double-click. I opened it and showed them. "Now, are you turning down aid to one of Sensenmann's hand-selected men? There are only six of us, and if this one loses his hand because of you I believe your death will not even be questioned—you losing a hand, hell that would be justice." The medic looked at my badge and then they started looking at my hand.

"I could not have known you were agents. I thought you were assassins," he said as he started to look at my hand. "Oh, my, this is not great, guys."

"No shit," Joshua said.

"Holy shot—he's shit too," the medic obviously was not used to this type of thing happening.

"I know. Let's deal with the hand first or there will be real damage." They continued following Joshua's orders. I think this may be because they did not think they could actually save my hand, and at least if they followed the orders of the senior agent, maybe the retribution would be less.

"We need to get him to the hospital; two of the tendons are cut completely. It is going to take a surgeon to fix it at this point," the medic said.

"I want to fly back to our base. What can we do to stabilize it?" Joshua asked.

"Sir, the tendons will continue to pull away from each other, and they will not be able to be fixed at all." The medic finally seemed to give a shit.

"I understand and so does he. The ambulance is going to take us to the plane. Let's go." As we rushed out of the building, Joshua was on the phone. I overheard him saying, "Get ready to take off". We jumped in the ambulance and the driver headed to the airport entrance. They did whatever they could to stop the bleeding in my hand, and bandaged my shoulder. When the ambulance arrived at the airport, I saw Jinau outside the plane, a look of concern on her face.

"My god, Joshua, what happened? This was supposed to be a simple in-and-out questioning," Jinau said more as a statement than a question.

"I can't begin to understand either. I will fill you in on what happened when we take off. For now let's get all loaded in," Joshua said. I saw him remove his blood-covered shirt and start changing, as he was facing the table that had his suitcase on it. I remember thinking, that old bastard is built very well. I looked over at Jinau who was also staring at Joshua's butt, naughty girl. Just then, Joshua turned around.

"Holy shit," I said out loud. When he had turned around, not only did the six-pack abs throw me off, but the huge tattoo across his chest blew my mind. "Come here — let me see that ink."

"I remember when you got that tattoo," Jinau said.

"No you don't," Joshua said.

"Come here," I said again. He walked over so that I could see it.

"You need to hold off on the pain meds, you're stoned," he said as he stood there. On his chest was Atlas, having thrown the world off his shoulders. The earth was cracked and magma flowed out like blood, and Atlas with his shoulders dripping blood was flipping the bird to the broken earth. Under the tattoo there were four letters, W I J G.

"What is WIJG? A radio station from the old days?" I laughed.

"Can't say — copyright issue..." he turned to Jinau. "Okay, smarty, when did I get it?"

"Sometime after you read that book and it changed your perspective," Jinau said.

"Well, duh... you made it sound like you actually remembered the day," he said.

"I do. It was the day that Ronald Reagan died. I was in the Philippines on assignment and you were in Denmark," she replied and thumbed her nose at him.

"Damn, you are crazy ripped for an old bastard," I said.

"You," he said, looking at her, "are right. I am impressed." Then he looked at me, "I work at it," Joshua said, buttoning his shirt.

"Shows," I said. "How long did that tattoo take?"

"About twenty-four hours, but he did it in three sittings because the muscle details were so crazy he wanted it to be perfect," Joshua said in a remembering kind of way.

"But I only saw it that one time, before today," Jinau said, sounding a bit disappointed.

"Not in front of the children," I said. "Especially the injured, bleeding children," sufficiently throwing water on the fire — maybe.

Chapter 7

The plane trip was rather quick to me, listening to him explain the situation and watching her reaction, seeing her grow as old as the color of her hair under the stress of what she had just learned.

"So he killed them both," I heard her saying.

"He did it real well, too. It was a clean shoot, but it's going to end up a big, fat hairy deal," Joshua was saying, while I attempted to stay awake. The focus had gone and Joshua had advised me not to use it again. I was starting to get a bit nauseous and the concern that Jinau and Joshua were showing was a tad disconcerting. The pilot came over the PA saying we were on final approach, but that was the last thing I remember.

"Judas, it's time to wake up. We patched you up and you are going to be just fine." I looked into the eyes of the one-armed doctor—what was his name? I couldn't remember. It's like a song—do-da-do or something. "Can you hear me? I need you to get your focus."

"Joshua said not to use it any more today," I said.

"Well, I am not sure that you have actually talked to Joshua today; you have been unconscious for about thirty-six hours," Dr. Strandtov said from the other side of my bed, kinda scaring me. "And you can use it as often as you need—there is no side effect." Double-click...

"Very good, I see you are more focused already," Dr. Kadodadeh said. *See, kinda like a song.* "Okay, so tell me, how are you feeling?"

"My head is clearer, but I feel crazy weak, and my hand is tingling," I said. "Does that help? Oh, I needed to tell you, there is a side effect..."

"Joshua told us." Strandtov interrupted me.

"Tingling like you punched a wall, or it fell asleep and is waking up?" Dr. Kadodadeh asked.

"Neither. I got shocked once as a kid, and that is the type of tingle—kinda hurts," I said.

"Oh, for pity's sake, stop whining." I heard Joshua's familiar voice over a PA.

"So they did not let you in this time. Ha ha," I joked.

"Apparently your hand is more sensitive than your testicles. Says a lot for you." Joshua got the upper hand on that exchange. *Not cool.*

"Zing," Dr. Strandtov threw in. "Great—now him for a burn also." He laughed to himself.

"Careful there, Doctor Chuckles, that young *ma'un* is a killer." Joshua gave a little zing back to him. I smiled and nodded my head.

"Oh, he would not hurt me, I am an important man," he smiled.

"He killed a governor." Joshua really did like shaking a bone when he had it.

"That was you?" Dr. Khera, who was over by the computer asked in shock.

"Yes but I wouldn't hurt any of you. I like you. That governor tried to kill Joshua," I said.

"Well then, good job," Dr. Strandtov added.

"So about the electric shock feeling?" I asked

"Well, that is most likely the electrical current we are using to stretch the tendons," Dr. Khera said from her perch across the room, she pushed a few buttons. "Better?"

"Yes, that is much better. Ouch. Oh, wow," I said as she turned it back on.

"It just so happens that you are our guinea pig again, Judas," Dr. Khera said. "We are trying the right frequency and amplitude to allow the tendons to conform to the stretching and the prepping for reattaching."

"Well, I put your first experiment to a good field test, anyway. Did you get good data from them?" I asked.

"Actually the logger really did give us amazing data. We could see exactly when you got shot and everything. It is amazing," Dr. Strandtov offered.

"What did it show?" I asked.

"Well, you show as very calm right up to a minor adrenaline increase, then your pain blocking kicked in on its own, and then your adrenaline kicked into overdrive," Dr. Khera said with her limited excitement." *Not cool.* "Dr. Strandtov was obviously sad that he did not get to report on it."

"Fascinating," a new voice sounded over the speaker. I recognized it to be Sensenmann. "Doctors, I do think this is all interesting. Please tell me the status of his hand."

"Yes, sir," Dr. Kadodadeh said. "After Judas was given your blood…" "

"Sensenmann gave me blood? Why?" I asked.

"He was the only match, and you needed it. As I started to say; in the first hour after his blood count was satisfactory, we had enough length to make a minimal connection. We wanted to see if we could get more. We have had no chance to put this new equipment to the test."

"Have you seen any positive outcome of the testing?" I was actually surprised Sensenmann asked that.

"Yes, actually, but not until we caused a modulating frequency, which surprised us," Dr. Khera said.

"Excellent. So when is it exactly you are going to be putting my agent back together?" Sensenmann asked.

"We are having the operating room prepped. We had to bring him around so that we could explain the procedure," Dr. Khera said.

"Is that the only reason you actually woke him? Because I find that reasoning abhorrent." Sensenmann said with incredulity.

"No, that is not actually why I woke him; I needed to verify that he was stable. I did not wish to use anesthesia on a patient who may accidently slip into a coma due to the pre-surgical issues," Dr. Kadodadeh explained.

"Thank you for the clarification. I need someone to get word to me when I can speak with Judas face to face, no matter what time it may be," Sensenmann stated, and then he was gone. The doctors recognized that there was no answer required.

"Judas, we are going to put you under anesthesia. We will be repairing your flexor tendons in your left hand. The goal is to put it back to an original state. Should this fail, we will once again be performing an experiment on you. Do you understand?" Dr. Khera asked.

"Yes, ma'am, I do understand," I said, as the injection that they put into my IV tube hit me. I relaxed and wondered if my body could float, if I tried real hard. But then I started chasing a puppy into a cloud and the world went out altogether. I woke again and they were wrapping my hand and someone explained that the wrapping forced all the blood out of my hand. I think it hurt, but it could not hurt, I was anesthetized—is that the word? Hmm, I like... hmm... it tickles my brain. "Where did that puppy go?" All went black again.

"We were able to repair three of the four with conventional sutures; the viscoelasticity will have no significant reduction. The problem was with your fourth finger; the sheath damage was so extensive that the tendon could not have slid evenly within the sheath." The voice belonged to Dr. Strandtov. I opened my eyes.

"So what did you do about the sheath?" I asked, and heard other voices. My throat was very dry. I looked around the room and saw Joshua was there, along with Sensenmann.

"Doctor, we asked what you did to correct the problem." It was Sensenmann with his distinctive leader voice.

"We had to use a substitute, and due to Judas's hand size that was not humanly possible without serious concern of the outcome," Dr. Khera ventured.

"Ma'am? Humanly possible?" I inquired.

"An English Bulldog's leg tendon was used," Strandtov said in his overly excited voice. "It was the right size and canine tendons have characteristics that make them uniquely adapted for this requirement." He cocked his head, uniquely looking like a dog's confused look.

"So shall we rename him Bulldog?" Joshua joked.

"Wait, I got it — Dog Leg Left," Sensenmann said and started to laugh. The leader of the country just made a joke at my expense. "So, doctors, when will Judas aka DLL be able to return to full service?"

"This is not an easy recovery; the stimulation of electricity will continue for a week. We will then put a cast on his entire arm, which will remain in place for at least two weeks, and then he will have a traveling cast. That will be required for probably thirty to forty-five days," Dr. Kadodadeh finally spoke up.

"So we have a week before he can return to his class?" Sensenmann asked.

"Yes, that is our best guess," Dr. Khera answered.

"Okay. Doctors, I need you to leave for a few moments..." Sensenmann ordered and the doctors of course followed his request. He then walked right up to the bed. "Judas, you understand what happened with the shooting is going to get a lot of attention. I do not wish to silence this attention; however, I do not want you in the middle of it."

"Yes, sir. What do you need from me?" I asked

"There will be another agent standing trial for it," he said quite simply.

"Trial sir?" I asked

"The public voted that person into office, and we put him in the ground. Now, giving them answers will allow this to pass, whereas hiding it or sweeping it under the rug would be simple enough to do. I want the entire thing to be in everyone's face—and to do that we need a trial," Sensenmann explained.

"So then who will stand trial?" I asked.

"DLL," he said. "It's not for you to worry about, Judas: if I let you burn out over a good shooting, oh, what a sin that would be. I have several hundred agents and only six who I have personally chosen into service. I had a man tell me once, "Every person is given gifts, and the object of life is to discover the gifts and then to utilize those gifts for the betterment of all." Well, I feel that one of my gifts is to be able to see the best in people, and those who have unlimited potential, well, I need to harness that for the country," Sensenmann said looking into my eyes. "And as I said, I have personally picked six, The Four—the selfless, and the Two—the Truth and the Sword. I was not aware that the Truth and the Sword were interchangeable."

"Sir, while I am greatly honored, I am going to need to think about everything you have said, although it does not feel I have much of a choice," I said.

"Joshua, the boy gets it," Sensenmann said, patting Joshua on the back as he walked out.

"Judas, you do understand that this is extremely, well, unprecedented," Joshua said.

"Yes, I do understand that, but I do not know how I could live with myself if 'DLL' is put to death," I said.

"Judas, you do know that Ursula can digitally produce a punishment—a video that will show any form of capital punishment that we want it to be. DLL may be decapitated, or shot, or it may be just injection. Either way,

DLL will be as fine as he was when he walked in," Joshua said.

"If you say so," I said. "I am just going to sleep for a while now," The world seemed to crash in on me and I elected to eject.

"You do that, but before you go, you have anything you want this bullet made into?" Joshua asked.

"That orb that the governor threw at you, what was that?" I knew I had ignored his question but needed an answer.

"The orb was the original practice remote that was used in a famous movie, encased in acrylic," Joshua said.

"I think I would like the bullet encased in there with it." I do not remember the reason I thought that, but it was my last thought, and I allowed myself to drain into a steady darkness.

"So what would you like for breakfast today, Judas?" The quiet voice asked barely above the machines.

"A dozen egg whites with a pound of turkey, a half cup of Chi seeds and a half cup of hot peppers," I said, not opening my eyes. "Hi, Miss Molly, is it the *early* early morning?" I cracked my eyes open.

"Judas, I have never heard that one before." She giggled, "Well not from someone who just heard my voice after sleeping for almost seventy hours, and pulled that out of their ass."

"Molly?" I said in shock, opening my eyes.

"Boy, I am fifty years old and I take care of three hundred agents and a couple hundred wannabe agents. I think I can curse every now and then," Molly said.

"Yes ma'am, yes, you can." I of course thought of Gram. *Not cool.*

"So do you want salsa added to the eggs while I cook them?" she asked with a smile and a quick wiping of a tear off my cheek.

"Please," I said, as I closed my eyes again.

"Oh no, don't you think of going to sleep if I am making you more food than I should have to cook for ten people," she said as she walked out.

"Not a chance Molly. If I am snoring when you come back, just kick me. Although if I'm drooling, don't waste your time," I said.

"That sounds like a practiced comment," Molly said with a sad smile.

"Yes, ma'am, every Sunday morning, Gram would wake me and make breakfast; when she would leave, she would say, 'Don't you drowse and make me waste this good food on a bad boy.'" I laughed, "And I would say that to her."

"I had a feeling it was something like that." She came over and wiped my cheeks, "Blow it away, you do not want Joshua seeing that." Molly said.

"Oh, my goodness, no ma'am," I said, getting my head together. "It must be my medications."

"I will let you have that one," Molly said as she walked out.

I pushed the call button. "Yes, do you need the doctor?" the person on the other side of the line asked.

"Not really. I could use some paper and pencils though," I said.

"I will have someone bring you a tablet right away," she said.

"Thank you." The line had already gone dead. About fifteen minutes went by, when a woman in an orange pair of scrubs walked in, setting in front of me a portable computer, a tablet. She reached down and plugged it in, stood the tablet on a small pedestal and then started to leave the room. "Thank you," I said. She turned and looked at me oddly.

"You are very welcome," she said in a strange voice.

"I am Judas. I really did not expect this. I just wanted paper and pencils," I said.

"I am Sonya, and we do not use paper down here. We need to control our garbage," she said.

"I guess I should have known that. Thank you for the clarification," I said.

"You are an odd agent," she said.

"I think I will take that as a compliment," I said, smiling.

"Yes, you should. We," she swept her arms and moved her body in such a manner as to take in all the other people, "are invisible to most of the agents."

"Not cool," I heard myself say aloud. "If my Gram was around, she would set them all straight." As I said that, Joshua walked in.

"Good morning, Sonya," Joshua said.

"Ah, he is your partner? Now it is all making sense. You, who have never had a partner, find the one who would treat us like people," Sonya said.

"Sounds like you got the measure of these two boys," Molly said as she entered the room with my breakfast.

"Oh that smells really good," Joshua said.

"You already ate," Molly said as she pushed playfully past Joshua.

"Yeah, but not anything custom," he said.

"Everything I make is custom," she said, smiling. "You just eat the stuff that is available when you walk up."

"True. So, Sonya why were you down here?" Joshua said, turning from Molly to her.

"Your boy wanted some paper and pencils," she said.

"We don't have those things down here," Molly and Joshua both said.

"I know that now," I said. The room at large chortled at my expense.

"He is a good boy, Joshua. You need to do a better job protecting him," Sonya said.

"Hell, I would settle for me not having to protect *him*," I said.

"Yup—if he had not taken up that mantle, I would be in the ground," Joshua said to the women. "He loves me, do not let him fool you," he said as the women both were cooing about how sweet I was. "Yeah, yeah. Now leave the sweet big oaf to eat his breakfast. Sonya, seriously, though, what is all this crap?"

"It's a tablet." She saw his blank face. "It's a computer, and they have been around for like thirty years."

"Oh, I know *what* it is. I am asking *why* it is," Joshua said with a slightly defensive tone.

"Like I said, Judas wanted some paper and pencils," Sonya said

"We don't have those things down here," Molly and Joshua both said.

"I know that now," I said. The room at large chortled at my expense. Again.

"Someone smack the damn writer—he is in a loop," Sonya said, looking irascibly in the direction of the writer.

"I need something to take down my ideas. I am going to be stuck here for quite a while and I have some things I want to have for our next mission," I said.

"Well, okay then, ladies, let's leave him be. And by 'let's' I mean goodbye," Joshua said.

"And I said he was nice," Sonya said as she turned to leave.

"Part-time nice Joshua is a far sight friendlier than the majority of the others," Molly said as they left walking passed Dr. Strandtov.

"So any of these ideas you got bouncing around — something that you want to talk about?" Joshua asked.

"Not just yet. Let's see if I can make it clear first. I am not an electrical engineer nor electronically trained, but I can follow circuits — you know, like what I did with that sight-testing unit," I said.

"Ah, is someone making new gadgets?" Dr. Strandtov asked.

"I'm thinking about it," I said.

"You know I am inventor, I have several patents. I love this stuff. You need to collaborate?" I just really love this doctor's energy. Yeah, I know I said it before, but come on — he's awesome. Admit it.

"I have a feeling that I will be saying yes eventually. Let me get my initial concept down on paper," I said.

"Let's give you a look over first and then we can let you get to it," Dr. Kadodadeh said as he put a stethoscope against my chest, "Need to make sure your lungs are okay. Take a very deep breath and then release it." I did. "Once again please." I did. "They sound good. That food smells good — you going to eat it?"

"If everyone leaves me alone for ten minutes," I said.

"I have seen him eat; he only needs two minutes," Joshua said.

"True," I added. "Can someone roll that tray up here and then y'all bounce."

"Really? You're going to talk like that..." Joshua started.

"You heard me all of you: I am starving, so bounce," I said, they all smiled and walked out — leaving the eggs just out of reach. "Okay, very funny. I did ask for help with the tray first. Please." Joshua poked himself in just enough to push the rolling table over to me. And I finally got to eat my eggs, and they were even better than they smelled. As I finished, I took the tablet out and started to doodle on it.

The drawing function was easy enough to make the overall rough designs. The glasses were a simple design. I managed to pull up the design to Joshua's glasses. This launched another application that showed the electronic side of the camera to storage device. I could use this. I interrupted the signal and brought that into a CPU. I could put a resident program on the CPU to capture a still frame each time the program recognized a change not associated with speaking. I put a "Q: How hard is it to interface with Ursula?"

When I finished drawing these plans up and outlining the program, I added an icon into the lower right of the lenses, to turn on a remote keyboard. The concept here was to allow small stickers on each finger to, after homed, presumably on the 'ASDF' and 'JKL:' keys, transmit the movement of the fingers and the thumbs, being the space bar. The reason to allow text messages between glasses was so that I could communicate with whomever I wanted. I outlined this idea the best I could and listed what I felt it would require to bring this idea to fruition. When I finished the ideas, I lay my head back to try to go ahead and enjoy some solace.

"These are pretty interesting." It was Joshua, sitting in a wheelchair reviewing my plans.

"What happened to letting me finish the designs first?" I asked.

"Well, I figured you would not sleep until you at least got the ideas out of your head into this tablet." He silently patted himself on the back for naming the device in his hand.

"I will not comment on the immense amount of pride you just showed at remembering what that device is called. Oh wait—maybe I will," I said mockingly. Joshua simply turned his head, raised his eyebrow and then, surprisingly, stuck out his tongue. "Too much! Don't you put that thing by my tablet." As I said that, he licked the screen and then burst out laughing. So did I.

"You know, this actually tastes terrible," Joshua said, laughing even louder, as he handed me the tablet back.

"Okay, that is enough making my patient laugh. We do not want him hurting himself," Dr. Khera said.

"I thought laughter was the best medicine," Joshua said through his laughing.

"I would have to believe a doctor did not say that," Dr. Khera said. "So, Judas, tell me, how do you feel after eating solid foods?"

"Well, other than having to use the bathroom, I am doing well," I said.

"You should go ahead and do that," Dr. Khera said.

"Ma'am, I really want to get up and use the toilet. This cast should stop all the movement," I said.

"All right, but you need help getting in and out of bed—do not let me hear that you are doing that alone," she said.

"Yes, ma'am. Joshua, a little help, please." He got up and tried to determine the best way to help me out of the bed. "Dude, just stabilize me," I smiled.

"You either forget how big you are or how old I am," he said.

"We got this," I said as I swung my leg out of the bed, noticing that my leg was bigger around than his waist. "But just be careful. I don't want to hurt your old ass."

"What position did you play? Those legs are like damn tree trunks." I was up and he was holding my right arm as we crossed the room.

"I was the little wimpy quarterback. I got this," I said when we got to the bathroom.

"Well, that makes sense," Joshua said. "I will be right out here if you need any help."

"Just be happy that this cast is not on my right arm because you would be in here doing some dirty work." I looked back at him, making a scrunchy face as he sat back down into the wheelchair. I turned back and closed the door and pulled down my boxers (yes, I wear boxers if I wear any undergarments). This being a one-armed bandit was going to take some getting used to.

"Hey, you drowned in there?" Joshua yelled through the door.

"Oh sorry. I was trying to save you from having to do this wiping thing," I poked back as I opened the door.

"I'm sorry—you seem to think I'm someone who is *that* grateful. I *am* grateful enough to help you out of bed, and even tie up your silly hospital gown, but wiping that big ass of yours, I think I would have rather taken the block to the head," he said as he reached up and tied my gown.

"Yeah, yeah," I said as I started back to the bed, "Hey, Dr. Khera, can I go for a walk?"

"Judas, I would prefer you wait until tomorrow," she said.

"So tomorrow it will be—okay?" I asked.

"I think that tomorrow you are not going to want to but yes, I am fine with you walking the hallways, a bit," Dr. Khera said, as she walked over to the door.

"Thank you, ma'am. Am I allowed to eat again today?" I asked.

"Of course. I can talk to Molly and have her come take care of that," she said as she left.

"You're trying to push yourself too hard; this is going to be a long recovery. Just relax," Joshua said.

"I feel like I have not been able to exercise and I am going to get fat," I said.

"Well, maybe you should cut down some of the food intake until a time when you can work out again. But maybe not," Joshua said.

"Oh, leave the boy alone. What can I get you to eat tonight?" Molly asked.

"Maybe he is right—how about one pound of turkey and a pound of green beans, tossed in a skillet with vinegar," I said.

"Boy, if that is dieting, I have been doing it wrong for quite a while," Molly said as she started to leave.

"Hey what about his distinguished partner?" Joshua asked.

"I figured since you were saying 'no eating until you could work out,' I figured you were sticking to that," Molly said over her shoulder.

"See, again you are missing the crux of what I said— 'until a time when you can work out *again*.' I can *currently* work out so I can eat whatever I want," Joshua said.

"But you don't," Molly answered.

"I did not say anything about actually working out, just being able to," Joshua said.

"You crack me up. What can I get you—and if you say 'the usual' I am spitting on a peanut butter and banana sandwich," Molly said.

"I think what he asked for sounds good. Make me half of that," Joshua said.

"I will be back shortly," Molly said as she disappeared.

"So in regard to these items that you drew on your tablet, I have a few ideas, if you are ready to look at doing this," Joshua said

"Oh, yeah, I am at least ready to talk about them," I said.

"So the big question that you had — how hard is it to tie into Ursula? My glasses have the ability now. So we do not have to tackle that hurdle," Joshua said.

"That's great. So is there an electronic lab where we can get some help on this?" I asked.

"So has Dr. Strandtov been in yet? He really is amazing," Joshua asked.

"I completely forgot he said he wanted to help. No, he has not been in yet," I said.

"Well, let's give him a call," he offered up.

"After we eat," I said.

"Good plan. He did seem to be eye-balling that omelet you had the other day," Joshua added.

"No, Joshua, that was you," Molly said as she walked back in with the food.

"That was impossibly quick," Joshua said.

"It's a damn book — she did not actually cook the stuff," I said.

"Good thing. I am kinda hungry," Joshua added, as the food was placed on the rolling table.

"So do you want me to get hold of Dr. Strandtov when I get back to the kitchen?" Molly asked.

"Thank you, Molly, that would be great," I said.

"Well, I will take off then, how is the food?" she asked.

"Mmrrph," I said.

"Hm MM rr ee," Joshua added.

"It's turkey and green beans... why would it have gravy?" she said incredulously as she started out.

"Well, I would think after this many years you would know I could not eat this..." Joshua stopped as she walked back into the room with a gravy boat. "Ah, you do love me..."

"Is that a tear in your eye, Joshua? Over gravy? You're supposed to be the Sword; swords do not cry — well at least not over gravy," I said.

"I think we could name him the Wailing Sword," Molly poked.

"Really?" I asked.

"I have known this one too long to not know he is more like a rainforest than a desert. But I think that is what makes him who he is and why he can do what he does for all of us. If he ever had an epiphany and determined that what he was playing at was wrong, he would not cry again, least not until it was all set right."

"The word was Raintree, kids," Sensenmann said as he walked into the room.

"Sorry?" both Molly and I inquired as we turned to the new visitor.

"Never mind," Joshua said, quite short. *Not cool.* Molly left the room rather quickly when she saw who was entering.

"I did not mean to break up this little roast of Joshua, but I was hoping to hear more about Judas's recovery plan and these new ideas I have heard about," Sensenmann said.

"You did not interrupt anything, sir. I was expressing how much I like Molly's gravy, and that turned into a couple comments. Anyway, Judas has a couple extremely interesting ideas that will bring our work straight into Ursula. Additionally, the new communication device is something I'm surprised hasn't been invented before," Joshua said.

"So I guess I know what you're going to be doing during your recovery," Sensenmann said.

"I think it will help me get through the few weeks, having a project," I said.

"Weeks?" Sensenmann looked around for a doctor.

"I told Judas he is already pushing himself too hard," Joshua said.

"Well, young man, you need to start thinking more on the long term, and understand that if you are here, studying, inventing and getting better, then we" — air quotes — "are okay with however long it takes to get you back together." He turned and gestured to Joshua to join him outside. They walked out, and I heard his comments very clearly, "The fact that he has mentally bounced back as if nothing happened — this boy is more than you said. You need to help him slow down." The voices stopped and Joshua walked back into the room with his arm around Strandtov.

"Have we got a challenge for you, Dr. Strandtov!" Joshua asked.

"Oh, this is a good one, yes?" Dr. Strandtov said.

"From what I hear, it is *so* good," I said.

"Then we are ready to tinker. Oh, I love this stuff," Strandtov said.

"Well, I am going to leave you two to tilt lances, or whatever it is that you are going to be doing."

"I do not know this term, but sounds a bit — not what I wish to do," Strandtov said.

"Tilting lances — jousting like knights who wish to become tournament champion," I said.

"Tournament champion. Okay, this sound I like. Let's tilt." The last thing I heard from Joshua was his laugh fading down the hall. "So let's connect that tablet to my overhead projector and see what you came up with," Dr. Strandtov said as he took my tablet. After a few keystrokes — *poof!* — my screen was up on the wall. "Here now, you drive this bus. Oh, wait — you guide the horse actually. I do not know what it's called to drive a horse."

"Reining," I said.

"Good, then you rein this stallion," he said smiling.

"Well, the ideas I had were based on the glasses that Joshua was wearing," I said.

"Those are mine. I enjoyed making those," Strandtov added.

"Okay. So this is going to be fun. The video input needs to be rerouted, to allow the program to catch changes in posture, micro-expressions and any extremities, to be noted and cataloged by Ursula," I said.

"I see what you are getting at," Strandtov said.

"This needs to be filtered against the normal speech patterns," I said.

"I think we can determine that and filter it, just a slight change in the program." Dr. Strandtov started making notations in the margin.

"How long have you been doing this?" I asked.

"Judas, how old do you think I am?" he asked me.

"I could not even begin to guess," I said.

"I am old enough to be Joshua's father. I was a microbiologist. My job was to make poisons that would cause illnesses, viruses and even cancers. I never knew the ramifications of what I did. In 1977, I was asked to create one that would be slow-growing, causing no major pain. Judas, do you want to know something? It is not really that hard. The illness would present in such a manner as a hang-nail that just kept coming back. It may present like a toe fungus that comes and goes until it is strong enough to simply kill the music that he sang about freedom for everyone." I watched his face; I saw so much remorse on his face, I knew not to ask for more information, seeing that, even this many years later, he could not discuss it. "After I figured out that my invention had been used to silence an advocate for human rights, I quit, I left my position in the intelligence agency. When I did, I was given a choice: if I simply shut up and moved on, all of my schooling to start a new life would be paid; if not, I was promised by the

President of the United States that if I did not take the offer, my defection would be made very public and I would be handed over to the leaders of my country. Which of course would have meant my death," Strandtov said. "So I simply buried it and went to school for engineering. I have been both an inventor of life-saving items, and a doctor to save people from death." He paused and rubbed his eyes, "I guess, in my previous life, I may have shot the sheriff but I am dedicating my life to saving the deputy."

With that clue, it jumped into my head, the death of a reggae singer, "Are you saying acral lentiginous melanoma is a manmade disease?" I blurted the question out.

"If a disease has no preference — man, woman, or race — it is quite often manmade."

"So diseases are either racist or sexist?" I asked

"Yes, they are. Several are single-race: cystic fibrosis, sickle cell anemia, thalassemia, Tay-Sachs, hereditary hemochromatosis. While others can attack multiple races, including HIV, but in reality if you look at the way HIV converts to AIDS, black men who are diagnosed fare worse than both Hispanic and Caucasian men who are diagnosed," Dr. Strandtov said. "Perhaps we are done tonight, yes?" His eyes had lost their entire normal spark.

"I think that would be fine," I said. He helped me shut down the overhead projector and then he started to leave.

"Judas, I am sorry; I was looking forward to taking this invention on together, and I hope you understand that there is no way I am going to be able to tilt tonight," he said.

"Of course I understand. There is always..." I paused. "I could not even force myself to say it," I said and he started to laugh as he walked out, singing that song. I remember smiling and then getting myself into bed and thinking that Strandtov had gone through his life carrying so much guilt. But when I sat back and thought about it, I saw no reason for him to feel that way. I don't think in reality I would have felt the guilt he did, but that was his penance to pay, not mine. I closed my eyes and drifted off into a slumber that was a haunted sleep, dreaming of diseases that were made by our government. I kept hearing Strandtov's voice saying, "So I simply buried it," and then my words to Joshua, "I am very compartmentalized." I woke feeling less rested than when I had lay down.

Chapter 8

"Good morning, Judas. How did the inventing go?" It was Molly.

"Was going great and then Strandtov got very upset," I said.

"Did you say something to upset him?" Molly asked.

"I don't think so. We were working away and I asked him how long he had been inventing stuff, and then the night was over," I said.

"I am not trying to tell you what to do, but around here everyone has a story. More often than not they are painful memories. I try to stay in the here and now, and let the rest take care of itself."

"Thanks, Molly. That is probably great advice," I said

"Probably?" she said looking at me sideways.

"See, I am a person who people like to talk to; I do not know why..." I started.

"Because you sincerely listen. Not a lot of people do. That along with your puppy eyes," she said and let out a giggle.

"But as people talk to me, I ask questions and..."

"That is different, dear. Follow-up questions are different than direct questions," Molly said.

"See, now that *is* great advice," I said, smiling.

"I must be getting sloppy. I had to work too damn hard at that. Dr. Strandtov will be fine today, you watch."

"I sure hope you're right. He really looked off when he left," I said.

"See, here he comes now. So, breakfast?" Molly asked as she started toward the door.

"I am really starving today. I think fifteen egg whites and two pounds of turkey with mushrooms and jalapenos. Please," I said she put her thumb up and zipped out of the room.

"Good morning, Judas. I got halfway home and remembered I did not help you into your bed. I am so sorry; I got so caught up in some memories that I could not stop the movie that was playing in my head," Doctor Strandtov said as he walked in.

"It was not an issue; I stood next to the bed until I passed out, and then fell into bed." I watched his eyes get big. "I got into bed without any problems—relax. By the way, I am sorry I pushed you into that bad movie review you went through," I said.

"Judas, what I did in my past, I cannot let it go. You did not do anything wrong; I do not want you to worry about it," Strandtov said.

"Doctor, I..." I paused, "do worry. Period. I wish could help you get through your guilt. I know I can't. So I feel terrible that I caused you pain because I pried. I will not do it again, I promise," I said.

"You did not pry; you asked a simple question. I thank you. How about we start again?" Strandtov asked.

"I was contemplating the secondary invention," I said.

"Secondary?" he said.

"I did not quite get a chance to explain this: I was trying to come up with a virtual keyboard that would allow me to take notes, send messages to Joshua's glasses, and multiple other uses," I said.

"Judas, there are multiple virtual keyboards like you are describing," he said.

"Not like this—there will be no laser to break," I said.

"Then how?" Strandtov asked.

"I was thinking one of two ways: a micro-transmitter dot on each finger sending signals to the glasses, or positioning grids on each finger to a main transmitter on the back of the hand. In either case, I would suggest gloves," I said.

"Okay. You are a damn genius, boy," he said.

"Well, that is actually true," Joshua said as he walked through the door.

"Where the heck have you been?" I asked.

"Well, the trial for the agent who killed the governor started today. And I was playing the role of lawyer," Joshua said. "All in all it went very well; the process that started out as a trial ended today by the judge changing the direction to a fact-gathering."

"So no one is going to get into trouble?" I asked.

"Well, I think if Joshua tries to eat this breakfast I made for you he is going to get into trouble," Molly said as she walked in with my food.

"I think that you should let him have a go at it before you give it to me," I said.

"I do not think so—I can recognize a trap when I hear one," Joshua said.

"What kind of trap? I was just going to let you try my food, my lovely spicy food that Molly made for me," I said.

"Spicy food? That is your trap?" Joshua said.

"Joshua, I did not say it was a trap—*you* did," I said as Joshua took up the fork and took a big mouthful of my eggs. After he chewed a couple times, his face began to turn red. "Joshua, are you okay?"

"I just remembered…" he mumbled through the side of his mouth as he ran out of the room. We all looked at each other and laughed.

"Molly, can you roll my breakfast up to me?" She did and I started to eat. "Thanks, Molly, the food is great. The jalapeno juice was a nice touch. Did you pan-sear the salsa?" I asked?

"I did—nice catch. I better get back to the kitchen. Don't be too mean to Joshua when he gets back," Molly said and then she burst out laughing as she left the room.

"Doctor, is there any reason I can't head to class today?" I asked.

"I think taking a walk around campus is one thing," Dr. Kadodadeh said as he entered the room, "but the stress of actual training and what Ursula may put you through emotionally is a definite concern."

"Well, here's my thought: I will stop by the class and see what Andelos is planning for class; I just don't want my classmates to get too far ahead of me," I said.

"There is no concern of that, in reality. But I do understand what you're thinking; I will allow this exchange with Andelos," Dr. Kadodadeh said.

"That is great—thanks," I said as I started kicking my legs out of bed and then realized I did not have any pants on. "Do you think I can get some sweatpants?"

"Of course," the doctor said, pushing a button to make the request. A couple minutes later, Sonya came in with a pair of sweatpants, undergarments, socks and puffy baby-blue slippers. Dr. Kadodadeh looked at the clothing, nodded his head in approval, and left the room.

"You listen to me, little big man," Sonya said. "I do not want you to push yourself too hard. There is no reason for you to put on pants yet." Her tone of concern came through very clearly. I took the clothes she held. I put them on my bed and then turned around, taking her two hands in my giant hand.

"Sonya, thank you. I know that your concern is coming from a good place. I will not put myself in harm's way, not here, and definitely not in those slippers." I looked down into her brown eyes, which were outlined surprisingly audaciously for a day at The Shop in scrubs. I looked around the room and whispered, "Did you have a good time?"

"What?" she asked.

"You were out on the town last night," I said. Letting go of her hand I imitated a dancing move. I watched her closely. "And you were not alone."

"Now you need to hush up there, mister." This time she looked around the room. "You are right. That is insane—how did you know?"

"That is not important. Did you have a good night?" I continued.

"Judas, it was so great. It is so stupid that people can't date here. Please do not turn me in." Sonya, whose eyes were twinkling a little while ago, now had the lines of fear outlining them.

I leaned in a little closer, "They could not torture it out of me—promise." I grabbed my clothes and whispered, "I would change up your mascara." She quickly started to move her hands to her face, which I stopped. "Later." I winked.

"Good call," she said, turning and started to leave, and then turning back to me she smiled, wordlessly having said everything she wanted to.

"Anytime," I said simply and set about getting dressed as she left. The elastic top on the boxers and pants made it possible for me to not have to yell for help. I had no choice but to leave my gown over them, as it was tied over my shoulder and I did not have a shirt to put on anyway. Sliding my feet into my puffy slippers she had brought for me, I started out the door.

"Hold up there, cowboy," Kadodadeh said as he jogged up and pinned a small locket onto me with a button on it. "Push the button if you need anything."

"Shall do. Thanks," I said as I headed to the classroom. I did notice that I was feeling lightheaded. I gave a double-click and gained focus, continuing to the class.

"Judas, what are you doing here?" Andelos said, greeting me at the door.

"Reporting for class," I said.

"Seriously?" Andelos was blown away.

"Technically I am supposed to ask you what you are covering and if you thought it was okay for me to be back," I said sheepishly.

"We are still covering shortcomings of previous administrations. This week we will touch on welfare reform and sequestration," he said. "I do not see any crazy things occurring. I will say this: Ursula is not going to know or care you are hurt; if you are feeling controversial, do not say anything," Andelos added with concern.

"I will censor myself. Thanks," I replied.

"Well then, welcome back." I walked into the room, being the last one present. "Class, you remember Judas, our bullet-riddled agent in training." The class laughed and welcomed me back. "So, as you recall, last week we were discussing the shortcomings of the final few presidents' administrations. This week we will jump into some very interesting topics — welfare reform versions one, two, three, through a million. And then we will finish the week with sequestration." Andelos cleared his voice, drank some water, and then said, "Ursula, you ready to get started or you need a drink?" he smiled.

"You continue to see if I have a sense of humor, even though you know I do not. I can at least recognize the inflection in your voice. Yes, I am ready," Ursula said.

"I would have to say that's better than most people," Andelos said. "So, class, in the early days of welfare, 1935 or so, there was never a need to kick people off it; the human condition of the day caused people to do everything they could to get off the dole." He paused, looking around the room. "I said that pretty harshly — no retorts?" He waited again. "Okay. The largest contribution to the welfare group, staying in the system or becoming systemized" — air quotes — "was that the more kids they had, the more they got; the more they got, the harder coming off welfare became. President Blythe took it on, modeling his policy much like those of some large cities across the United States, determined to force capable people to get off the dole by imposing the need to work for their welfare check. The people were required to work a certain number of hours each week, month, year." Andelos paused again.

"In that regard, the outcry from the people and community leaders accused the government of reinstituting slavery. Does anyone in the class have support for or a statement of deference to that claim?" Ursula added.

I looked around the room and waited for the rest of the group to discuss. I raised my hand and looked at Andelos who was shaking his head at me and trying to signal me to put my hand down. "Oh, for pity's sake," Ursula said. "If you do not call him I will."

"Ursula, if you shock me I may die." There was silence.

"I think I just laughed," Ursula said, "The simple honesty made my program back up a sixteenth of a second. Interesting."

"My answer to your question is that of deference: if a person has to work for what they get, then we are all slaves. As an aside, those who take welfare with the expectation that they should not have to do anything to earn it — or, worse, they propagate to earn more — aren't they in fact holding us, the earners, as the slaves?" I said. No shock.

"Do we have a counterpoint?" I looked around the room. "I will not shock anyone on this one as The Shop has no vested interest in this topic." A hand quickly shot into the air, Sebastian. "Please proceed," Ursula encouraged.

"When people went on welfare, they were not holding anyone hostage; they were simply people down on their luck. Welfare was made to help those who could not help themselves." Sebastian sat up straight; his face looked like someone set a plate of pickled herring and limburger cheese in front of him. "What the hell is that?"

"I am not certain what you are referring to, Sebastian," Andelos said.

"The smell—it's terrible, like nothing I have ever smelt." Sebastian looked like he was going to…

"Do not throw up in here," Andelos yelled, helping Sebastian out of his seat and rushing him out of the class. "Find a bathroom," he said as he closed the door behind him. "Did you do that?" he said, facing Ursula's speaker.

"Of course I did," Ursula said.

"You said you would not do anything if he spoke out," Andelos said in an admonishing voice.

"No—what I said was I would not *shock* anyone. And I did not," Ursula said. *Not cool.* Funny as hell, but definitely *not cool*.

"Well, I had a lot more to cover but that will do it for today."

"There is no reason to stop," Ursula said.

"Sure there is: one of my students is missing the class," Andelos said.

"He will not be returning. He has informed me, between waves of vomiting, that I have won. I was not trying to win anything, Andelos; I am not clear on the exact reason for this comment."

"He felt you were picking on him and trying to drive him out," he replied.

"That is not based in fact; if I were trying to drive him out, I could do much worse things, like making him urinate or defecate his pants, or even ejaculate while sitting in class."

"Well, I am very glad you did not do that," Meglar said, obviously because she sat next to him.

"You are welcome, Meglar. The actions that I took should have served as a dissuading factor based upon the initial psychological profiling I did. His reaction is making me question some things. Andelos, I am going to be going offline. I will be performing some diagnostics," Ursula said and then went silent.

"Okay, let's touch on an even more sensitive subject. The continuing reform of that was signed into a law that allowed states to petition to remove the work requirement. This requirement could be removed only if the state showed they had a plan for a twenty percent increase in welfare exits. Can anyone explain what this means?" Meglar raised her hand. I like this girl's confidence.

"When families come off welfare?" she said.

"That is right; however, what does it have to do with the number of families that are on welfare or how long someone is on welfare, or even the relationship between people coming onto welfare versus the number coming off?" Andelos asked.

"It does not have any relationship to those items. It does not even need to be employment exits," Meglar said. "As a matter of fact, there could be an increase from twenty thousand people on welfare today, with an average of one thousand coming off monthly, and next week there could be one hundred thousand, and as long as they show an increase in welfare exits by twenty percent, so from one thousand to twelve hundred exits, they claim a percent reduction in welfare. Even though the net is an increase in people on welfare by nearly eighty thousand in that example."

"Very good, Meglar. Yes, that was the 2012 version of fuzzy math," Andelos said. "The truth is the TANF or Temporary Aide for Needy Families program that was established in 1996 was an interesting approach to controlling how long people stayed on welfare, and by 2012 it was a widely accepted program, with numbers ranging from the high eighties to high nineties in approval numbers. So why did the Federal Government elect to remove the work requirement, which was the basic tenant of TANF?" Billings raised his hand.

"The premise of your question is not exactly correct; what I think you are looking to know is why did the Federal Government accept the petitions from states to waive the record-keeping side of the Workfare program which was part of the 1996 TANF. My answer to that is that the request was made because the paperwork involved in tracking the work requirements for those on welfare was constraining the state's ability to develop better methods to get people off welfare. The Federal Government may have actually been following the Founding Fathers' wishes. For the record, I am not saying that," Billings said.

"And it is a good thing," Ursula said, surprising everyone by coming back online. The class all turned their heads to Billings. "Actually, Billings, there was a lot of dissidence in both parties during 2012 reform debates, and when the petitions were granted, by presidential decree, and there were many on both sides who cried that laws had been broken. Very good, Billings."

"And with that, today's class is at an end," Andelos said. Everyone got up and started to leave. Billings and Meglar stayed around to talk to me.

"Dude, I thought for certain, when I heard Ursula on the PA, you were going be shitting yourself for sure," I said.

"I did too," Billings said.

"And me," both Meglar and Andelos said.

"It was close," Ursula said. We all laughed.

"I think you are developing a sense of humor," Andelos said with affection to Ursula.

Chapter 9

Joshua, Jinau and I ate dinner together in my room. We talked about the interviews they had done that day. It was funny that I was jealous that they were out on my mission, and listening to them laugh about a joke I didn't get, I felt left out. I watched the video and noticed very little facial and body-posture reactions that caused me to question the answers that they gave. When I watched it a second time, I saw a couple discrepancies in the words compared to their postures. "Jinau, I am seeing something that is odd," I said.

"Go ahead," Jinau said, looking very interested.

"The man is standing with his shoulders back and chest out. It is reminiscent of the alligator puffing up its backside when threatened. Am I seeing that correctly?" I asked.

"I saw the same thing," she said.

"But the speaker's posture doesn't extend to his face, vocal patterns or to his words," I stated.

"Two things we need to be conscious of: first, he is very well-trained in public life; the shoulders probably would not have shown up nine times out of ten," Jinau said.

"And second?" Joshua asked.

"These signs, gestures, postures and expressions, they are not admissions of guilt. They are something for us to take notice of—we are humans and humans do these things—but if you see them, it should make you watch deeper for more," Jinau said.

"That is an excellent point. One of my coaches, er, well um, you understand, he crossed his arms instead of letting them fall to his side, simply because it hurt him to allow his shoulders to hang down. He looked like he was posturing aggression but he was typically the nicest guy you could meet," I said.

"Exactly, Judas—and if you didn't know that, you may get bowed up at him thinking he was being aggressive. Very good point," Jinau said.

"All in all, I don't think he is lying; I think he hates the shit out of you guys," I said.

"If only you would have been there, he would have had a completely different posture," Joshua said.

"I would say so—a horizontal posture," Jinau added.

"Ouch," Dr. Strandtov said as he joined us. "Okay, enough teasing my patient, let's be off with you."

"Good night. We will be in town tomorrow; we have meetings with Sensenmann, and he wants us to get involved in finding the hacker," Joshua said.

"He is still getting hacked?" I asked.

"Yes. This person must have a serious death wish. That is all I can say," Joshua said.

"Well, good night," Jinau whispered as she bent down to give me a hug. "Get some sleep."

"Not tonight—the boy has some explanation of parts of his experiments," Strandtov said.

"I need my tablet. Can you get it out of the locker please?" I said to Joshua.

"Sure I can," he said as I heard him try to open the locker. "It's locked. What is the word code?"

"It's 'For my children,' no spaces," I said.

"*What?*" Joshua asked in a wtf voice.

"Well, they said pick something no one could guess," I said

"Okay, that is a password that no one would guess for you my friend. You really do compartmentalize a little too well," Joshua said. He retrieved my stuff and brought it to me.

"Thanks. Good night, guys," I said. As I looked up at him, reaching out for the tablet, I noticed his eyes were shiny like he was fighting back tears. He patted my shoulder, nodding his head.

"Too well," he said, walking out of the room wiping his eyes.

"What the hell was wrong with him?" Jinau asked as she watched him walking out.

"Judas here had an accident, which is how he joined us. He has a shiny new pair of testicles," Strandtov said.

"And?" Jinau asked and then it dawned on her. "Oh, Judas, oh." Then, as if the recognition of what I had said my password was came into full meaning. "Oh, Judas, good night," she said I thought I saw her wiping her eyes as well.

"So that was interesting," I said.

"You do understand that their reaction would be considered valid—they have feelings for you," Strandtov said.

"But what is the difference? They don't have any kids," I asked.

"There is a huge difference: they chose this life—your life was stripped away and this life hit you when you were down. It is not right when young people in love have their life stripped away. We all feel it; because we see how you are and it only lets us know how much of the world was open to you. The way you are handling it is kinda scary. I hate to see it," Strandtov said, placing a hand on my shoulder.

"I do understand that, but when I see Joshua and Jinau together, I wonder why don't they leave this place and celebrate the life they have left? I know I am not going to have that again," I said.

"There is really no way that could happen. Internal relationships are not allowed and they are strictly policed, and those who violate it, well, they have serious time to consider their actions when they are sitting in opposite ends of the world from each other," he said.

"Enough girl talk. Let's talk about the questions you had," I said as I tried connecting to the overhead projector. "Could you turn on that thing so I don't feel so stupid?"

"Of course," he said, trying not to laugh. I connected and projected the glasses on the screen. "Okay, so here are the questions I had. How did you propose to pull up the applications?"

"I thought in the same way Joshua does now: his eyes direct the cursor of sorts. And looking acts like the click of a mouse," I said.

"Yes I agree. My concern, however, is as we start adding all these applications to the glasses, your display may get crowded and you may inadvertently launch an application," Strandtov said.

"True. What if we added a button on the frame to activate the cursor?" I suggested.

"That is an easy solution. Next question: do we want the captured image to show on the glasses?" he asked.

"I think that may be confusing. Could we have a specific list of captured gestures that would appear on your 'heads up' display?" I said.

"That is another easy solution. I like the way your mind works — very Ockham's Razor-esque," Strandtov said.

"So then I am like a premise which states that among competing hypotheses, the hypothesis with the fewest assumptions should be selected," I said, as pompously as I could muster.

"Actually I was going for the simplest answer is usually the right one." He laughed. "All right — now, about the keyboard; do you want the words to show on your display always? Or did you want them to vanish?"

"I like the scrolling-away affect. I think messages would need to be limited to a certain number of characters, creating a sort of 'page down' function. Same with replies," I said.

"Last question: should we make gloves that would store the transmitters?"

"I would say as a model, yes, but in the long run it would be great if we had an opaque cover on the fingernails that would hold the transmitter," I said.

"So it would simply look like fingernails?" Strandtov asked.

"That is what I pictured — or perhaps it would look like the white half-circle on your nail," I said.

"Oh, the lunula. So you would simply have a false lunula. I like that answer. Let's target that for the trial, I didn't like the glove idea. Agents with gloves are kind of a cliché," Dr. Strandtov said with a wink. "I think I have enough information to take these ideas forward if you are okay with that."

"I think it sounds exciting," I said.

"Okay, let's take a quick peek at that arm," Dr. Strandtov said.

"I know that everyone was freaked about my hand but I am still in shock that I actually got shot," I said.

"Well, speaking as your doctor, your gunshot wound would have been considered far worse on a person less substantial in size than you. As your shoulder is so large, it looked like a small wound, which mistakenly led those treating you to not worry about it. The stabilizing of your arm due to your hand allowed the damage to be lessened," he said.

"So it was actually bad?" I asked.

"It could have been. As it was, not so much. But speaking as a person who has also been shot, it is strange to have a part of your body penetrated by a projectile," Strandtov said.

"Look, I know I said I would not ask about your past, but that was a type of opening I cannot ignore," I said.

"Well, I was shot during my attempt to defect from my homeland the first time, and on my second, and again on my third attempt. But the fourth time I made it without any interaction with officials or their bullets. The first time I got shot was in the same place you were," Dr. Strandtov said. He pulled up his sleeve, showing a nasty scar.

"I will let you end it at that. I didn't mean to pry," I said.

"As you said, I left quite an opening. You know, it is funny; my scar looks so big and yours so small—it is an optical illusion. You have huge arms and me not so much." He put his hand almost around his entire bicep, and then showed he couldn't get his hand around one side of my arm and he laughed. "Good night, Judas. Would you like help from an old man with tiny arms, getting into bed?" Strandtov asked.

"I am going to walk over and see if Molly is still around or if there is any food I can pilfer," I said, smiling at his self-deprecation.

"I will walk with you then," he said.

"If you wish, but it's not necessary." He did join me and we walked down to find Molly preparing the sweet rolls for the morning.

"Well, I will leave you with Molly. Good night," Strandtov said.

"Good night, my friend." I started to turn to Molly but I caught a hesitation in his exit, followed by a smile, and then he seemed to walk away into his own memories.

"Judas? Well, Li'l Sexy, what brings you around my kitchen tonight?" she said.

"Li'l?" I inquired. "What is it with you and Andelos and 'Li'l?"

"Aigh, Li'l Sexy. It's a pet name—you don't like it?"

"Molly, have you been, well, drinking?" I asked.

"Gee, I give you bad nickname and I am a drunk! Okay, how about Pan's Tail?"

"Are you calling me a goat's ass? Okay, I like Li'l Sexy much more than Pan's Tail. What's up with you if you haven't been grabbing a nip of the cooking sherry?"

"I didn't say I wasn't drunk; I deflected your question with a defensive objection. You should have caught that—you're a tier-four agent now," Molly said. Her words really were a bit slurred.

"No, ma'am, I am only a three. But no one is supposed to know that I am a three," I said, and noticed her smile; it was crooked, endearing. "What do you know?" I asked.

"Sensenmann was telling Joshua that he was giving you the opportunity to move up," Molly said.

"Interesting. Why?" I asked.

"Well, as I understand it, you have a knack for everything, and the ability to diagnose a situation correctly nearly instantly," Molly said.

"Whoa—I am amazing," I said. "What can I steal from the kitchen? Amazing me is really hungry."

"Well, if you weren't my favorite agent, I would tell you to wait until morning." She winked. "Let's go see what we have."

"Yeah! And if I need to be Pan's Tail…"

"Stop it. I was joking about that and the Li'l Sexy name!" Molly said.

"Oh, come on, I like that one. I have not been called Li'l since Andelos welcomed me into his class, back when I had two hands," I said.

"I was being ironic. Did you want a sandwich? I did buy licorice, and cranberry juice," Molly said.

"Do you have avocados?" I asked.

"We do. Actually my fresh guacamole is really good."

"Awesome. Can I get a turkey, bacon and guacamole sandwich on a hard roll?" I asked.

"You are so specific on what you order, it is crazy. Yes, I can make that and bring it to you. Do you want some licorice?" Molly asked. Looking at my face and seeing the huge smile, she simply tossed the bag on the counter. I promptly put it into the elastic band on my sweatpants. "Well, that is worse than licking all the cookies. I am guessing you didn't want to share those," Molly said. "I will bring you a glass of cran…"

"Jug?" I said.

"Are you high? You seem to have the munchies — should I order a drug test?" Molly teased.

"I think you should, but give me the jug of cranberry juice and I will head back to my room and enjoy the solace of my buzz dying." I winked as she handed me the full container of cranberry juice.

"I sure hope these late-night raids don't go on any night when I am not here," Molly said.

"Molly, would I do that? By the way, why *are* you here?" I asked.

"Every Sunday morning I have fresh hot sticky buns…" she started.

"Does that happen because of the alcohol?" I poked. She turned slowly to face me.

"As a matter of fact, not since I turned twenty-five," Molly said, raising an eyebrow.

"Oh, so last year?" I said.

"Fine — Pan's Tail it is. Cinnamon rolls… I make them on Friday night so the yeast has time to rise," she said.

"Makes sense. That's how Gram used to do it. But she only let the yeast rise a few hours," I said.

"I have found that by putting the buns in my giant refrigerator and allowing them to rise for nearly thirty hours, the buns are perfect," she said.

"Wow, you take this stuff serious," I said.

"Oh, who am I kidding? I don't have time on Saturday night to make all these buns," she smiled. "I play cards with Cookie and Sonya on Saturday night. All right, you get to bed. I will get this sandwich order in and Cookie will knock it out a.s.a.p.," Molly said, shooing me away from the kitchen.

"Thanks, Molly—and tell Cookie thanks as well," I said as I started toward my room. I got back and turned off the overhead projector. As I started to shut down my tablet, I noticed that I was on Strandtov's home directory. *Not cool.* I shut down the file manager application, launching a movie viewer and looking for some old movies that I may have watched with Gram while she made sticky buns. I guess I was feeling kind of nostalgic. Odd, that is not like me. I opened a word processing program and started typing a journal one-handed, then stopped, took out a licorice, whispering to myself, "Mmm, writer food," and began by summarizing the weeks that had led up to this point, of course leaving out the Article Eighty-Seven stuff. Next, I started a new file called "Why The Shop is needed." About that time, Molly came in with my sandwich. "Oh, boy, that smells good."

"I brought some hot sauce and some dry mustard for you to try on it." She left the sandwich. "I have about three hundred more cinnamon buns to make," Molly said and started to leave.

"Thanks again," I said.

"Judas," she said, turning to face me as she stood in the door. "I know this is not fair to others but I feel you are different." She took a breath. "You have three challenges that you will be facing. The first could come at any time now. Ursula will issue this challenge. I do not know what it is, as it changes for each person. The second will be given by Sensenmann; he will assign you a project to complete. The last is Gypsy; her training is very specific. Take it seriously — it may save your life someday. I was not here, and didn't tell you," Molly said and left just as quickly. I had a very hard time single-hand-eating that wonderful sandwich. I decided it was time to switch to salads until I had a second hand.

Chapter 10

The next few weeks brought new eye-opening class discussions, and while I had understood and agreed with the view The Shop took on many of the topics, what we did not discuss was the human psyche. How were the people in America during the second decade of the twenty-first century changing from their predecessors? Did the diminishing progress of freedom lead us into a second Dark Age? Were the people's imaginations restricted as they were forced to rely on the government for help and subsidies? The more I studied, the more I began seeing that those who produced things were being sued — which resulted in a reduction in the number of companies to hire people, and a sense of importance to the companies that remained. This new swagger allowed them to declare, "For us to have our business in your state or city, we will not be paying income or property taxes." The additional tax burden was then forced upon the working man, causing these tax-paying citizens to become race- and class-centric more so than ever before. The Nationalists hated those who were coming to America to steal jobs, steal schooling opportunities, hating each other for their skin color differently than in the past. Now the goal of the hate was to allow equality for all, knowing that there was no way the other guy was actually going to understand what each was going through. My reading showed that the government was at the center of every problem that was occurring in the country. What I couldn't get from my reading was an understanding of *why*. What possible good could come of causing your countrymen to live in discord? And then one night it hit me: they were doing it to stay in power. They were doing it to be important.

My arm during this time was getting better; they took off the bandages and started my physical therapy. If women like scars, I was turning into a real chick magnet. I really don't like scars—now I am rethinking the gloves for my wireless keyboard idea. When this started, the pain that I felt in my shoulder was a surprise, especially since everyone (less Strandtov) had ignored the gunshot wound over the hand injury. The physical therapy really sucked, and the doctors said the full recovery was based on how hard I worked at it, which would depend on my pain tolerance. My hand, by comparison, just didn't work and the recovery for ligament damage was a mind-over-matter battle trying to make a group of spare parts work. Shit, I couldn't teach my dog to sit when I was a kid—how can I teach one to bend? I am not sure which was worse—the physical pain and agony of the shoulder physical therapy or the mind-numbing marathon physical therapy sessions for the hand.

"Young *ma'un*, we are going to be meeting with Sensenmann today," the voice pulled me out of reverie.

"Wait—what?" I said. "I am not ready to go back on the road yet," I don't know why I said that.

"Relax, we are not going on the road," Joshua said.

"Sorry, I don't even know why I said that," I said, a bit embarrassed.

"I do. The challenge of getting past the wounds you sustained is more than just the physical side. You will be starting some other training today. This is a surprise—as the rest of Sensenmann's update to you will be," Joshua said.

"When do we meet?" I asked.

"He wishes to break bread with us this morning," Joshua said, "so get dressed." I got up and went to my closet and drew out my suit. "I would not advise that, in case he wants the training to start immediately," Joshua said. So I drew out khakis and a collared golf shirt. "That is a good choice." I walked into the bathroom and changed. We walked out of the room and right up to the elevator that I knew took us to Sensenmann's office. When the door opened, Deces stood in the elevator with another, the last, of The Four.

"Good morning, Joshua, and good morning, Judas," he gave a slight head movement toward his comrade. "This is Hungersnot," the man was third in height but thinnest of all The Four; his face was almost sunken.

"I have thanked each of the others and to you I also say thank you for what you have committed to do." He said nothing, but reached his hand out. His eyes softened only slightly as we shook, yet as we broke, the cold dead eyes returned. The elevator doors opened and I looked into the room. Guerra and Sampar were at the other doors, and there at the table was Sensenmann.

"Good morning, gentlemen. I am pleased that you were able to accept my invitation. Please, sit," he indicated the two chairs, I walked to the far side of the table. As I did, I gave Guerra a slight nod of my head; he of course did not move nor did his eyes lose focus as they monitored Sensenmann's hands. It appeared as if his eyes moved in rhythm with Sensenmann's gestures. I reached the seat and waited until Joshua sat, then I did as well. "Judas, do you have any idea why you are here?" he looked intently at me.

"I have some idea," I said.

"You do?" Sensenmann said incredulously.

"Well, I believe you want to discuss my rank in The Shop," I said.

"That is partially correct," he looked interested and then looked at Joshua.

"Not me, sir," Joshua said under the scrutiny of Sensenmann's gaze.

"It matters not," Sensenmann said, showing his truth.

"Sir, when did you start wearing glasses?" I asked.

"Can't sneak anything by you," Sensenmann said, removing the glasses. "These glasses are amazing," he said as he slid them to me. "These are of your mind I understand," I greedily picked them up and placed them on my face. I looked at Sensenmann. "My name is Sensenmann and I am the leader of The Shop." He paused, "Nothing? Good. My name is Daravan. I am the leader of Local two thirty-three," the glasses picked three specific images and flashed them on the screen. I smiled. "It worked. Very nice."

"Have you had many chances to use them? How do they work?" I said excitedly.

"Interestingly enough, you two are the first that I have used them on where it showed no lying. As I would expect of you, but I expected more of others," Sensenmann said.

"If I may, sir," I said.

"Please feel free to speak as you will," he said. I noticed Joshua was enjoying this.

"As Jinau counseled me when I started this, indications of lies are not proof of guilt, just as the lack of indicators is not necessarily proof of innocence," I said.

"I appreciate the piece of advice. So are you saying you and Joshua were lying?" he said, hesitating before his face broke into a large grin. "I have to say this is an extremely impressive invention, Judas," Sensenmann said.

"Thank you very much," I replied, feeling a bit full of myself I must admit. As I reached up to take them off I felt an inlaid button on both sides. Wondering if the second button was just another to activate the heads up display, I pushed it. Instantly everything in the room was gone and I could see the display as clear as a computer monitor.

"What the heck just happened?" Sensenmann asked. I pressed the button again and I could see through the glasses again.

"Strandtov must have added a function for making it easier to review things while wearing the glasses." I said.

"I love how you give credit where credit is due." Sensenmann stated.

"Thank you sir, Gram made that a point never take credit for what isn't yours." I said as I removed the glasses to see what it looked like to others when pressing the button. It appeared that the glasses frosted over, just as the privacy glass in expensive offices did when electricity was applied.

"As I understand it, there is a bit of a challenge with the keyboard; the small positioning transmitter battery is too weak to transmit to the glasses," he stated while I was looking at the frosted glasses.

"We could add a repeater to a watch, then it wouldn't have to go as far," I said cutting him off.

"That is amazing. Does your mind always work so quickly to solve problems?" Sensenmann marveled.

"If I hear a problem, I am instantly thinking about it. Gram always said there wasn't a problem I didn't have a solution for," I said.

"The thing that I find amazing," Joshua added, "is his adaptability; when his first idea doesn't work he can apply his solution to the new problem and adapt his initial solution, almost instantly."

"That is what Strandtov said as well," Sensenmann added. "All in all I have continued to be impressed with your devotion and drive, your innovation and successes. I am going to be moving you up to a Level Four..."

"Thank you, sir," I said, interrupting in my excitement.

"Slow down—you may not wish to thank me. Of those who have been promoted to Level Four, only ten percent stay there." He waited. "That's better. It is a very challenging rank in our organization. The vast majority of our people will stay Level Three for their entire career. The training will start immediately. But first let's have some breakfast," Sensenmann said as he pushed a button. The elevator opened and Deces and Hungersnot stepped into it. "They will be back with Molly in a moment. Tell me, Judas, do you remember when the purchasing of over-the-counter prescriptions was made illegal?"

"I believe it was made illegal by the appointed President Blythe, the beginning of her second year," I said.

"That is correct. Do you know why?" Sensenmann asked.

"I believe it was as a result of the aquatic flu that came about following the accidental overflow of several million gallons of waste during hurricane Sandy. The initial concerns for the waste and its containment went unanswered and all the experts felt that there was no cause for alarm, but the algae in the Hudson River mutated and over the next few years continued to mutate. This mutation in their food caused several types of fish to begin a slight change which brought about a variation to the avian and swine flus; they referred to it as aquatic flu. The Center for Disease Control and Prevention was all over it, and they ordered the nation's flu vaccines to fight what they classified the most deadly flu of all time. The first group of vaccinations went to the elderly and the sick, per orders..." I explained, pausing to take a drink as the elevator opened.

"Please continue," Sensenmann said, and then noticed I was looking at Molly walking toward us. "Go ahead and order first, and then continue. Molly is what I would consider our 'inner circle.'"

"Well, aren't you sweet," Molly said, mussing his hair. "What can we get you today, Joshua?"

"I will have exactly half the size order of whatever Judas has you make for him," Joshua said.

"Seriously?" Sensenmann said.

"He orders the best food. No matter what I think I am in the mood for, I steal some of his," Joshua said.

"But half?" he replied

"He eats a lot," Molly said.

"So do I," Sensenmann proclaimed.

"He eats more than Deces," Molly said, deflating him.

"Oh, well, give me three quarters of whatever Judas orders," Sensenmann said.

"Okay, then, Li'l Sexy, it's on you," she said.

"I will have an egg," I said, deadpan.

"Okay, that makes one egg for you, half for you and three-quarters an egg for you. Got it." Molly winked and walked out. Everyone laughed until the elevator closed.

"I hope she is coming back," Joshua said. "I am quite hungry."

"So, the vaccine was to go to the elderly and the sick — go on," Sensenmann said.

"As it ended up, the plant for the egg incubation for the vaccine was sabotaged by a group that identified themselves as Aquae Mortem Fieri. The vaccines were filled with HIV. As a precaution to the mass spreading of the virus, the Interstate Health Awareness Act Document was passed, which forced all people to get tested for HIV. Additionally, all highways leading out of a state had verification stands put up; anyone crossing the state line was required to have the IHAAD paper. Shortly thereafter, it was reported that there were several similar acts of sabotage. This caused Congress to pull all over-the-counter medications." I completed the story as the elevator opened with the serving cart being pushed by Molly.

"So, breakfast is served," Molly said. "First we have the half egg, followed by the three-quarter egg, and lastly one full egg," she said, setting covered plates down in front of each of us, "Please enjoy the food."

"Thanks, Molly," we all said together, removing the covers.

"What we really have is egg whites with turkey, broccoli and pepper jack cheese, cooked with jalapeno juice instead of milk in the eggs. On the side you have salsa and minced jalapenos, in case you want a little extra fire." Molly smiled and then placed milk and cranberry juice on the table and then left again.

"Well I am guessing you have a standing order?" Sensenmann said.

"Pretty much the only variation is the amount of turkey," I said.

"Bon appétit," Sensenmann said as he took his first bite. "Damn, that is good, Judas."

"I told you—the boy picks out some amazing food," Joshua added.

"Nice and spicy too. Tell me what the real reason was for the ban on over-the-counter medications," Sensenmann asked.

"It seemed to me it was a control move to slow down all the end-of-the-worlders, the doomsday preppers," I said.

"Once again—right in one," Sensenmann said. "So tell me this: should they be legal, should the ban be removed?"

"The manufacturing base for these items has been greatly affected, and should this ban be removed there would be a rush to market. The safety of the people, the welfare of the worker would need to be observed with forethought," I said.

"You really do have an answer for everything," Sensenmann said. "So let's test the answer machine again. What can we do to make the process better?"

"As it's been seven years since the ban and the general public has been without this medication stream, we should introduce a public service class, or have the pharmacist hand them out and make certain they have either gone through the class or they need to get that advisory that no one ever listens to." I smiled and waited for feedback.

"Well, that seems like the perfect solution. You should make that your Level Four project. Put together the press junket for the removal of the ban on non-prescription and over-the-corner medicines." Sensenmann said, looking at me and then at Joshua. "As Judas's shadow partner, you will assist him in this, Joshua." Turning back to me, he continued, "We will be starting the first phase of your Level Four training." Looking at his watch, he indicated towards the elevator as it toned and the doors opened. A six-foot-tall muscular American-Indian woman with blue hair walked off. "Gypsy, I am pleased you made it." As she approached the table, we all stood. "First, you already know Joshua."

"Nice to see you again," Joshua said extending his hand. As they shook, I noticed that she had small hands for such a tall person, and while her features gave away her nationality, her skin was far lighter than Joshua's.

"And you, Joshua. What has it been—six years?" Gypsy said.

"I believe that is correct," he replied.

"And this is Judas, the one I was speaking with you about." I extended my hand. She briefly shook and then reached for my left hand.

"Pleased to meet you. Let me see the dog hand," she said as she began examining my scars. As she turned my hand over, I noticed her entire inner forearm was tattooed with a gold ink; there was a totem pole with a crow, a fish, a coyote, a badger and a lynx, although the color of the ink was such a light color that the tattoo artist really had to know his stuff. As I stopped examining her arm, I looked up straight into her inquiring eyes, "So? Did you get a good enough look?" Gypsy asked.

"The work is amazing, isn't it? I have seen several gray-scale tattoos that are not as detailed," Sensenmann said. "Tell him what they mean."

"I am sure Judas doesn't..." she started.

"I would love to know," I interrupted.

"He is Mr. Trivia, after all," Joshua added.

"The fish represents a person who is graceful, sly, open-minded and has the ability to change his mind quickly. The badger represents a person who is courageous and aggressive, and who is a healer, and an energy conduit to others. The coyote represents a person who is a trickster, intelligent, a master of stealth, wisdom, folly, guile and innocence. The lynx represents a person who is a keeper of secrets, a guardian, a listener, and a guide to help others. And finally, the sky end of my personal totem is the crow, which represents justice, shape-shifting, change, creativity, spiritual strength, energy, and balance," Gypsy said as she indicated each of the symbols. "Each of these represent the animal guides that I have experienced in my life. I had this tattoo done in New York, which is where my first assignment with The Shop was," she finished.

"That is some amazing information," I said.

"I am glad you enjoyed the explanation. So, let's see you bend your hand into a fist." I held my right hand up and made it into a fist. "Amazing."

"That was amazing, Judas. Now, how about you do it with the hand you hurt?" Joshua said.

"Fine," I said, this time raising Dog Leg Left, and folding the fingers as far as I could.

"That is actually pretty damn good—as was your ploy before; you already have the quick wit and cunning of a fox. Let's begin your training and see if you have the other skills of the fox," Gypsy said.

"Well, if that is what I am targeting, being sly like a fox, I am ready." We bid Sensenmann and Joshua farewell and then we left through one of the side protected doors, which led to a fireman's pole that went down at least a hundred feet. "I can't imagine there are many people who come up this way." Gypsy reached up and grabbed what looked like handle bars from the wall.

"Hook this on the pole; this is brake," she indicated the grip that rotated the opposite way of a motorcycle accelerator. "Wrap your legs around the pole and use this brake to slow your slide. Or you can do it the old-fashioned way. It's just quite a long way and friction stopping or slowing on the pole is not great."

"How the hell am I going to work the brake or hang from that thing with my hand like this?" I asked.

"I am certain that you can figure it out," she answered—and she was gone. I looked up at the wall and saw a set of handlebars that had a sling under it. And on the bars there were lanyards for the arms. I took the larger sling and fashioned it around my butt and hooked the lanyard around my left arm, to secure it in. Hooking the handle bars to the pole, I went for it. The majority of my weight was on the large sling under my butt. I was sitting back on the sling like a swing, and modulating my fall with my right hand, my left arm simply tied to the bar.

"*Wheeeeeee*," I said—the yell of excitement simply masking the fear that was ripping at my soul. After what seemed like an hour, I saw Gypsy at the bottom waiting. I touched down and looked at her. "Where do I put the bar?"

"Small basket behind me," she said pointing to the basket that I saw her bar sitting in. "I knew you would figure out a way down. Follow me." What we were walking in was a cave with a river running through it. There was illumination coming from small lights along a path that we were walking on.

Chapter 11

I looked over the ledge into the river; the lights lit up the riverbed. I was surprised to see there were large fish down there. "So where exactly are we?" I asked—then looked up to see I was alone. *Not cool.* I started up the path looking for turn-offs. Where the hell did she go? I stopped and looked back. The path was no wider than one person so she hadn't gone back toward the pole. And there were no turn-offs. I saw nothing, heard nothing and just because I couldn't think of anything else, I took a big sniff. Nothing. I took about five steps back in the last direction she was headed. "Gypsy?" I didn't exactly yell, but in a totally silent cave it sounded pretty loud.

"What?" The voice was less than a foot behind me.

"Holy shit!" I almost jumped out of my skin. "Where the hell did you come from?"

"This is what I will teach you," Gypsy said.

"That would be awesome. I could not have believed that someone could do that," I said and turned away for a second. "So where are we going?" I turned around again, and of course—poof!—she was gone. I held my breath and once again listened, looked back toward the pole and even smelled. Still nothing. I sat down and looked at the edge of the ledge to the river. Just water. Then I looked at the rock-wall side; there were small spots for feet but no ledges to hide. "So does this hiding thing work in the light too?" I asked.

"Yes, it does." She was behind me?

"How the hell did you get by me?" I said while looking at her standing next to me. Had she squeezed by me? No, one of us would have ended up in the river. Looking closer, her feet were still dry. "Seriously, how did you get by me?"

"I wanted you to see two different skills—first the hiding, second the disappearing," Gypsy said. "Okay, no more tricks. Let's get to the base so that we can start this training." We continued to walk along the path and she started to teach: "The first thing about stealth — you need to control your walking and movement, your breathing and eye positioning." She paused and looked about. "The last thing that you should know is sound: a person who is a master can use any sound to their advantage."

"How so?" I asked.

"A rhythmic sound is the best but a loud noise will make those around less willing to listen closely, allowing someone a great opportunity to make a lot of distance quickly."

"How can you know when there is going to be a loud noise?"

"Typically we set it up ahead of time."

"I should have guessed that," I smacked myself in the head. "This has been just a bit freaky."

"I understand. So let's look at the training facilities and then get you back up for your interface with Ursula," Gypsy said.

"I am sorry — for my what?" I asked.

"Well, as a part of your Level Four, there is an Ursula challenge, something like the challenge you had to go through to become a Level One." Gypsy said.

"Oh, the whole mind-fuck thing? Oh, my goodness, I am so sorry — it just popped out." I said.

"It's fine — and yes, that whole thing again. She will devise a challenge that will meet the requirements established by The Shop," Gypsy said as we continued down the hall, reaching a large cavern in which there was a lake the size of a hockey rink, stalactites and stalagmites surrounding it and some rising out of the lake. We spent what seemed like ten minutes doing exercises, a sort of walking Tai Chi parkour with the goal of no sound. "Okay, it's been three hours. I do not want to get in trouble for allowing you to overdo it."

"I just got here," I said.

"Yes, you did, three-plus hours ago." She laughed.

"This place is amazing," I said standing up and looking around. "I could spend hours in here."

"It really is a mystical place. You will have many hours in this cave simply reflecting on how sound works, how light reflects and how the way that you walk allows you to move in ebbs and flow instead of a herky-jerky. As a matter of fact, when you are finished you will be able to walk across that lake and not even scare the trout," Gypsy said.

"I look forward to that. Two questions: first, what time tomorrow am I to be down here to start? And second, where is the way to get back up to my room?" I asked.

"I did not mean to make you nervous about the Ursula challenge. Let's get you up top." We started in the same direction we were walking in all along, past the lake and following the river about fifty yards to what looked like a grain elevator manlift. "As the belt turns, you grab the handle and then step on the small platform as it comes around. You ride it up until you pass through three floors, step off the platform at the third floor. Be careful to not step off until the top of the platform and the floor are even, and don't wait too long after that to get off—the belt does not stop. Then just walk out the door. When you return, a little before eight a.m. tomorrow, the door will remember you. Do you understand?" Gypsy asked.

"One more quick question, if I may," I said.

"Please," she replied.

"Of the ninety percent of the people who fail to complete their Level Four training, which of the parts trip up more students? Your training? Ursula's challenge? Or Sensenmann's project?" I asked.

"I would have to say it is about even," Gypsy said with a wry smile.

"So if I pass Ursula's challenge I am up to about a forty percent chance of passing this training?" I asked.

"Well, I said that we fail out about the same; however, of the people who fail Ursula's test, the majority would have failed my class, and those who don't make it past me, none would have passed the project," Gypsy said.

"Well, that makes me feel *so* much better," I said, stepping onto the platform and grabbing the grip. "See you in the morning." The lift bounced a bit when it took my full weight but it was obviously more than up to the test. And after what seemed like a minute, I passed the first floor, and then rather quickly the second and after another delay of twenty seconds I passed the third, stepping over as the platform top was even with the floor top. I didn't trip or slip, but I could easily see how people could do that. I backed away and then turned to see where the door to leave the elevator was. I saw it and walked through it right out next to the gun range. Damn, it was loud; the entire class was standing ten feet from me and it happened to be the automatic rifle exposure day.

"Judas," Ursula's duo voice overpowered the gunfire. "You need to walk to Primary lab. This is where you first met me."

"I am on my way," I thought. I walked out of the firing range and through the hall. At one point after I passed the classrooms, two agents walked up to me. But before they even opened their mouths, they stopped, obviously having received instruction from Ursula, and then they parted to let me pass. I walked to the end of the hallway and waited. After a few minutes the barred door opened and I walked through it. "I am here."

"That you are. Please make yourself comfortable," Ursula projected a picture into my head of me sitting in the recliner and placing the bike helmet next to the chair on my head. I brought it home by sitting on the chair and putting the helmet on to my head. "Judas, welcome back home." I sat back and watched as the entire room went blurry, and then when it focused again, I was sitting in Gram's house, looking into the kitchen. "Alec, you need to come in here and give your Gramma a kiss." I walked in and kissed her on top of her head.

"Gram, why am I here?" I asked.

"It's simple, Judas. Everyone thinks you are this amazing inventor and person who can solve problems. But can you invent something frivolous — like a game — and then sit down across from you and play the game?" Gram said.

"So I need to invent a game, and challenge Judas?" I asked.

"You have the basic idea, yes. But will you challenge Judas or Alec? And what kind of game do you want to invent?" Gram asked.

"I would challenge Alec. I want to see if I am more than I was. Also, it would have to be a board game that is a combination of luck and skill, combining chess with backgammon perhaps," I said.

"People work their entire lives to come up with a game that combines those two games, with the concept of skill and chance," Gram said.

"Perhaps, but I haven't," I said.

"Interesting comment. So you have some early thoughts?" She smiled and it traveled up to her eyes. She waited.

"Preliminary thoughts: the board will be a checkerboard style, five columns across and twenty-one rows. The game is played head-to-head, like the earliest games of skill, chess, or backgammon. Each player has five tiles; there is a black-and-white side — this is the starting side for each tile — while the opposite side has a red circle. This will be important later. The tiles are moved using five six-sided dice." I paused.

"So what is the goal of this game?" Gram asked.

"The first player to get three tiles across the board into the opponent's base, effectively capturing a column, wins. But this has to be done without crossing over any of the opponent's tiles, in any direction," I answered.

"Without crossing the other player's tiles? How can you accomplish this?"

"The tiles can go forward, backward and sideways, but no diagonal moves. When you move to the side, this forces the other piece in that column to move along its original row to the vacant column. Only one tile of each team is allowed in a column," I said. "Additionally you can end on the other player's tile…"

"What happens then?" Gram asked. Her prodding was helping me just like it did when I was growing up with her. Each and every harebrained idea I had, we would work out all the details, outlining the rough edges, and then Kat would sometimes jump in and help with the finer details. I anxiously looked around for Kat. There she was against the door opening.

"Depends; if both tiles are base side up, the tile that is landed on is sent to its base and turned over to its red side."

"Or?" Kat asked.

"Well if the tile that you land on is red side up if you are on base color you go back to your base and both tiles flip." I said.

"What if you are both red side up?" Kat asked.

"Well if your tile is on its red side is up and your opponent's red side up tile; this sends you both back to your base — it flips both tiles back to their base."

"Why would you do that?" Gram asked.

"Two reasons—the first being a tactical move to defend your base, and the second if you have no other choice, as all dice need to be used or you lose. This pulls another rule: at the end of a move, that tile cannot be moved on that turn. An exception would be pieces that are forced to move when a primary moving piece makes a side movement," I said.

"So how do the dice work? One for each tile?" Gram asked.

"I don't think that would be challenging enough. I want the dice to have the opportunity to work together; matching dice and sequential dice can be used in different ways," I said.

"Interesting. So where would the different ways come in?" Kat asked as she pushed off the door jam, walking over to the table and taking Gram's chair as she had got up and walked over to the oven.

"Well, let's say I rolled three, four, and five. And let's say I have a red piece I am moving and you have a piece in my column that is in your base. I can move to the side three and then advance nine. The only exception to side-to-side movement is when your piece is at home position, in your base, and your opponent brings a piece to your base and it is in the column you would move to, as there is no way to move that piece."

"So there is no interacting with pieces on either end of the board?" Kat asked and leaned back in the chair.

"Correct—due to the inability to clear that tile, as once you have reached your opponent's base those pieces are safe," I said.

"When I roll the dice, all five could go to a single tile?" Gram asked from the sink.

"Yes, as long as the dice go together, like a roll of one, two, two, three, four; you can tie them to a single tile via two, one, two, three, four, allowing one tile to move twelve spaces," I said.

"Nice touch, but won't the game go fast after you have the first tile in base?" Kat asked. "I mean as you have five dice for four tiles, and then three, et cetera."

"Good point. You will lose a die for each tile in the scoring position," I said.

"What is this game called, Alec?"

"Un Sukiru." I said answering to my old name.

"So are you ready for the challenge?" Kat asked. I looked at her in confusion, then back down at the table. There was an amazing replication of what I had described as the game. The board Ursula had generated was mirrored stainless steel and carbon fiber. The tiles were the same construction, stainless steel and carbon fiber with a red inlay on the back side.

"Sure. Bring it, Alec," I said. It was a strange sight to see me walk through the kitchen entrance, walk up to Gram and give her a kiss, and then pull a chair up and give a side-of-the-mouth-grin.

"Well, I'm white; my assumption is I go first," Alec said.

"Standard to most games, I believe this should be the same," I said. He took the dice and started the game. As the game was reaching the halfway point, I realized I was looking at his pieces and thinking what move I would make, and was basing my next move on that. While that established a good defensive ploy, it did not allow for good offense because my counterpart was doing the same thing. I altered my game play by trying to throw Alec off a bit. It worked and I won the game. The room instantly went blurry and when it came back into focus, I was once again in the lab.

"Congratulations, Judas, you have advanced past my Level Four challenge. Please proceed to your room," Ursula said. I got up and headed out of the lab knowing that, while mathematically I still had a huge opportunity to fail the overall Level Four orientations, I was walking out proud of myself. As I got to the door I saw a wrapped box on the table; there was a card with my name on it. "Please take it as a small congratulations gift from us." I opened the box; in it was a jewelry box which contained a ring. It was gold and had The Shop insignia. I tried it on my finger it fit perfectly, they seemed to know every last detail. *Not cool.*

"Thank you," I said

"Please do not wear the ring until you pass the final test. Only certified Level Fours get that ring. We are however, confident you will pass." Ursula said.

"No pressure there." I said taking the ring off, placing it in my pocket and walking out of the room.

I walked past the class room as they were letting out. Andelos stopped me and inquired about the challenge. "I just completed it," I said.

"Way to go, brother. Did they give you your project yet?" Andelos asked excitedly.

"Yes, it's…" I started.

"No," both Andelos and Ursula said.

"I didn't know you couldn't discuss," I said.

"The actual project you cannot discuss; you can, however, ask others questions to glean insight," Ursula said.

"And when it's over, and you pass, you can freely talk with others who have passed it and compare notes," Andelos said.

"Well, I look forward to hearing about your study," I said, and excused myself. As I walked away, Meglar and Billings walked up. I quickly started thinking as loud as I could, "Ursula, what can I say?"

"Simply tell them that you are testing for Level Four," she boomed in my head.

"That's it?" I thought.

"Tell them the test is made up of three parts; the training is secret. But Sensenmann's project and my challenge are okay, but remember the details are Article Eighty-Seven," she again answered within my head.

"Judas," they were saying as they ran up.

"Howdy," I said, stopping my progression to allow them to catch up.

"Where were you today?" Billings asked. "Saw Andelos talking to ya—did you get in trouble for ditching class?"

"I didn't ditch class. I was assigned out of it," I said.

"Okay, spill," Meglar said.

"Well, I am starting my Level Four testing."

"*Four?*" they both said.

"When they took me out to the field, I had to complete Level Two gun proficiency," I said.

"Okay, cowboy, how about you start at the beginning."

"Ursula... what can I share?" I thought while I held a finger to ask for a minute.

"For these two I will allow you to talk openly, less the specific questions and target of the investigation. Let me brief them first," Ursula said and then she went silent. A moment later, they both went completely still and then they both said out loud that they understood. "Take them to the cafeteria. There is no one in there right now."

"Come on, you two, let us adjourn to the cafeteria. We can talk there," I said as I headed off with them looking open-mouthed. Apparently Ursula talking in their heads wasn't something that happened to them every day—and here I was starting to get used to it.

"There have only been three others who have adjusted to me as fast as you, Judas." Ursula projected.

"Actually several people have thrown up the first hundred times I did this."

"Boy, I guess I am too polite to throw up just because a woman talks to me," I joked, she went silent again. When we got to the cafeteria, there really were no others there, less Molly. "Hello, Molly. Can I get some food?" I asked.

"Of course you can—do your friends want anything? Billings and Meglar, right?" Molly said.

"Right in one as usual," I said. "Did you guys eat?"

"I could eat," Billings said.

"Something small if it isn't too much trouble," Meglar said.

"Oh, no trouble at all, dear," Molly said. "What would you like? A salad is light but I am looking at Judas and I know I am going to be making a huge pasta salad with about three pounds of turkey and two heads of broccoli. I think I have a fresh block of feta in that giant fridge," Molly said, poking.

"Greek dressing on it?" I said, thinking I sounded like a kid in an ice cream shop asking for a cherry on top.

"Li'l Sexy, would I disappoint?" Molly said.

"Li'l what?" both Billings and Meglar said.

"Sexy," Molly said. "It was that or…"

"Molly!" I interrupted.

"Oh, come on, that or what?" Billings said.

"Pan's Tail," I said.

"Oh, I let that one go. I was going to try a new one," Molly said.

"I heard that others call you DLL," she said.

"Molly, that's…" I started.

"Article Eighty-Seven?" she said. "These two are read in, Judas. Well, they will be when you get your order in and tell them." She smiled, winked and then looked at the others. "So, Greek pasta salad?" she said.

"Sure," they both said. I started over to the tables, glancing back to make sure they were in tow as they appeared to be in shock. They had obviously known who DLL was, and their surprise and confusion obviously tickled Molly who turned from us and burst out laughing. We walked over and sat down. "Dish," they both said.

"It started the night Andelos freaked out on me at the range. I ended up getting put before Sensenmann, and he decided that my eyes needed to be checked. After I showed that I wasn't lying and actually could see the lasers they gave me another test, which I passed, that being seeing Andelos twitching in class, micro-expressions. After I got my gun qualifications completed, I ended up in the governor of Washington's office. I stopped him from killing Joshua and then ended up killing him. When his assistant came in, I was in the process of seeing if the local Washington agent was okay, when the assistant shot me. I killed him too," I said.

"So let me get this straight: less than twenty-four hours after being certified shooter, and after taking a wound to the hand that would have put most humans on the ground in shock, you took out a governor and his assistant?" Meglar asked.

"That's about correct," I said.

"How many shots?" Billings asked, trying to get clarification.

"Two in each," I said.

"With a hurt hand and a shot shoulder? Four shots, two kills—not bad," Meglar said.

"Thanks. Stupidest part is until my qualification, I had never fired a gun in my life," I said.

"Wait—and you qualified Level Two on your first time at a range?" Billings about shit himself.

"No," I said.

"Well that isn't anything to be embarrassed about. How many attempts did it take?" Meglar asked.

"Look, I qualified Level Ten master marksmen in the first hundred rounds. And then spent nine hundred more rounds proving it wasn't a fluke," I said.

"That is unbelievable," they both said.

"The fact is I am really good at it, and let's leave it at that," I said.

"Okay — left," Billings said. "So what happened after?"

"Well, after the doctors put me back together, I had a meeting with Sensenmann and I was promoted to Level Three immediately. The saving of another agent gives him that ability. When I gave the plans of my inventions to Dr. Strandtov, they were built and now they are going to be used. This apparently put me in for the opportunity to test for Level Four," I said.

"So what happens with this Level Four testing?" Billings asked.

"Well, I can't tell you everything, but I can say there are three parts, and Ursula creates a challenge just for you."

"Kind of like when we first came here and there was complete sensory deprivation for an hour before it started?" Meglar asked.

"Not completely. But I can't say much. I passed that part today," I said.

"Judas, you really are amazing," Billings said.

"Hey, I did mean to tell you congratulations earlier for passing that," Molly said as she brought our lunches out. "That entire conversation with Ursula about these two as you were walking up kind of distracted me. So please accept it now." She extended her hand and I shook it. "And you two think about this: I have not heard of Level Ones being read in, ever." Molly said this as her hands lay on both

Billings and Meglar's shoulders, removing her hands she walked back to her kitchen.

"The second part is called Level Four training, and I really can't say much more. I met the instructor and I know what the final exam is," I said.

"Are you nervous?" Meglar asked.

"I know if they gave me the test today, I would fail," I said. "Although, as Meglar said earlier, that would not be anything to be ashamed of, especially as ninety percent of the people who take this advancement test fail it."

"Holy shit! Well, do you get to take it again?" Billings asked.

"No," I said, although I actually wasn't completely sure.

"The way the levels work, you can be a Level Ten without passing each of the other levels. I would say it is a rather stupid system," Molly said, bringing back extra feta and Greek dressing. "The interesting part is you don't need to take the *final exam*, as you called it, until you feel you are ready. So you could stay in training for that level indefinitely, since you have been nominated for it. If it means that much to you to pass that part, no one will question it. They may ask you to allow someone else to take the training while you practice, as there is only one person permitted to be training within each category of Level Four. The other interesting part is, you can be promoted to levels above four while still taking the Level Four qualifications." She looked around, and apparently saw no questions in our eyes, so excused herself again.

"The final part is a project that Sensenmann gives you." I paused to see if they had any questions. With none coming from them, I ventured on. "I obviously can't tell you much but based on my project it is not a surprise that ninety percent of the people fail."

"You'll do fine," they both said.

"So that is where I have been and what I have been doing. Although that was quite a concise version of events," I said.

"DLL?" Meglar inquired in a way only she could — one word asking a very lengthy question.

"Ursula?" I thought and waited. "Ursula, is this too deep? Or can I read them in on this too?"

"You are fine; you have come this far," Ursula projected.

"After the incident in Washington, it was decided that a trial was needed for the public, but that showing my face at this point was not warranted."

"So what or who is DLL?" Meglar pushed.

"I am," I held up my left hand. "Dog Leg Left, it was a joke about the dog tendon in my hand," I said.

"But the trial, that wasn't you," Billings said.

"And I don't know who it was. I was promised he would be okay," I said. "Any other questions?"

"I wish you were in the class," Meglar said.

"It's odd how close we all have become; we haven't known each other that long but I really was bummed that I couldn't share with you two what was going on," I said.

"I am glad that it is mutual," Meglar said and she held out a fist. Billings and I both bumped it, forming a fist triangle.

"Can either of you draw?" I asked.

"I can, I'm pretty good," Billings said. "Why?"

"I would like a drawing of this," I said indicating the three-fist triangle. "I have always wanted a tattoo, and with everything I have had in my life, I have never had that epiphany that made me want to ink it on me forever. I just did."

"I can capture it," Billings said.

"I can't wait to see it," Meglar said.

"Well my friends, I need to get to my room. I have a huge project that needs starting. Molly I am going…" as I turned my head, I saw a blur coming at me. I reached up and pulled a bag of licorice out of the air.

"…to need some writer food," Molly said.

"As always, right in one. Love me some writer food," I said as me and my bag of licorice headed to my room. When I got back I pulled out my tablet and started to outline my project.

Chapter 12

Level Four Project—Removing the Restrictions on Non-prescription-strength Medications.

I. Understanding which medications were both made restricted and are going to stay restricted after this change.
    a. Cold and flu.
    b. Allergy.
    c. Aspirin and derivatives.
    d. Sleep aids.

II. Manufacturing:
    a. Which plants are still manufacturing the medications that will no longer be restricted?
    b. Which plants were mothballed and would be reopened?
    c. Plan for staging the startup of shutdown plants vs. the increase in production of operating plants.
    d. Can any other manufacturing plants that have been closed down be easily modified to produce these medications?

III. Training and awareness
    a. Preparing the training
        i.   Determining what the public may have forgotten about these medications.
        ii. Communicating the limits that can be purchased.
        iii. Training the pharmacists
            1. Understanding how to know if people have been trained.
            2. Understanding the recording process.

3. Understanding the limited amount they can sell.

iv. Training for Shop inspectors.

1. Inspecting plants that are increasing production prior to speed- up.
2. Pre-inspection of mothballed plants.
3. Production verification and statistical verifications.
4. Shipping and Transportation

a. What are the interstate travel increases and the burden this will place on verification booths?

i. Do we need to impose night shipping only?

b. Preparing awareness

i. Writing the Public Address.
ii. Recording the TV spot—first choice, actor Doogie Howser.
iii. Airing the TV spot.
iv. Determine how the general public can prove they watched the TV spot.

1. There is a number at the end of announcement that is only good for 12 hours.

c. General Public

i. To purchase the medications, people need to have either:

1. Followed class offered in high schools or in college and some large businesses;

2. Watched the public service announcement, and then spoken with pharmacist;
3. Attended training which can be rolled into the DMV as part of getting driver's license.

As I completed my typing, Joshua walked in with Jinau. "So what is in the works today?" Jinau said.

"You first," I said.

"Fine. We went and visited two more governors today," Joshua said.

"Did you bring movies home? I got some licorice..." I started.

"Not just writer food anymore?" Jinau said.

"You got that mostly right—movies and writing, the perfect food," I said.

"Yes, we brought home movies for the kids to watch," Joshua said. "Get that projector booted up." I did, and he gave me his glasses to connect. While I was hooking it up, he looked at the outline I had done for the project. "Hold up—Doogie Howser?"

"Yeah, come on, who doesn't like Doogie Howser," I said.

"Oh, for pity's sake, you can't even stay serious when your career is riding on it," Joshua scolded.

"So are you saying Sensenmann doesn't like Doogie Howser?" I asked.

"How the heck do I know if he likes..." Joshua started

"As a matter of fact, I love Doogie Howser. I have the first season on Green Ray," Sensenmann said, interrupting Joshua.

"Seriously?" Jinau asked.

"Well, not really, but it felt like the right thing to say," Sensenmann said. "I was coming here to congratulate Judas on passing Ursula's challenge. And I walked into a discussion about me—what am I..." he paused and looked at the wall. "Oh, I see. 'First choice for actor, Doogie Howser.'"

"I figured we could digitally make a twelve-year-old Neil Patrick Harris to give the public address. I didn't think Doogie was real," I said.

"Thank goodness," Joshua and Sensenmann said. Jinau just shook her head.

"Thank you for coming down to congratulate me," I said.

"Actually it looks like you are already done with the project too. You covered everything, even transportation issues. Can you walk across the lake without disturbing the trout?" Sensenmann said. "You could knock this Level Four out in record time."

"I don't think so," I said.

"Well, you can take Andelos's final and count that while continuing Gypsy's training as your continuous education training for the year," Sensenmann said.

"He can?" Joshua and Jinau said.

"Only because he already passed his Level One and there is no reason why not. There are no hard rules other than the ones I laid out, and I just write this down for the next person who jumps out of Level One. That final exam isn't exactly easy; sixty percent of those who get to Andelos's final fail it," Sensenmann said.

"I really want to take Gypsy's course. What she does just seems amazing to me," I said.

"And you will, I promise," Sensenmann said. "I will let you get back to the home movies. Can I have a licorice stick?"

"Of course." He took one and then left. "So how hard is this final?"

"Comparatively, sixty percent fail Andelos's final while ninety percent fail Gypsy's course," Jinau said. "I would have to say you have been given an opportunity to get back on the road sooner."

"Is that a bad thing?" I asked.

"Not even a little bit. It says a lot about what you have accomplished, and who you have proven that you are," Jinau added.

"I don't want advantages," I said.

"Judas," Joshua said—and as he never said my name, it got my attention—"you take what is given you. This life which you are entering into is not easy. You will never know the feeling of home and hearth, and you will not have normal holidays or vacations. Those who have relations in this place can be killed for simply falling in love with each other. There is no reason to simply roll with this," Joshua said, and I read a bit of remorse and resentment in his comment.

"Yeah, what he said—well except home and hearth, I wouldn't have used those words," Jinau said, and while she tried to add levity, her eyes did not meet Joshua's as his were looking at her.

"Okay, I understand," I said.

"I still need to review that project. I may end up with questions at some point," Joshua said.

"Okay. I saved it to your glasses. You can review it while you are on the plane," I said.

"Perfect. Okay, so let's get to the movie." I started the first file. I wasn't long into it when it became obvious that this was a different situation than the other interviews.

"Who is this governor?" I asked.

"Why do you ask?" Joshua replied with his own question.

"He is a liar. And the agent in the back, he is extremely confrontational—look at that posture. I don't like the feel here," I replied.

"Well, that didn't take long," Jinau said. "Go to the next file." I did and we watched but this was much like the first visit.

"He had much the same reaction as the first visit—no real emotions at all here," I said. "Back to my first question: that first governor, where is he from?"

"That was the governor of Alaska," Joshua said.

"What can you tell me about The Shop agent who was with him? When he left, he gave the governor a look that was really sharp. If he isn't in charge, I will be surprised," I commented.

"That is so perceptive; I have to say I really am impressed Judas," Jinau said. "I believe, as you stated, this agent needs to be understood."

"I will pull all the records on this agent. Determine which governors are in his rotation," Joshua said. "Perhaps then we can see if there is a group."

"When we started on this, was there a plan or specific group we were targeting? Or, moreover, did Sensenmann suspect there was a plot?" I asked

"Plot? I am not sure we can say that yet; that sounds a bit conspiratorial. Let's wait for this to unfold before we say something like that. It could simply be a bad egg," Joshua said.

"If I didn't ask, I wouldn't be doing my job," I said.

"True. Very true," Jinau said. "So we will reconvene tomorrow to discuss the other governors this agent has on his rotation and..."

"What about The Shop agents who would be in the same rotation?" I asked, interrupting Jinau. "Sorry." I winced as I saw Jinau's face contort into a scowl.

"And the other Shop agents as well. I was about to say that, but I will give you two points for that," Jinau said, pulling her face back into a grin.

"Thanks," I replied.

"All right. Well, I need to figure out the best method of doing that without leaving a trail," Joshua added. "Good night. See you after your day tomorrow." He smiled broadly.

"What?" he had piqued my interest—he never smiled like that.

"Well, you need to ask Andelos to stay after class and give you the final early, *and* you have to tell Gypsy that she is your yearly continuous education instead of Level Four... And when she hears that, it will probably cause her to throw you in the lake." Again he had a huge toothy grin. "I wouldn't bring any electronics that you want to use again." This time Joshua burst out laughing and walked out of the room leaving Jinau and me dumbstruck.

"He thought that image pretty amusing," I said, breaking the silence.

"I kinda do as well. Think you could sneak a video camera down there and set it on the rocks?" she asked.

"Sure, why not? I live to make you two laugh." I started dreading the conversation. "Is she really going to freak?"

"She does enjoy the role she plays," Jinau commented as she started to walk out the door.

"Spoiler?" I asked as a follow-up.

"Well, yes, I think that is a good word for it. *Spoiler* to some, and *Inspiration* to others," she said.

"Did you pass her class?" I said as I started packing my tablet. Looking up, she was gone. I looked to see if there was a shadow in the hallway of her leaving. "I will take that as a yes," I muttered to no one.

"I did," from the other side of the room Jinau answered.

"Holy shit... how the hell did you do that?" I stammered.

"Take her class seriously. It is something that you will use the rest of your career," Jinau counseled.

"I promise you, I mean to," I said.

"Let her know that, and show her that, and she may not throw you in the lake." This time she did walk across the room and leave.

I woke early in the morning knowing I had several important things that needed to be accomplished and in a manner that I was not accustomed to doing things. I had a bit of groveling and ass-kissing to get some of it done and good old ingenuity to do the other. Ingenuity, check; ass-kissing, not my strong suit—but everyone needs to add to their toolbox. Let's start with food and exercise, and then move on to growing my toolbox. I got dressed and went down to see if Miss Molly was preparing food at four-thirty in the morning. She wasn't there so I figured I would go to the elevator that led to the underground lake and see if Gypsy was down there. When I arrived there, the door did not acknowledge my presence. I quickly gave up and started walking past the gun range as Andelos was heading in with a different helmet than the one I had used when I fired on the range.

"Judas, that door doesn't turn on its reader until six a.m. What are you up to?" he asked.

"I need to talk to Gypsy, but I also need to talk with you," I said.

"Me and Gypsy? Strange. Well, I am here—what can I do for you?" he asked. The early morning hour seemed to result in his accent being more pronounced, or perhaps it was that he was getting more comfortable with me.

"I had a meeting with Sensenmann last night and I am to ask you if I can take the final exam for your class," I said.

"You have already been given a passing grade for my class," he said.

"The final exam is to take the place of Gypsy's training in my Level Four," I said.

"Oh, shit, she's going to throw you in the lake," Andelos said.

"I keep hearing that," I said.

"As far as my end, that's easy; you can take it when the rest of the class takes it," he said.

"He wants me to take it today," I said and watched his eyes bug out of his head.

"But you are friends with others in the class. I can't have that," Andelos said.

"Andelos, I will not share the information — Ursula will torture me if I do," I said.

"Today or tonight?" he said, musing on that image.

"What about right after class?" I answered.

"Okay, right after class then," Andelos said.

"Do you know what time Gypsy gets in?" I asked.

"She is down there now. She lives down there. Right about now she is doing Tai Chi," Andelos answered.

"So how can I get down there?" I asked.

"Well, if I badge in, the door will read you."

"Could you do that then?" I requested. And he walked with me over to the door and touched his badge to the glass. The door scanned us and opened up.

"If you can sneak up on her while she is doing Tai Chi, you may not end up getting tossed in the lake," Andelos said.

"Thanks. See you in class," I said and walked through the door.

"Not if you drown you won't." He gave me a thumbs up and turned away as the door started to close.

"Andelos," I said, touching his shirt collar and changing my voice to a whisper, "Sonya and you need to be more careful." I winked and I went through the door leaving him looking at the dark makeup that had obviously been transferred there when she kissed his neck.

I walked over to the conveyor belt and watched as it rotated. When it came around I stepped on and started the long descent. As the platform got close to the bottom, I stepped off as silently as I could. I started into the cave.

The water was reflecting the light from the other end of the lake. While it was pretty, the lighting was not very good for orienting myself in an area I had only been in once. Still, I moved as quietly as a mouse, picturing myself scaring her on the other side of all this sneaking around. I allowed my senses to feel that the rocks were next to me, without actually reaching out and touching them. After a few minutes of creeping through the darkness, her silhouette moved quite gracefully in the darkness as she performed the martial art with expertise. I stepped on a rock and it skidded out like a rocket, making a slight click, the bounce of the rock on my right. She stopped in mid-motion, listening to the cave, as I stayed silent as I could. While I stood there, I noticed there was more light than a moment before, and as she started to move, so did I, throwing myself flat against the rocks, finding a slight indent in the stone.

"Who's there?" Gypsy said in an even tone, to which I did not reply. A moment later she shut off her light and went back to her exercising. Now that she was listening for me, this was going to be really tough, I thought. Another ten feet—find a cubby. Wait. Repeat. After what must have been ten minutes of repeating that process, I was close enough to her to spit on. For the first time I noticed that she was doing Tai Chi in the nude. *Not cool.* Andelos set me up. There were very quiet rhythmic bells playing on a boom box that sat on the rocks. My plan was to shut off the boom box bells and scare the shit out of a naked woman. She was going to throw me in the lake for sure. I had come too far to chicken out now. I took the next few steps after I saw what her pattern was—strike, strike, step, step, stretch, overhead turn. While I was certain the moves had a name, I didn't know them; I just knew that it was a repeatable cadence and perhaps I could use that. On the turn, I moved and found a cubby. Strike, stretch and turn. I moved, reached the power button and pushed it to turn it off. I felt myself being pulled and then thrown and then splash. "Judas," Gypsy said as I stuck my head out of the water, and I noticed she was reaching for her robe.

"Yes, Gypsy, it's me," I said.

"What the hell happened to you back there?" she said indicating back where I'd sent the rock flying.

"I stepped on a rock," I answered.

"So you didn't step on any more after that?"

"I stepped on a bunch; I just noticed them before I transferred my weight from the other foot," I said.

"Nice. You learn quickly. How did you fit that huge mass in my rock wall?" she asked.

"I can honestly say I have no idea; about the time I needed to hide, I simply didn't let myself feel the rocks," I said.

"Seriously?" Gypsy said.

"Yes, seriously. Why?" I asked

"Go back out and start again."

"But you're going to know I'm coming in," I protested.

"Judas, I knew you were coming when you kicked that first stone," Gypsy said, laughing. "Now run—go." I didn't run but I did go. When I got to the end, I waited until she started to do her Tai Chi again. Although the fact that she was doing it nude again did surprise me. I started down the path again, from the beginning. I made the commitment to hit a cubby periodically—fifteen steps, cubby, fifteen steps, cubby, then feel the bells and see her pattern, stretch and turn. Ten steps cubby, ten steps, feel the bells and see her pattern stretch and turn. I was close enough to turn off the radio. I decided to push my luck—and the bells, stretch, turn. I went into the water and went to her other side and waited. Stretch, turn, get out, cubby. I grabbed her robe and waited until she turned. Yes, my eyes were closed—almost. *Wink*... "Judas, how did you do that?" she said as she grabbed the robe. "Open your eyes, moron. How did you get around me?" Gypsy was truly freaked out.

"Well, I felt the bells, like you said. I watched your pattern, like you said," I answered.

"Wait—I put compression marbles all over the last twenty feet while you were running back," Gypsy said, taking me forward and shining her flashlight across the walkway, showing hundreds of small marbles on the ground. "Watch this." She poked one lightly with her toe; it made a bright flash and let out a whine. "You couldn't have missed all of them."

"I definitely didn't miss them. I didn't allow my foot to move them. I found purchase around them," I said.

"Okay. As impossible as that sounds, I will let that go. There were marbles and the bottom of the lake right there to there," she indicated the area I just walked through. "That is a slide straight to the deep water—you couldn't have missed it without making some splashes."

"When I got to it, I felt how the angle was and knew I was in trouble so I used my arms to hold me above it," I said.

"I can't wait to see what you can do in a few weeks," she said.

"Well, that is actually why I came down here. I am going to be taking this incredibly seriously as I just think it is probably going to be important to me for the rest of my career," I said.

"But?" Gypsy prompted.

"Well, I was told I needed to get into the field, so Sensenmann wants me to take this as continuous education and take the final exam frommmmmmmmmmmm." Splash. *Not cool* – she threw me again. This time I hit marbles – *flash!* – and then hit the slide – wheeeee into the deep water.

"So I am just continuous education now?" she said – actually *screamed*. She was really loud.

"Please let me explain," I said as I swam back to the shallow water.

"I don't think it's for you to explain. If I am not important to the future of The Shop..." Gypsy started.

"How about you turn your melodramatic bullshit down just a tad?" Did I really just say that? Out loud? Good thing I was still in the water.

"Excuse me?" Her hands went to her hips and her head cocked.

"I am sorry but I know you know how important you are, and I will be back. I have already learned so much from you," I said as I climbed out of the water and waited to see if I would go back in. I didn't.

"I will let you leave on that note," she said. "I have to finish my morning ritual." I turned and started to walk away. "Judas." I paused. "You really are amazing, and I have never had a guy down here who didn't allow his eyes to wander, even the couple who are homosexual – until now."

"Well, don't be so amazed. I failed too. When I got behind you, my eyes weren't closed tight," I said as I left.

"Well, thank *goodness*. I thought I was losing a step or two," she joked.

"No comment," I said as I walked with my back to her. I got on the lift and rode away, dripping the whole way up. Of course when I got off and walked through the door, it wasn't just Andelos. Andelos, Joshua, Jinau, Meglar, Billings, and Deces were all there — and, oh yeah, Sensenmann, and they were all belly laughing... "All ya'll don't have something better to do than stand around and wait for me to come up so you can laugh?" I asked.

"Well, I was going to watch over the free world sleeping, but this definitely was more fun," Sensenmann joked. Nothing like the leader of a nation having a horselaugh at your expense.

"How many times did you go in the water?" Jinau asked. I looked around. Joshua was holding three fingers down his leg.

"Three." A fresh round of laughing and then money changed hands. All ended up with Joshua.

"Young *ma'un*, let's go get you dried off." I started walking away and the jokes and the laughing continued. "Well, that wasn't so bad, was it?" Joshua asked.

"No, it wasn't that bad. By the way, half that money is mine — one of the times I jumped in," I said, smiling.

"Well, let's hope the rest of your day has less disappointment," Joshua said as he took the money out of his pocket and placed it in his wallet. "So when you take your final exam, you should remember there are no real right answers — there are wrong points of view." And with that he changed the subject. "I am headed to the vault to pull the hard copies of records for the assignments. I completely forgot we keep such things, but that is something that people still are afraid to give up. I will see you this afternoon." I finished getting dry clothes on and headed down to get some food, feeling pretty good about everything that had happened thus far, less the Judo flips of course.

Chapter 13

"Good morning, class," Andelos said, in a different shirt. "Today is an interesting day. Today we are going to discuss taxes. And everyone has opinions on this subject. And today Ursula is not allowed to zap anyone; Sensenmann wants to get a true report of what every Shop agent and agent-in-training feels about the taxation topic. This allows several things to occur: The trainees are just coming from university, and so your views are quite often followed by others from whence you come. The other thing it does is give a continuous smell-test as to the current state of the tax code, including where it needs shoring up from the sneaky bastards who try to beat it," Andelos said, looking about the room. Not liking what he saw, he started again. "I give you my word: if anyone gets zapped, free punch in the nose by the student of the class's choosing." Of course everyone smiled and looked at me. "Yes, even Judas." The class physically relaxed. "Okay, Ursula, let's not get my nose broken."

"I promise — no games," Ursula said.

"All right. First let's ask this: who understands what the tax situation was pre-Shop?" Andelos asked. Several hands shot up. I waited.

"It was tax-based upon earning. Most businesses and individuals filed the taxes once a year," a girl who had never raised her hand before stated.

"Very good, Tierney. Anyone have more to add to that?" Andelos asked.

"The taxes were collected by the companies from their employees. This would then be matched by the companies to a certain extent," Billings added.

"There were several taxes withheld — FICA, Medicare, state, federal, and in some cases local taxes," Meglar added

"So when the people filed their taxes, what was it based upon?" Ursula asked.

"The tax tables, which were based upon the estimated earnings of the taxpayer," Tierney said.

"So not everyone paid the same percentage?" Andelos asked.

"No, it was a graduated table. The more you made, the higher the percentage you paid," Tierney said once again. I started thinking she must have been talked to about her lack of participation.

"So when things were thrown up in the air and it became obvious the country needed a new system, what was the concern about simply adopting a standard percentage of earnings going to the government?" Ursula asked. This time the hands stayed down — fear of the shock treatment I suppose.

"There was a large percentage of the country who still would not pay taxes," I said after Andelos pointed to me.

"How so?" he said.

"The people who were working illegally, under the table, weren't filing taxes, and some large businesses did not pay taxes on their earnings due to reasons of sweetheart deals they had worked out," I stated.

"So what about a value-added tax?" Ursula asked

"This is a tax that is a type of consumption tax I pay when I buy something, and then when I use the raw materials and make them into something better, like sand, cullet, utility made into glass and glass products. When I buy the sand, cullet and utilities, I pay a tax to the seller, and when I sell my glass I collect a tax and pay that tax to the government," Tierney answered.

"What is that tax based upon?" Andelos asked

"The total of the sale minus all taxable inputs to the product," Billings added.

"And what are the shortcomings of this?" Ursula asked. Again no one raised their hand.

"The need of the IRS is still implied in this in its full strength. Business can inflate the costs it took to produce the good. There are several other, less significant, issues. Who is actually paying the tax and who is deducting the previous tax? If I purchase a car and turn it into a limousine, I could technically deduct all the previous taxes on this product. It becomes very convoluted," I said.

"Correct. How about consumption tax?" Ursula asked.

"This is a tax on spending and service, much like the sales tax; however, it can also be set up as direct personal tax. All in all this is very complicated and, as Judas pointed out about value-added tax, the full-blown IRS is required to implement consumption tax. Also, many people would be hit with a large bill when they file once a year, which they would never understand and would never be able to pay. Lastly, people who rent are hit on this more so than any home owners," Billings said.

"I don't think I have any follow-ups to that," Andelos said.

"I have no comment to that either," Ursula said. "So that brings us to where we have currently set the country up—a Nationalized Sales Tax. Which of you wish to give some understanding on the NST?"

Meglar spoke up: "The NST is very much like the consumption tax, in that it is paid by the end user. Services are paid to the provider of the service, like the person selling a good. The largest complaint in relation to this tax is the larger burden is carried by the low-income to middle-income families. This was addressed in the Welfare Reform Act of 2023, which allowed the people who were signed up for welfare to get a consumption rebate. It was a flat amount, based upon a high level of consumption. Basically, if you made a hundred dollars on welfare, they figured eighty dollars of this would go toward the items that would fall into the NST. This allowed these people to get eighty dollars times the current tax rate of the country, which is thirty-three percent for federal and seven percent for the state, which would give them a check increase of twenty-four dollars for each hundred. The renter and imputed rent tax has been added and taken away. Currently it is back in, as I recall, but at a reduced level compared to the other NST.

"In the past, hospitals, churches and even Indian Reservations did not pay taxes. These areas were added specifically into the law. Hospitals were to collect a patient fee that was to be collected at the time of service. Patients who were brought into the hospital in a state of unconsciousness were allowed service without that being paid in advance; all others would be required to pay the twenty-dollar charge in order to be seen. Churches were to be viewed as a service and the parishioners were taxed accordingly. Incidentally, there has been a drop in attendance of church leading to a large number of churches in poor communities closing down. Finally, Indian Reservation taxes: some of the largest post-Shop rallies have been held on Indian Reservations as the tax was fully levied against their sales, the second largest being advocates for fair treatment of aliens," Meglar completed her comments.

"Does anyone have anything else?" Ursula asked.

"I had read that there was a large concern about predictions that black-market contraband would go into the National Sales Tax," Tierney offered.

"Ursula, you can take this one," Andelos said.

"Thank you. With the addition of state border monitoring for the healthcare concerns that arose a few years back, the policing of such trafficking became easier. Additionally, The Shop arrested the first few black marketers and made very public the executions of them for undermining the government and crimes against the Nation. The total number of people willing to deal in large-scale black market brokering fell significantly and thus the didactic nature of the executions was obviously taken at face value," Ursula completed with very significant finality.

"Point of clarification?" Tierney said, raising her hand.

"Go on," Ursula replied.

"Your statement of 'the didactic nature of the executions.' Please clarify," she said.

"I am going to reply with the assumption that you understand the definition of *didactic*. The meaning and intention of this comment was that we, The Shop, are not going to give you a slap on the wrist as the old government would have for such a crime against us. We, The Shop, will kill you," Ursula commented. "Does this give you the clarification you required?"

"Yes, thank you, Ursula," Tierney said.

"Are there any other questions or comments about the NST?" Andelos asked. When no one replied, he continued, "Okay, then we have a bit of time left; I would love to talk about Social Security."

"This is out of our normal coursework, Andelos," Ursula said. "But this is a very interesting conversation."

"One of our country's biggest challenges has been Social Security. In the past it has been suggested to privatize the entire system. Any comments on this?" Andelos asked.

"The biggest thing I have to say is if this would have been done when everyone was pushing for it, the country would be in even worse shape," Tierney said.

"I would like to comment on that," I said.

"Please," Ursula said.

"How is that it seems to be forgotten that part of that discussion included the method of making the entire account secure. There were no real methods to prevent the person having put their money into this account subsequently losing it. The reason it didn't get endorsement was due to the lack of support for the existing members on Social Security. The truth of the matter is, it is just as possible that, had they done it back then, it would not be in trouble now," I said.

"So, Judas, what would you suggest?" Ursula asked.

"There are only two real-world things that can be done for Social Security at this point, and neither are actually ever going to happen. First, you could raise the rates that people pay into it; second, modulate the amount people can get out," I said.

"And how would that work?" Tierney asked, rather aggressively.

"As I said, it wouldn't. Social Security as it is will fail; there are not enough people paying into it to cover the number of people collecting. What could be done is evaluating people's means and determining what they can get," I replied, then asked a question of my own: "Why does a millionaire need to collect Social Security?"

"I would like to thank you for the debate; this subject, as I said, always sparks a lively discussion. That will do for today," Andelos said. The class headed out while I remained in my seat. Billings looked at me; I indicated that I was staying. He waved as he left.

Chapter 14

"All right, Judas, I want you to come over to this side of the room, please," Andelos said.

"Sure. Do you want me to close this door?" I asked. He shook his head so I walked over and sat down.

"All you need is a pencil or two," Andelos said.

"I have a pen — is that okay?" I asked.

"That's fine. Here is your test document," Andelos said. I opened it and it was blank. "I am headed out; Ursula will be working with you. You must write the question as I will not know until I see the booklet later. Do you have any questions?" He waited.

"Are you grading on grammar, or are you restricting to content?" I asked.

"Primarily content. Any other questions?" he asked. When I shook my head no, he left the room.

"Judas, your first question." I got my pen ready. "During the transition from the old government to The Shop, there were two phases: the first phase was when the American people chose three potential representatives to come to Washington and represent them. During this time, the making of laws continued to be through the three branches of government: Legislative, the writers of the laws; Executive, the executor of the laws; and the third being Judicial. They determined if the law was unconstitutional. Together they were the checks and balances. As we went into phase two, which consisted of a review of all laws that were already on record, some were amended, others simply deleted.

"At this time, The Shop began requesting a law submittal from each candidate in order to move into Level Two. All will be submitted; only those that are made into laws will be given full credit. Do you have any questions of clarification? You will be given the next question in one hour — or, if you are ready, sooner. After you complete the other questions you will be allowed an additional hour on this question, and that will complete this test. Begin now."

My pen finished outlining the question. I sat back and thought. Thinking about music and entertainment, many things popped into my head, but each more obscure than its predecessor. Business and manufacturing — I didn't have much to contribute there. Death and the effect of the living… *Ding*.

"Judas… Are you sure?" Ursula's duo-voice pounded in my head.

"I am," I thought and started to write.

'Tearson Law — When a woman has an elective abortion that has no legal modifications; i.e., charges filed with the court for rape or incest. The abortion will be performed with the understanding that the woman will no longer be fertile.'

I sat back thinking of any broader-reaching ramifications. While fewer than forty percent of women have repeat abortions, around fifty-two percent of women wish to have children when they are ready, financially or older.

"What if the pregnancy could do physical harm to the woman?" Ursula prodded in my head.

"What will the difference be on the next pregnancy?" I thought.

"What if she has cancer and the baby could be affected. That brings up a question of what if there is something wrong with the fetus, as in disfigured," the duo-voice asked more softly this time.

"Point." I thought and started to write again.

'Tearson Law — When a woman has an elective abortion, the abortion will be performed with the understanding that the woman will no longer be fertile — provided none of the following exclusions are proven to be true at the time of the abortion. Exclusion one: Legal modifications; i.e., charges filed with the court for rape or incest. Exclusion two:

Verified Harm; i.e., health concern to the mother will cause the child harm or, conversely, health concern of the child that will cause harm to the mother. Exclusion three: Verified Compromise; i.e., a disfigurement of the child that will compromise that child's quality of life.'

"Would you like to think about it or would you like to move on to question two?" Ursula asked.

"Let's move on," I said.

"Question two: When The Shop took over, there were a great deal of documents from the old government that were opened. This was done to allow the general public to see how corrupted the old government really was. Some of these were: that the second shooter in the grassy knoll was CIA, that Watergate was a means to reduce the power of the president, that Bracken was a planted CIA agent, that Blythe was a Communist peace offering, and that Dhoulou was the first non-American President. Or at least these are what the actual official documents really showed. A lot of these were facts that the conspiracy theorists had known for years; The Shop simply allowed the true, un-redacted documents to be released. While you have been with The Shop, you have had access to several documents pertaining to the old government, the majority of which the general public has never, ever seen. The question I have for you is: Can you think of three pieces of knowledge you have come across that The Shop would like to use as proof of the previous government's shortcomings, or things that showed the lack of true concern for the people of the country?"

"Does the word 'propaganda' come into play here?" I thought.

"Be careful—my restriction to not use outside stimulation on you is no longer active," Ursula said aloud.

"Very well. Please ignore the thought. I was simply asking," I thought.

"Forgotten—in as much as it can be," the duo-voice said.

"Thank you," I said aloud and started writing the question down. I had to ask her to say it again.

'Answer one: During the first term of Dhoulou's administration, there was a large push for green energy; the country needed to reduce the cost of producing energy for the masses and the carbon footprint that the energy left on the planet. The government did not wish the people to have free energy—the cost savings for businesses and people would drive the people away from their control. The government gave several billion dollars to three companies that had neither true plan nor design on how to produce the green energy. The continued support of these companies by the government was done with the specific intent to damage the reputation of and take the legs out from under the Green movement.

Answer two: During the second administration of Dhoulou when the government could not put together a budget, Dhoulou himself determined that they must go under sequestration. Upon review of the documentation of how this sequestration was handled, and what happened shortly thereafter, it became obvious that the goal of the sequestration was to weaken the US military. Take, for example, having grounded thirty percent of the fighter squadrons in the country: not only did the planes fall into disrepair but, more importantly, the pilots and crews lost their battle-readiness and the edge that it takes to make the Air Force the feared aerial force that they were. When the war broke out with Israel, the sequestration took its toll on life and machinery in the US Air Force.

Answer three: In 2014 there was a thwarted assassination attempt on President Dhoulou. The plan was scripted to allow Vice President Robinette the opportunity to pursue a ten-year presidential reign. The group that had planned this was led by a group of foreign nationals who had been in support of Vice President Robinette for several decades. The assassination was to take place on a visit to Panama for the one-hundred-year anniversary of the Panama Canal. Prior to the president arriving at the celebration, he had taken some allergy medication. When the champagne came around for toasting, he elected to not actually drink his. The twelve people who were sitting around him all died from a dose of poison in the drinks. In the following months when the full plot came to light, the conspirators who were caught made clear what their goals were, and the fact that the vice president was in no way involved but that Dhoulou had outlived his usefulness.'

I sat back and read what had poured out of my head and populated the paper; I had actually never concerned myself with understanding how it would be received. "I think I am done," I thought.

"You think? Or you are done?" she said, her voice surprising me in the silent room.

"Well, let's go on to the next question and I can come back," I said.

"There are no more questions," she said.

"Give me a moment to review then," I said, and set about re-reading the answers that were going to determine whether I was getting my Level Four clearance. "I am done," I thought, a few minutes later.

"Excellent, Judas. Please sign each paper and slide it into the slot on the podium," she projected into my head. I signed each paper, realizing this was the first time I had actually signed the name *Judas*—my entire life I'd simply written a *J*. Finding the slot on Andelos's podium, I moved the blotter, revealing a slot, into which I put my test. Securing the blotter and making certain the lock was in place, I left the room, shutting off the light and locking the door.

I felt like I did after my first final exam in college. As I walked through the fully deserted halls I had a flashback that was too real to be happening…

"Alec, how did you do?" I turned and Kat was coming up from behind me.

"I'm sorry?" I said.

"Your test—you were so worried about the fluid dynamics test," she explained as she approached me.

Recalling the conversation, I fell into a memory. "The test went real fast. That could mean I knew the material real well."

"Or it could mean you didn't know it at all." She poked me in the chest.

"I'm going with the former." Grabbing her finger and kissing it, her nail had a little burr and it poked my lip.

"Oh, shit, I cut you," Kat said. "Here, let me give you a…" she reached down to her side to grab her purse. "Shoot. I left my purse in my room. Stay here—I will be right back." She turned and started away.

"Kat, leave it. Please just stay with me," I said, breaking away from the way it played out back then.

"Oh, you big baby, it's just a little blood, you'll be fine. Besides, I need my meal pass," she said.

"You can eat my lunch—I'm not hungry. Please don't go," I said.

"You know I have to go," she said. I saw the double meaning—both Ursula ending the simulation and Kat's personality. She needed to know where that ugly purse was. I found myself walking into the cafeteria, and Molly waved to me.

"Judas, your lip is bleeding," she said, reaching over, grabbing a napkin and dabbing at my lip. I lay my head on the table and started to cry. "She caught you off guard didn't she? Ursula can be a bitch sometimes. Now, blow it away, you hear me?"

"Thank you. I am fine now," I said.

"I know you are. I just didn't want those salty tears on my clean table," she smiled. "Go ahead and order some food. I think today would be a good day for a baked potato with turkey, broccoli, and I have this amazingly sharp white cheddar cheese. What do you say?" Molly asked.

"I would love that," I said as she walked back to her haven.

"Molly, why don't you make that two more," Joshua said.

"You got it. So is this J-cubed a permanent thing now or what?" Molly asked.

"Maybe. Seems this tri-team is pretty strong, I would hate to break it up," Joshua said.

"So," Jinau started, "we are a tri-team?"

"I just came up with that—pretty good, huh?" Joshua asked.

"It's lovely, Joshua," Molly said from the kitchen area.

"So, Judas, what happened to your lip?" Jinau asked.

"Ursula," I said.

"What?" Jinau and Joshua both jerked their heads to me, and I told them everything that had happened.

"You don't have to explain it to them," Ursula boomed in my head.

"Yes I do," I thought.

"Are you doing okay?" Joshua asked. I could see how much it worried him to hear the tale.

"Hey, it's been a really good day, and I would have been fine if the stress from the test wasn't making my nerves on edge. And I know that is why she did it, but if the shit that has happened in the last six weeks hasn't broken me, seeing Kat in a hallway isn't going to do it," I said.

"True," Molly said as she placed a plate with two huge baked potatoes in front of me.

"So tell us, Joshua, how was your luck today?" I asked, trying to get the attention off me.

"Young *ma'un*, such an obvious attempt to pull a red herring," Joshua said.

"Da," I said.

"All right. Enough playing with Judas. What did you find out?" Jinau said.

"Okay, there are four governors in his rotation and he crosses over six different Shop agents. This group of governors has been together the longest, and interestingly enough three of The Shop agents have also been in this rotation for over ten years."

"Then we need to review those agents as well?" I asked.

"I would leave that alone," Molly paused as we looked up, "for now." And she headed back to the kitchen.

"Agreed," Joshua said. "The governors of Virginia, Louisiana and Texas are the next interviews. I want to meet with the governor of Alaska again."

"Will all The Shop agents be covered in these interviews?" I asked.

"No, the third agent is currently in Minnesota," Joshua said.

"So we need to start with these four specific governors. How are we going to not look like we are targeting these people?" I asked. "You just flew to Alaska; now we will head to Texas, then Louisiana, then Minnesota, and then talk to Virginia. Where is the logic in that pattern?"

"I am not quite following what you are asking," Jinau asked.

"There was a comment that Sensenmann made that first time we talked: 'Nothing like targeted selection.' That is what I am questioning—are we violating what we were asked to do?" I said.

"I did not remember that but now I do—thanks. I am not too concerned about that. This is actually following a lead, this has nothing to do with their past behaviors," Joshua said.

"I am confused; when we go talk to them based upon this, it is targeted selection," I said.

"Targeted selection when discussing interviewing is a technique for getting information out of the person you are interviewing. Sensenmann was saying that is not the style of interview he was going for," Joshua said.

"Oh." I was embarrassed.

"Judas, this is a good conversation; don't be embarrassed or back off. This will make you two a great team," Jinau said.

"That is true. You need to remember, I have been doing this for a long time. It's okay to learn from me and I will continue to do my best to listen to you. It's good you're such a big behemoth—it will help me remember to do that," Joshua said.

"Thanks. I don't like when I am wrong," I said. "Okay, tomorrow morning? We head to Minnesota first then hit Texas and Louisiana on our way back here to Virginia?"

"I think yes, we can hit them all in one day, and then we can pull together a plan the day after?" Jinau said, looking over at Joshua.

"I would normally say no to this, but I have this burning in my gut..." Joshua started.

"You have a hunch?" Jinau interrupted.

"No, I have this burning in my gut; I don't think I have been chewing my food well enough with all this talking going on," Joshua said, standing up.

"Oh, sure—make the food I slave over the butt of your joke," Molly said as we brought the dishes up to the counter.

"Apologies, Molly, the food was awesome—thanks," I said as we departed. I was thinking back on the day as we walked. If someone would have ever told me I would be doing things like this, I would have laughed at them, I was a good ole corn-fed boy destined for working out my body to have a long football career. This stemmed into a thought: which would have been better?

"You are perfect for this role, Judas," Ursula said in my head. I really was getting too used to her doing that.

"So, Judas, you've had a hell of a day. Are you all right with five a.m.?" Joshua asked as we arrived at my room.

"Sure am—five a.m. at the lobby to leave for the airport. See ya then." After they said their good nights, I went in and laid out my clothes for tomorrow and then, without changing into appropriate night clothing, my lids crushed out the desire to do so.

Chapter 15

"Well, it looks like you were going to sleep through your departure time." I sat up. Kat was standing at the foot of my bed taking off my shoe. "These are not the shoes for today's activities."

"I know—I laid out my clothes," I said.

"So are these Shop-style pajamas?" Kat said, smiling.

"Only for important agents." I sat up and started to head to the bathroom. She followed me. "No, no, missy—you know when you go in here hours pass and I miss important events."

"Oh, come on, it was one time—and all it was, was getting your name on a stupid perfect attendance plaque that no one ever looks at anyway," Kat said.

"*I* looked at it," I said.

"I remember; you said, 'Look at all the commitment these guys had. I want my name on that plaque someday," Kat said in an interesting impersonation of me.

"Ya but it isn't, is it?" I said through the toothbrush cleaning my teeth.

"I already apologized for that, Mr. Perfect." She frowned.

"It's all good, Kat. I did things far better than that last year. That silly little thing…"

"May have been the only thing they would not have erased—they never even looked."

"What?" I said as I put my leg into my pants

"You know that Alec Tearson never existed, right? You know that you never got all those awards. And even Michigan Tech lost the title. It was the only way," Ursula's version of Kat said.

"I understand." I finished getting dressed and left the room, heading for the lobby. As I did, I thought about the hickey that came as a result of the missing that one practice and the comments in the locker room—those bastards got more mileage out of that simple hickey, and all in all it may have helped them see me as something more than 'Mr. Perfect.' I wondered if she knew that. She had never in our time together done anything like that. Interesting. Jinau was waiting and we chatted for a bit about the governor of Alaska and that trip they had taken.

"All right you two — what's the hold up?" Joshua said as he walked past us.

"Sorry to keep you waiting," I said as I got up to follow.

"Wait — what?" Jinau sputtered

"Come on, Jinau, we don't want to keep him waiting any longer," I said as she got up and started to follow. We got to the plane in what felt like no time at all, which was strange as none of us were talking.

"Sir, the flight plan that you filed has not come back yet," the pilot said as we got into the plane — which made sense; he couldn't have filed it more than five hours ago.

"I want you to contact the tower and tell them the plans have been filed and we are on Sensenmann's orders to get these interviews done today, and you can speak to him when we don't get our asses in the air." Joshua was on a roll.

"We will get the prep work done and perhaps by that time we will receive the completed paperwork," he said as he turned his back and continued to look into the cockpit.

"Ladies and gentlemen, we have all the necessary paperwork now and we will begin the taxiing momentarily," the copilot said over the PA.

"That didn't take long," I said.

"It is a good thing because I am not sure what would actually happen if I pushed harder," Joshua said.

"Let's not find out — shall we?" Jinau said.

"Sounds good to me," Joshua said as he sat back, pulling out his briefcase. "We have not changed anything from the last time you were with us but it has been a while so let's discuss how we will handle the questioning. And you should probably get your transmitters in place so we can chat."

"Sorry?" I said, and Joshua did a little jazz hands at me. "You're using my keyboard?"

"*Your* keyboard? Gee that is very selfish—it's The Shop's keyboard, and I mean they were part of your Level Four training after all," Jinau said.

"So if I fail the Level Four testing, do I get them back?" I asked.

"Why of course you don't," Joshua said.

"Not cool," I said. I opened my briefcase, which was again under my seat; there was a black glasses case with three silver circles on it. I opened it and saw my glasses; they were not the same as Joshua's pair, in that mine were actually more to my style. I put them on and clicked the inlaid button.

"It takes a bit to get the transmitters in place and then get them calibrated. You should do that while we are in flight," Jinau said.

"Good point," I said, clicking off the glasses and reaching back into the briefcase to grab the black leather box. I opened it and saw several semi-circle transmitters with double-sided tape. I started applying the tape to the back of my finger nails. I looked in the box after I had applied the last transmitter, found the signal amplifier and what looked like an O-ring that had been customized with a flat spot and two metal bands. I had to admit they'd done a good job of making this transmitter look innocuous. Once I had applied all the transmitters and put on the repeater, I clicked on my glasses and then squeezed both of the metal bands on the O-ring, turning on the repeater. Now the icon appeared on my glasses. I moved my eyes to look down on it twice and the words 'Calibrate keyboard Y/N appeared.' I looked at the 'Y' twice and words flashed across my screen, telling me which keys to push and words to type. Ten minutes after I started, I typed a text message to Jinau, 'test test test.'

She promptly replied back, 'received and replying… Hello… Now stop messing around with your new toy." *Not cool.*

The flight was very quick. Jinau had asked me about my visit with Gypsy, and before I could really get into the story of my experience, we were landing. "Current departure time is two hours hence," the pilot said as we were leaving, allowing his anger at Joshua for the scolding he had given him earlier to come through as sarcasm now.

"Are you looking to have a problem with an old man?" Joshua, who had already started off the plane in front of me, had now turned and was talking over my shoulder. It looked like an old game of "hold me back," but as I had witnessed how much Joshua wasn't an old man whatever he may appear, I knew that was not the game here, and I stepped aside. "When I return 'two hours hence' there will be a new pilot in that seat or we will be taking this out to the tool shed." He had his finger in the pilot's face – a man twenty years his junior, four inches of height and forty pounds of muscle on him.

"Yes, sir. I am sorry, sir, I meant no disrespect." The pilot blinked and Joshua stormed off the plane. I wondered briefly if I would ever see that pilot again.

The car that was waiting had an agent who looked to be around Joshua's age, and from the look upon his face they had a history. "Agent," Joshua said in greeting. Not waiting for a reply, he got into the vehicle. The agent knew enough about these visits to not ask any questions while we were in transit. We arrived at the governor's residence around seven-thirty Central Standard Time. He was waiting for us in his study. The rest of his staff was not in this part of his residence. "Governor, I appreciate you making accommodations to see us in this early hour. We have a long day ahead of us," Joshua said.

"Anything I can do?" the governor asked.

"Governor, I have six questions. To each I want a simple 'yes' or 'no' answer. Do you understand?"

"Yes."

"Are you currently plotting against The Shop?" Joshua asked

"No," the governor replied. As the governor was replying, Joshua sent a text to me asking if I had my facial recognition program running, to which I replied that I did.

"Do you know of anyone who is plotting against The Shop?" As Joshua started to ask, I adjusted myself so that both the agent and the governor were in my direct view.

"No."

"Are you willingly ignoring any laws The Shop has established?" Joshua asked.

"No," the governor answered but my glasses flashed on the agent as he pulled his shoulders back and flexed his fist.

"Do you wish to stay in the position that you currently hold, as an elected position within the government?" Joshua asked immediately upon the governor's previous answer, as he had before.

"Yes." The governor for the first time had a trigger emotion—fear—and at the same time the agent turned his head like a dog unsure of the sound it heard.

"Is there anything that we, as Shop agents reporting to Sensenmann, and only Sensenmann, should know?" Joshua asked his last question and waited.

"No," the governor said.

"Okay, now I want you to leave the room," Joshua said. The governor started to walk out. "Governor, my apologies, I mean the agent." The agent walked out and closed the door. I watched the agent very closely when he walked out, but saw nothing. "Sir, I am going to ask you six questions. To each I want a simple 'yes' or 'no.' Do you understand?"

"Yes."

"Are you currently plotting against The Shop?" Joshua asked again.

"No," the governor replied.

"Do you know of anyone who is plotting against The Shop?"

"No, I'm not," the governor said.

"Governor that is not what I asked you. Do you know of anyone who is plotting against The Shop?" Joshua repeated. The governor couldn't answer. He kept moving to the door and then he would look at the floor. "I think we are done here. Do you need anything from us?"

"No," the governor said.

As we started to walk out, Jinau stopped. "You need to hold it together. We will be back soon. Can you handle this?"

"Yes, thank you," he said.

"Thank you, sir. That was all we needed from you." As Joshua was talking, I opened the door. When the door opened, the agent was standing ten feet away and it did not appear that he had moved. When he looked at me I indicated for him to come in, closing the door after he entered. "This is considered Article Eighty-Seven. No conversations outside of this room regarding what just happened here. Are you one hundred percent clear on this?" They both acknowledged Joshua's question, and we walked out, not pausing until we were in the car, when Joshua surprised me by saying, "What a waste of time. Sometimes I wish I could do something that I felt was worthwhile." As he said this my glasses started flashing on the agent — and then I remembered I hadn't shut off my glasses and smiled. And no one said another word the entire trip.

"Good morning," the copilot said. "The other pilot has not arrived."

"Please tell Cartner to come back then; we need to leave." And then, looking under the plane, he saw a set of legs in pilot pants. "It shouldn't take you long," he said smiling.

"Yes, sir. I mean no, sir," the copilot said, coyly acknowledging the fact that the pilot was there.

When we were seated, Jinau said, "That was a strange thing to say in the car."

"Was it? It felt like the right thing to say," Joshua said.

"Well, it worked," she continued. "Did you see how his posture changed?"

"Actually, no, I wasn't looking at him," Joshua said with a tone of 'well duh.'

"I believe I got it," I said and stood up, taking off my glasses and racking them into our monitor. I jumped ahead in my video to the recording of the car ride, and froze it as Joshua's mouth started to move. "See how, when your first sounds were coming out, his entire body tensed up?" I started the playback again, this time at half-speed, as Joshua's mouth stopped moving, "See the slight grin touch the corner of his mouth, and there his shoulders relaxed and he even sat back a bit."

"Nice shot. How did you know...?" Jinau started. The plane took off.

"It was just lucky. I had forgotten to turn off the record feature," I said.

"Well, it's important. Let's make certain to record all the way to the plane here on out. Don't you love his honesty?" Joshua said, turning to Jinau.

"It's refreshing to see a new agent who is of principles," she replied.

"Garsh, I am all a twitter with your kind words, you two," I joked

"If you tweet anything about it, I will categorically deny any such folderol," Joshua said. I pulled a small jump drive out of my briefcase and plugged it in the front of the unit and backed up my glasses. After it was done, I purged everything and let them charge for the next visit. "The charge on this new model lasts all day and the memory is insane."

"Still, never know how things will go," I said, letting them stay on the charger. I saw his fingers move. "Boy Scout, huh?" I said, catching him off guard. Jinau laughed. The rest of the flight was spent talking about miscellaneous adventures that the older members of J-cubed had in the 'old' days; there was a lot of laughing until the pilot told us to prepare for landing.

"We need to be at our best—and, remember, no talking; this could get ugly and ugly fast. If it does, aim to disarm only," Joshua said.

"By that he means aim for the gun—not to take the arm off," Jinau clarified. I looked at Joshua; I wasn't so sure that was what he'd meant. We repeated the landing ritual that had superseded this visit and shortly thereafter walked into the Capitol building of Texas, then into the governor's office and the door was closed.

"Governor, I have six questions. To each I want a simple 'yes' or 'no.' Do you understand?" Joshua asked.

"I am here," the governor said.

"Please answer 'yes' or 'no.' That was the first question," Joshua said.

"Yes," the governor begrudgingly replied.

"Are you currently plotting against The Shop?" Joshua asked

"No," the governor replied. It was hard to get both the governor and the agent into frame. Just then I got a text from Jinau that she would cover the agent and that I should focus on the governor.

"Do you know of anyone who is plotting against The Shop?" asked Joshua.

"No." His face was turning red and he knew it. "I need to ask you why the hell this line of questioning is being pointed at me—I have been a governor for twenty years," the governor blurted out.

"Are you willingly ignoring any laws The Shop has established?" Joshua asked, ignoring the outburst.

"No," the governor answered. I was thinking that things were riding a tightrope.

"Do you wish to stay in the position that you currently hold, as an elected position within the government?" Joshua asked.

"What the hell kind of question is that? Who the hell are you to barge in here without an appointment? That shows no respect for other people's schedules. Do you know how many..." The governor was starting on a roll.

"Do you wish to stay in the position that you currently hold, as an elected position within the government?" Joshua asked again more loudly, cutting him off.

"Yes," the governor said through clenched teeth.

"Is there anything that we, as Shop agents reporting to Sensenmann, and only Sensenmann, should know?" Joshua asked his last question and waited.

"No," the governor replied, his sneer of derision clearly visible.

"Okay. Now I want you to leave the room," Joshua said, looking at The Shop agent, who went white as newly fallen snow. "Please depart." This time he did. "Look, Governor, this is where I ask you the same six questions, without the agent in here, to see if there are any issues between you two." Joshua said calmly.

"Six questions? I only counted five," the governor said.

"As I said, the first of the six is 'Do you understand?'" Joshua continued, unfazed although the governor was obviously trying to shake him.

"That is silly referring to that as a…" he continued.

"Shut the fuck up," Jinau let out. The governor's face went purple.

"Are you going to let your subordinate talk to me that way?" he asked.

"Better it was her than him or me. I wanted to smack you with the butt of my gun, and from the clenched jaw of Judas, I think he was going to find a cross to nail you to," Joshua said.

"I am the governor of Texas. I will *not* be spoken to in such a manner. You will leave my office at once." We didn't move. "Did you hear me? I said…"

"Yes, we heard you—and unless you wish to get arrested and taken to an undisclosed location where I will ask you these questions next week…"

"We have plans for abating the office next week," Jinau added.

"Well, it could be two weeks…" Joshua started again.

"We have the birthday for Sensenmann's pug, Bubbles," I said.

"Oh, yeah, well you may be stuck at an undisclosed location until I have time to talk to you. But understand this," and he walked right up to the governor of the great state of Texas and leaned in as if to whisper in his ear, "*You will answer my fucking questions!*" he yelled in his ear. The governor, to his credit, didn't even wince.

"Fine," the governor said, and Joshua stepped back taking his original area.

"Governor, I have six questions. To each I want a simple 'yes' or 'no.' Do you understand?" Joshua asked.

"Yes," the governor said.

"Are you currently plotting against The Shop?" Joshua asked

"No."

"Do you know of anyone who is plotting against The Shop?" asked Joshua.

"No."

"Are you willingly ignoring any laws The Shop has established?" Joshua asked.

"No," the governor said.

"Do you wish to stay in the position that you currently hold, as an elected position within the government?" Joshua asked.

"Yes," the governor said, once again through clenched teeth.

"Is there anything that we, as Shop agents reporting to Sensenmann, and only Sensenmann, should know?" Joshua asked.

"No," the governor replied.

I walked over to the door and let the other agent back in. When he got in the room, I closed the door started over to my place. About that time Joshua started again, "This is considered Article Eighty-Seven. No conversations outside of this room regarding what just happened here. Are you one hundred percent clear on this?" He was nothing if not repetitive. They both acknowledged Joshua's question, and we walked out and headed down to the car. I waited until the agent got in. He sat next to Jinau, back to the driver. We pulled out and headed to the airport. Fifteen minutes into the drive, Jinau pulled a Joshua.

"Why do we have to keep wasting all our time?" Jinau said. I continued to look at her incredulously as the agent was in full screen as well.

"Not now," Joshua said coldly. Again I saw the agent physically relax. We got to the airport, exiting the car without another word spoken, and we boarded the plane. When we sat down on the plane, Joshua relaxed and said, "Nice touch in the car." Jinau nodded, "So is there any doubt that both of them are involved?"

"Not in my mind," I said.

"I want to watch the film. I didn't see the governor while the agent was in there with him," Jinau added. I got up and plugged in my glasses and we watched the recording. Following the viewing, Jinau looked at Joshua. "There is no doubt, that man is one of the leaders in whatever is going on. I think he fancies himself as the next Sensenmann."

"I think he just fancies himself," I said.

"Why, Judas, what a truly terrible thing to say about the governor of the grayt stayt of Tayxus," Jinau said through a smile that usually appeared only on cats that have not only ate the canary but opened the fridge and took all the cream as well.

"What a terrible accent," I poked. The plane bounced as it took off. "Louisiana, here we come."

"I am going to grab a sandwich—you want something?" Joshua said as the plane got to a stable height.

"No," Jinau said.

"I will look. I'm also starving. I think I could eat an entire cow—not one of those free-range ones, I mean the ones from the old days of steroid injections and growth hormones," I said.

"Okay, now that is bordering on crimes against the state; you know that since the two-year Blythe/Dhoulou Administration, beef and chicken are illegal, and turkey can only be raised free range. Taking shots at free-range cows, very distasteful of you," Joshua said.

"Why did they do it?" I asked

"Do?" Joshua looked confused for a second, "Oh, you mean the meat—and I thought you were talking about this governor's plot. They made meat illegal in order to gain control of the land—the farmers who were raising chickens and cows took up too much land. They allowed free-range turkeys specifically because a turkey can grow on less land than a chicken. Had it been the other way, then we would have chicken on the menu. I expect that turkey will be made illegal very soon," Joshua said as he finished making a sandwich.

"Joshua," Jinau yelled from across the plane. He turned and saw her rooting through the drawers of the conference room.

"What are you looking for so crazily?" Joshua asked as he walked back to the seats where he had been sitting.

"I need a new ink ball for the printer." She sounded frantic.

"What the hell are you talking about?" Joshua asked, then looking over at the table he saw the electric typewriter sitting open with the head removed. "Sorry, I still call it a ribbon. You remember the good old days where we just replaced the ribbon? And the keys would stamp on that ribbon and we would complete our letters to file?"

"Come on, the ribbons always had to be burned after a single letter was written, and the damn keys would stick. This is so much better—all the keys on a ball and a ball that contains ink. So there is no other record of the document besides the document itself. So if some idiot forgets to burn the ribbon you are still safe," Jinau said, still digging around in the drawer.

"Maybe, but if the ribbon ran out, you could always rewind it a little. These simply run out and it's out, it's done," Joshua said.

"Did you try shaking it?" I said.

"What?" Jinau asked.

"Try shaking the ball—you may get enough ink spread around to finish the letter," I explained. She took the ball and shook it, then placed it back in the typewriter. She started to type then gave a resounding thumbs up. "What is the classified letter for?" I asked looking at the blue ink on the paper.

"How did you know the letter was classified?" she asked.

"It's the blue ink—that color blue is not copier-friendly, so you can't photocopy them," I said, sitting down and starting to eat my sandwich.

"So Jinau, is your seal still a dove with an arrow pinning its wings above its back?" Joshua asked.

"Yes it is," Jinau said, pulling her orange and blue wax, loading it into the melter and pushing the button until the melted wax pooled over the closed side of the envelope she had addressed and placed her typed letter into; surprisingly, the wax was a gold color. She allowed it to sit for a bit while she turned her stone in her Shop ring over, and pressed it into the cooling wax. Where her emblem pressed in, the unmixed blue and orange wax showed through, "I really think this is stupid." As she said this I reached in my pocket and removed my ring.

"I, on the other hand, think it is fantastic—no different than the days of squires running letters for their knights or kings. The letter is assured to make it without being read," Joshua said.

"But the entire process—why is it that classified letters are no longer allowed on computers?" she asked, knowing the answer full well.

"Well, there are secrets that are to be kept. And anything on computers can be read by others, even if you erase it," I said as the plane touched down. When it stopped I took Joshua's plate and mine and walked over to the sink.

Jinau had grabbed my briefcase, which I forgot. "Pug? Bubbles?" she said as she gave my briefcase to me and we all stepped off the plane. I fumbled with it as I was still holding my ring. The car was not there. We stood outside the plane and Cartner went back inside. "What's in your hand?" Jinau prodded.

"My ring I am not supposed to wear it until I pass Level..." I started.

"Your stone... what is your seal?" Jinau said jumping around excitedly.

"I don't know I didn't look." I said.

"Sir, the car will be here in five minutes," Cartner said as he returned from the plane a few minutes later. "Would you like to step back in?" he asked.

"No, we will wait here; I do not want that driver to think for a second that we waited patiently," Joshua said. The pilot said nothing but he did get back on the plane himself. "Well young *ma'un*, turn that stone."

"I don't want to jinx myself," I said.

"Give it here then," Jinau said grabbing at the ring in my clenched hand. I raised my hand over my head. She jumped once and realized that she could not possibly reach it and kicked me in the shin.

"Ok," I said handing it to her and rubbing my leg.

"I thought she was going for the tiddlywinks." Joshua laughed at my discomfort as Jinau turned the stone and showed him.

"Let me see," I said. She waited a moment; I reared my leg back pretending as if I were going to return the kick. She gave it back and I looked; the stone had a broken cross outset on it.

"I like it." Joshua said. As he showed me his it was a long horn sitting across a wall. "Joshua's trumpet and the walls of Jericho," he said.

Chapter 16

When the car pulled up, the agent in the back opened the door and stepped out, waiting for Joshua to get in, and then stepped in behind him, sitting next to him. Jinau jumped in ahead of me, winking.

"Sir, my apologies. The..." the driver was saying.

"Just get us there and be ready to leave as soon as we walk out," Joshua said, and Jinau raised her eyebrow at him. A moment later the text 'Did Joshua's cold heart melt in the sun while we waited?' arrived. He replied, 'Look at his eyes—something happened.'

"Yes, sir," the driver said. We stopped at the capitol and got out of the car. The agent still had the look of a schoolboy when the substitute teacher who just walked in the classroom ended up being the principal of the school. We rode the elevator in total silence and looking straight ahead. I started to feel bad for the kid, who was at least five years my senior.

"Governor, we have six questions and we need six 'yes' or 'no' answers. No explanation is required nor desired." He paused, "Do you understand?"

"Yes," the governor said.

"Are you currently plotting against The Shop?" Joshua asked

"No," the answer from the governor came right on the final syllable.

"Do you know of anyone who is plotting against The Shop?" asked Joshua.

"No."

"Are you willingly ignoring any laws The Shop has established?" he asked.

"No," the governor said.

"Do you wish to stay in the position that you currently hold, as an elected position within the government?" Joshua asked.

"Yes," the governor said.

"Is there anything that we, as Shop agents reporting to Sensenmann, and only Sensenmann, should know?" Joshua asked.

"No," the governor replied. Joshua sent us a message, 'I am considering not sending the agent out.' Jinau replied, 'Consistency first—don't want to vary.' 'Excellent point,' Joshua replied.

"Agent, I need you to step out of the room," Joshua said and the agent practically ran out of the room. "Now, Governor, I am going to ask you six questions and I want a 'yes' or 'no' answer to them—okay?"

"Yes." He looked a tad confused, showing emotion for the first time.

"Are you currently plotting against The Shop?" Joshua asked

"No."

"Do you know of anyone who is plotting against The Shop?" Asked Joshua.

"No." This time he sounded perturbed.

"Are you willingly ignoring any laws The Shop has established?" he asked.

"No," the governor said.

"Do you wish to stay in the position that you currently hold, as an elected position within the government?" Joshua asked.

"Yes," the governor said.

"Is there anything that we, as Shop agents reporting to Sensenmann, and only Sensenmann, should know?" Joshua asked.

"No," the governor replied. Jinau walked over to the door and beckoned the agent back in. When he got in the room, Joshua started again, "This is considered Article Eighty-Seven. No conversations outside of this room regarding what just happened here. Are you one hundred percent clear on this?" They both acknowledged Joshua's question, and we walked out. During the car ride, the recording continued, just as it had been each time before. I did not feel this agent had any part in the governor's "plot," as Joshua had called it.

"Sir," the agent said to Joshua when the car had stopped, "can I speak to you alone for a moment?"

"You can step on the plane with the three of us. It is needed for us all to hear the same thing," Joshua said, and the agent did.

"There is something going on at the capitol — I don't know what but the governor has had other governors visiting him and I looked in the records; there is no precedence for this number of visits," the local agent said.

"Thank you. I will most likely follow up with you on which governors, but for right now, I don't want you to tell me — understand?" Joshua said.

"Yes, sir," the agent replied and then got off the plane. When he had left, the pilot and copilot got on board.

"Back to Virginia now, sir?" the pilot asked.

"Yes, thank you, but not home — to the capitol." Joshua said.

"All right. Give me five to hit the air," the pilot said with a tip of his hat.

"Cartner, did my communication get out okay?" Jinau asked.

"Yes, it did. Should be arriving at the airport about now. Fifteen minutes after that will be to target," the pilot said and this time he left.

"This has been an odd day," Jinau said. "I haven't had to send a confidential sealed communiqué in at least three years."

"I wasn't even going to ask you about it," Joshua said.

"Well, we'd better get some ink balls if we are going to get those requests," she said.

"Where did the request come from?" I asked.

"Ursula," she said pointing to the glasses.

"Can she hear or just monitor texts and stuff?" I asked.

"*They're* your invention—how would we know?" Joshua said.

"Well, I haven't used them for talking to her, but the program for the facial recognition is linked to her," I said. Then I sent a thought to Ursula: 'I have a question on the statement that Kat made this morning.' To no avail. "I don't think she can work like she does in the Mill."

"Why do you think…?" Jinau's comment was cut short as the pilot came over the speaker.

"Everything is set; we will be leaving momentarily."

"… She can't work like in the Mill?" she continued.

"I just tried to talk to her with my mind, and she didn't reply," I said.

"She never replies to me that way," Jinau said.

"Even at the Mill?" I asked

"Even at the Mill," she said.

"Joshua, how about you?" I asked

"The relationship between Ursula and you is your relationship—but, yes, she replies to me sometimes," he said. As the plane took off, the pilot said we would arrive in about one hour.

"So," I said, getting up and plugging my glasses into the unit. "You ready for some high-class POV porn?"

"Oh, *ya*," Jinau joked with a fist pump.

"Grow up you two. Do you really even need to watch that? That kid is about as guilty as a bull frog is for croakin'," Joshua said.

"Good point," I said.

"What is it with you two and not being consistent?" Jinau said.

"Fine." I pushed play and the movie started. Then I walked over to the kitchen area and made a sandwich. "You know," I said, taking a bite of my sandwich, "it's amazing how every time you ask the six questions, it's almost like an exact cut and paste. So if they make this a movie, do you think they will shorten it by having you talk to all the governors at the same time? You know, like a little square with a face shot of all of them one on top of the other?"

"I personally think you should just shut up before..." Joshua started

"I know—like that old show with the guy with kids who married the lady with kids..." Jinau interrupted me.

"I don't think you could get any closer to violating copyright," Joshua said, cutting her off. "So where do we stand on the governor of Louisiana?"

"It's a guilty from me," I said.

"Myself as well," Jinau added.

"And me. What about the agent from Louisiana?" Joshua continued.

"Not a chance. I would be interested to see which other governors he says visited the Louisiana capitol building," I said.

"I agree he is clean," Jinau said.

"So we are still unanimous on our selections. The governors from Alaska, Texas and Louisiana are definitely involved. The governor from Minnesota not involved. The Shop agents from Alaska, Minnesota and Texas are also involved, and the one from Louisiana definitely not involved," Joshua summarized.

"Well, let's hit the capitol in Richmond and see what we get," Jinau said with a bit more punch than she meant to. Joshua and I both turned to her with an eyebrow raised, "What?"

"We are getting ready to land," the pilot said.

"Saved by the bell," I said to her.

"What?" she said innocently.

"Damn car better be there," Joshua grumbled as we started to taxi.

"It is—I can see it up there. Besides a car waiting for you may be a bad thing someday," Jinau said.

"I didn't even get a chance to eat my sandwich," I pouted and tossed it out as we walked off the plane.

"Agent," Joshua greeted the man at the door of the car.

"Agent," the local agent acknowledged Joshua. We all got into the car and headed to the third capitol of the day. Another quiet trip. We walked into the building and the place was bustling.

When we got to the governor's office, the assistant stood up, "Gentleman, I am sorry. The governor is meeting with someone. He should be done any moment."

"I understand we had no appointment, and that those who do have probably had the appointment for weeks. Is it okay if we stand?" Joshua asked.

"Of course," she said. A few moments later, the door opened.

"Mr. Danvers, it is so exciting to have members of our community wanting to put their hard-earned money into an endeavor such as this," the governor was saying. "All we need is a final name for the business and then we can both sign the documents we have put together."

"Thank you, Governor Kincade. You can't..." he smashed his model straight into Joshua and me. Pieces crashed to the floor. We all scrambled to pick them up, "Gee, you Shop guys destroyed my business." He was obviously nervous as he stood up with the model and started for the elevator.

"Sir," Joshua said. The man, Mr. Danvers, turned as Joshua held out a small piece. "The Dive." He took the diving board from Joshua with a gleam in his previously nervous eyes.

"The Dive." He smiled and handed me his model, and walked back up to the governor who extended him a pen and turned around. Mr. Danvers took the pen, smoothed the paper on the governor's back, wrote something on the paper and then signed it, handing the pen to Governor Kincade then turning around. The governor put the paper on Mr. Danvers' back and signed it as well.

"The Dive," the governor said, shaking hands very enthusiastically with the man. "Rachel, please help Mr. Danvers get those papers filed at once."

"Yes, sir," she replied, and she led the man to the elevator. Joshua made an odd face as we walked into the office, and typed a message, 'Jinau, create a disturbance to get me five minutes with the governor.'

"Oh, shit, I'm going to throw up." Jinau grabbed a trash can and made heaving sounds into it. "Can you help me to the…" another heaving noise. The local agent grabbed her and they ran off.

"Does your door seal from the inside?" Joshua asked as he walked into the office with the governor and me.

"Yes, it does."

"Please do it," Joshua said and the governor complied. "Governor, what was your reason for your comment a moment ago? 'At once,'" Joshua asked.

"It was just a…" Governor Kincade started

"Look, your agent is going to be here in a moment."

"Look, I don't know what you're here for but there is some serious shit going down and I need to get it out…"

"Are you being threatened?" Joshua asked.

"My family is, yes."

"I am going to ask you questions. You need to say only that you are being blackmailed about a sex scandal and you want out—nothing about the rest. Do you understand?" Joshua continued.

"Yes," Governor Kincade said.

"Open the door. Quick, they are coming back." The door opened and Joshua and I stepped out of the room. "Are you okay?" he asked Jinau as she rounded the corner.

"Yes, sir. Sorry, sir, just too much flying today, I guess," she said, wiping her mouth with a towel. "Governor, I left your assistant's trash can in the bathroom. Sorry about that."

"It's okay. Please come in," the governor said. When we got into the room the doors shut and sealed.

"Governor, we have six questions and we need six 'yes' or 'no' answers. No explanation is required nor desired." He paused, "Do you understand?"

"Yes," the governor said.

"Are you currently plotting against The Shop?" Joshua asked

"No," the answer was quick from the governor.

"Do you know of anyone who is plotting against The Shop?" Asked Joshua.

"No."

"Are you willingly ignoring any laws The Shop has established?" Joshua asked.

"No," the governor said.

"Do you wish to stay in the position that you currently hold, as an elected position within the government?" Joshua asked.

"Um. I'm sorry?" the governor asked, looking put out.

"Do you wish to stay in the position that you currently hold, as an elected position within the government?" Joshua repeated.

"I am not sure," the governor said.

"Is there anything that we, as Shop agents reporting to Sensenmann, and only Sensenmann, should know?" Joshua asked.

"I am being blackmailed. I was involved with this woman and she is threatening to go public," the governor replied.

"Governor, I am not certain what Sensenmann would say about that. It wasn't his action that caused this. Are you saying you expect us to deal with your little problem?"

"I don't know, I guess not. I..." he waited, perhaps uncertain what to do. "No, I do not wish to stay in the office I was elected to," he said. The agent was looking around like the Easter Bunny had just hopped in the room and mooned him with his fuzzy little tail.

"We will need to return tomorrow to discuss what exactly this means This is the first case of this since the reformation of the government under The Shop," Joshua said, and we all walked out. The ride to the airport was definitely different than the others. "How did you not know about this? Who is this woman? Is the governor married? Does he have kids?" Joshua was barking out questions and the agent was still transfixed on that fuzzy little tail. We got to the plane and Joshua was yelling into his phone to get him Sensenmann right away. The agent never even got out of the limo. We sealed the doors to the plane.

"What in the hell just happened?" Jinau asked.

"We got the governor's' Plot, if we can get Kincade out without them knowing it," Joshua said, almost reaching out and kissing her.

"I've got an idea — can I run with it?" she asked.

"Of course. Okay, leave me here." She walked over to the door and let herself out. Joshua closed it behind her.

"Home, boys," Joshua said to the pilots. "Agent Jinau is not coming with us." He came over and sat down as the engines started up.

"How did you know?" I asked him with awe, and even reverence.

"He gave too big a shit about that guy. No Governor does that. I knew something was up," Joshua said.

"I got a lot to learn," I said.

"Young *ma'un*, we all do," he said simply. It wasn't even ten minutes and we were home. The car drove us to the Mill. Halfway there Joshua's phone rang.

"Joshua. Hold on, Jinau, let me put you on speaker." He pushed a button, and at the same time I rolled up the window to the front.

"Hello?" Jinau said.

"We are here," Joshua said. "Go ahead."

"I have a reporter who is meeting me at the governor's car after he leaves tonight. Watch the news — you're going to love it," she said and hung up.

"I figured she would do something like that," he smiled.

Chapter 17

We got back to the Mill and went straight to my room. Being in the hospital wing had a couple advantages: for one, my TV was big. The news was starting and the anchorman was saying something about a shock at the capital. The scene cut away to the governor's exit. "Governor Kincade, I am Dot Buchanan, with News Service 17, Capital City's Certified News Network. I am following up on the allegation that you are involved in a sex and blackmailing scandal, and looking for a comment." The girl was tenacious, following the governor and his lieutenant governor, Shop agent. As she had stated, she was a *Certified* journalist, and the agent could not forcibly remove her — what a great plan; this young reporter is going to go far, I thought as the car door shut in her face.

I looked over at Joshua as he made a phone call. "Governor Kincade, this is agent Joshua. Yes, sir, I saw the news. Yes, sir, I understand that was embarrassing. Yes, sir, we were the only ones who knew about the sex scandal. Tomorrow afternoon you will announce that you are stepping down. I will have a full press conference set up. Afterward you will have a one-on-one interview with that reporter who just scooped this story. Do you understand?" Joshua said. I could hear the governor being insane on the other end, an obvious show for the agent, and then he said he understood, loudly. Joshua hung up. He then dialed the phone again. "Mrs. Kincade."

"I am not talking to the press," she shouted.

"I am not the press." She stopped yelling. "My name is Agent Joshua. I need you to understand that your husband is a hero. Do not believe any of what is about to happen. Goodbye." And he hung up.

"That was good of you," I said.

"You need to hush up. I have to determine how to fill this last hole." Just then Sonya walked in. "Sonya, I need a blackmailing bitch," Joshua said.

"Well, I am a black female bitch—does that help?" she said.

"Probably not, unless you still have your identity outside The Shop?"

"I do. I'm a clean-cut accountant in New York City," Sonya said proudly.

"Oh, ya, you are my bitch," Joshua said.

"If you need it that bad..." she started

"We are trying to save a governor and his family," he said humbly.

"You got me. I am your blackmailing bitch," she said, smiling.

"Sonya, what brought you down here?" I asked.

"Oh, ya, Molly had asked me to check in on you and let you know to come say hello when you can," she said.

"Thanks, Sonya," I smiled as she turned to leave.

"Sonya, a Dot Buchanan is going to be setting up an interview. I need you to play the scornful lover. Remember, only talk to Dot Buchanan," he said.

"How about this: you lost your love child to cancer and that's when he dumped you. We need a bit of hate for him to get him out clean," I added.

"Okay, young *ma'un*. You're a bit of an asshole, aren't you?" Joshua asked but did acknowledge that it was a good plan.

"You got it, sweetie," Sonya said, then turned and left.

"Well I guess we go see Molly and then turn in and wait for the chips to fall," Joshua said. We shut off my TV and left the room.

"Judas, what the heck kind of trouble are you causing now?" Molly asked as we turned the corner into her café.

"Why, who did I piss off now?"

"Ursula. She has been broadcasting all day about this and that. Apparently the first thing was a new law that is going on the books—the Tearson Doctrine or something like that. Then all these items that were released to the news wires, and I heard your name being involved in them," Molly said, trying to stare me down.

"Molly, it's all good. I didn't do anything wrong," I said.

"But then in the last twenty minutes Sensenmann and The Four rushed out of here and I swear they said something about J-cubed starting Mount. St. Helen all over again," Molly said.

"Well, we did that," I said.

"Do you boys need anything, because I am going to turn in early. I have a feeling there is going to be yelling, and I always feel like I am going to pee myself when there is yelling." She winked and walked off, not really caring if I wanted food.

"Joshua, Judas, please join me upstairs. *Now!*" Sensenmann barked from the elevator. That was why Molly had disappeared. We walked over to the elevator and waited. When it came back down, Guerra and Hungersnot were inside, we joined them and went upstairs. The elevator doors opened to show Sensenmann pacing the floor. "I feel left out. I feel a major decision was reached and I have no idea what it was. As a matter of fact, it sounds like I lost a governor today, a popular governor whom I actually knew outside of here." Neither of us said a word as he continued to pace around the floor. "Oh, and this on the day that Judas set a record for getting through Level Four examination faster than anyone ever has. So instead of being happy and enjoying an illegal prime rib dinner with you both, I am sitting here trying to determine exactly what the Sam Hill happened today. You need to start talking," he inclined his head to me this time.

"We are very close to determining what the governor's Plot is..." I started.

"I feel like you are bringing me in at the end of a long story. Read me in earlier." Sensenmann said slowly.

I looked at Joshua and he gave me the go ahead. "There was an interview with the governor of Alaska, the results of which showed a very strong problem with both the local Shop agent and the governor." I paused. There were no questions so I plowed ahead. "We had a long-view concept meeting and determined, upon checking for any interface with the immediate rotation group, the governors the agent rotates through and the other agents who rotate on that loop." I took a moment to allow questions—still none. "We set out this morning to meet with each of these players." This time I saw questions coming.

"So you elected to pursue this 'targeted selection'? Didn't I specifically say 'No targeted selection' on this mission?" Sensenmann asked.

"Yes, sir, you did." I was considering turning and kicking Joshua in the balls. "We did not target this group based on past behavior—this was current behavior."

"That is as close to the line of directly disobeying me as possible. I will allow this slip. Go on," he said.

"Governor Kincade has information, but he is afraid to share it; his wife and daughter have been threatened," I said.

"Okay, we can't have that. Have you seen his daughter? What a gem she is. Her name is Jealousy. Anyway, I digress. What is our plan?" Sensenmann asked.

"This reporter is going to let the entire story of his sexual misconduct out. This has actually already started. He is going to do a very public resignation from the governor's post and then he will do an interview with the reporter, and so will his girlfriend," I said. "When he is out and safe, he gives us the plot and all the information that he has."

"I am going to let this stand, mainly because I don't have much I can do now. You should have come forward as this unfolded," Sensenmann said, looking at me. Just then the elevator dinged, The Four all drew their guns, as did Joshua, so I did as well. When the door opened there was an agent with a purple stripe; he looked a bit like a crossing guard except his sash was not orange. Everyone put away their guns, so I once again followed. "This is a classified letter from Jinau." Sensenmann looked confused.

"That is just getting here?" Joshua blurted out. "We sent that from Louisiana when we landed from Texas."

"Why the delay?" Sensenmann asked, facing the courier.

"I was ordered to California to deliver the letter from you to the Mayor of San Diego," the courier stated flatly.

"And a letter addressed to me, marked Confidential Urgent Priority Alpha, didn't seem more important to you?" He reached up and tore the sash off the agent and sent him on his way. "Report to Andelos for Level One training, immediately." The sashless man left. Sensenmann examined the seal — I assumed he was looking for signs of tampering — and then broke it open and read. "Well, my boys, it seems that the system failed us both. Jinau tried to read me in early on. You need to keep me in the loop as often and as quickly as things happen."

"Yes, sir," Joshua and I said.

"Now I think we need to get that prime rib," Sensenmann said. I looked excitedly at Joshua.

"Sir, we have a whole lot to do in order to get Governor Kincade safely out of his post," Joshua said.

"That is probably best. But I will share your cuts with Andelos and Gypsy. I can't let this beautiful meat go to waste," Sensenmann said.

"Understood, sir. I hope you enjoy the meal," I said and Joshua and I started toward the elevator.

"Oh, and Judas," Sensenmann said as we were walking away, "you are going to need this I believe." He tossed me a wallet. I caught it and looked at it—my new ID; the previous red stones were now green and there was one in each corner. "It's time to put on that ring as well. Congrats!"

"Thank you, sir," I said and we left this time. When we got on the elevator I took the ring from my pocket placing it on my finger. Both Guerra and Hungersnot shook my hand and congratulated me. Even Joshua shook my hand. I thanked them all.

"Jinau," Joshua was talking into his phone, "where are you? We have a few updates."

"I am with Dot. She has set up an interview with Governor Kincade, which is immediately after his press conference," Jinau finished.

"We have located his love interest. She is going to be available for an interview—I would suggest prior to the press conference so she can lambaste our governor during the interview," Joshua said.

"Sounds like a plan. Contact info?" She asked.

"Judas is sending it now." I took out my phone and texted the number we had given to Sonya.

Chapter 18

"Ladies and gentlemen, I stand before you today as a man who has strayed from my responsibilities — to both my family and my post as governor of this fine state. Concerned about continued distraction and dragging multiple people through this, I am stepping down as governor, effective immediately. I would like to introduce you to your new governor and he will then answer any questions that you may have. I will not be answering questions at this time. Without any other information to delay this, ladies and gentleman of the *Certified* press, please welcome Governor Anthony Pense." With that, he stepped off the podium and walked over to a limousine that was idling nearby. Dot Buchanan was waiting inside and, as they drove away, the interview took off. We were to meet the governor at his house in an hour.

"That was a pretty shitty storyline," Governor Kincade said. We gathered around his kitchen table. "I would hate me." His wife sat poised as silent as a china doll. His daughter walked into the room and grabbed an orange. She was, as Sensenmann had said, a gem. I was reflecting on how this was going to change her for years to come.

"We needed a clean break from the office. You are most definitely going to have a lot of fallout. You will of course stay on The Shop's payroll. It will be handled in a new way. I will get you all the details. Ma'am, I have to say this is going to be very difficult and your daughter is going to most likely have quite a lot of challenges that you and your husband will not even know about. For this, your country is grateful," Jinau said. Mrs. Kincade didn't say anything. The governor simply put his head down. "I would actually advise moving."

"We have already talked about it, and there is no doubt that is the only way we can get through this," Mrs. Kincade finally spoke.

"Governor, it's time. We need to understand exactly what is going on," Joshua said.

"I know. Last week I was cornered by my local Shop agent. He told me that I was going to be visited by the Governor of Texas, that he was coming to discuss a plan that would help the entire country. I was told that this was not a plot against the government, that it was a matter of removing a large amount of burden on the country." He paused and took a drink. "When the visit came I was told I needed to make certain that the border checkpoints were doubled and to revisit the containment of the airfields and airports."

"So whatever is being planned is going to need you to be ready to isolate your state from it?" I asked.

"That is what it sounded like, yes. I spoke with him only once more and this was last week. He asked me how the plans were coming along. I reported the progress. He let the word 'virus' slip and he tried very hard to make me believe he didn't say it." He wiped his forehead and looked at us expectantly.

"So, Governor…"

"Look, I gave up that post. I am simply Landon, Landon Kincade now," he said.

"Well, Landon, do you know of any other governors who are involved?" Joshua asked.

"I went to a couple conferences with a few other governors, but the only clue I got there was the largest supporting states are needling to get rid of some of those that simply take. From that I extrapolated Alaska and Louisiana…"

"That is interesting," I said. I was trying to really gather my arms around this when Joshua stood up. "It was nice to meet you, ma'am—and good luck on the move." I shook her hand and then his and we left. I wouldn't see Landon Kincade in person again for nearly twenty years.

We watched his interview with Dot Buchanan and hers with Sonya, only Sonya was now Selena Washington, the mistress. The interviews went as we designed them. He came off as the biggest villain since the Mendez brothers. The newspapers reported the suicide of Selena Washington, mother of one, that night. The backlash on the governor was that of driving all memory of him out of everyone's minds, at least every good memory.

Chapter 19

"Wake up." It was Joshua. "Judas, come on, young *ma'un*, we have to meet with Sensenmann; Jinau just got in." We had talked for a while after we saw the interview the previous night, and after Joshua had gone to his room I had watched some of the late-night news shows. The main point of discussions on these shows was the need for Governor Kincade to step down, and specifically what exactly the personal life of the man had to do with his ability to run the state successfully.

"I'm up—do we have time to eat? I'm ravenous," I asked.

"I have no issue with that. I will get word up to him that we would like to meet—by the time he gets back to us we will have had breakfast," Joshua said. We walked down to the cafeteria and met up with Jinau. "Molly, can I get a half-Judas," Joshua said.

"Absolutely. How about you, Judas?" Molly asked.

"Um, what?" I said.

"He will have a full order," Joshua said.

"Okay, go sit down. I will bring it over shortly." Molly smiled and went back to the grill.

"Jinau, the way you pulled all that together, I just wanted to say, wow, I have a lot to learn," I said.

"Me too. You jumped right in and made the moves quicker, far quicker than I ever could have. I'm impressed," Joshua said.

"Gee, guys, thanks," Jinau said. "So, tell me, what did we find out from Governor Kincade?" Joshua brought her up to speed. Halfway through the story, our food showed up. Molly congratulated me on the Level Four promotion and then she left. "Judas, I am crazy impressed— how did you get through Level Four that quick?"

"I have no idea. This has been a hell of a week," I said and I took a bite of my breakfast. Joshua continued to explain what happened with Landon Kincade. When he finished I asked, "So if we know only those who may be involved, and that they want to reduce the overall impact of those who do not contribute to the system, what is it that we really learned?"

"I think the confirmation of what we had learned seems to be the most important piece," Joshua said.

"I agree. I was just hoping for more," I said.

"Joshua, Jinau, Judas, come up," Ursula communicated to us. We all stood up and started to the elevator, which opened as we walked to it. This time the elevator was empty. *Not cool.*

"Where are The Four?" I said.

"You now carry a Level Four, so if Sensenmann calls you up, Ursula will allow the door to open for you," Jinau said.

"Interesting," I said as the doors opened. The Four were in the room, and Sensenmann was sitting at his desk. He indicated for us to join him there instead of the conference table.

"Good morning J-cubed."

"Sir," we all said.

"The last twenty-four hours has been quite an explosion of events. Tell me what we have learned." His eyes never left Joshua.

"Well, sir, it is apparent that Governor Kincade was not in the upper level of this plot as they did not share with him the details of what they are planning," Joshua said.

"So I lost a good governor for nothing?" Sensenmann asked.

"With all due respect, sir, he was tangled into something that would have caused you to lose him in a different way. This way he is safe, and we have confirmed some valuable intelligence," Jinau said, much to the chagrin of Joshua.

"Yes, I am certain that is correct. I would have lost him in the end. Tell me though, what new knowledge did you get?" Sensenmann said.

This time Joshua started talking without a delay that Jinau could step into. "Landon said that they let slip that they were looking at using a virus, to reduce the number of those who are not contributing to the nation," Joshua finished and looked to us to see if he had missed anything.

"Virus?" Sensenmann asked, and while his voice showed no change in pitch or emotion, his eyes opened just a bit wider than normal, and they bounced from Joshua to Jinau to me and then back to Joshua. Then he closed them tight and held them shut for a moment longer than normal. When he opened them, he was back to himself. "All right, thank you for the information. I want you to get back to your initial project and I will take this ball and run with it."

"Yes, sir," we stood up and started to leave.

"If I may, do you have a plan?" Jinau asked. Her white hair and gray eyes seemed to pull all the color away from the area to make them her personal aura. It was very disarming, leaving you feeling like you could trust her with your innermost secrets. *Not cool at all.*

"Well, my plan is to sit down with Landon and see if there is anything that he's remembered since you spoke with him," he said.

"That sounds like a sound start. We will leave you now," Joshua said, and, stepping in behind Jinau, he ushered us away. We stepped into the elevator and Joshua turned to her. "Jin, I am surprised we didn't end up with escorts out of there."

"If he demotes me for asking what his plan was, at least I gave him all due respect," she smiled.

"And trying to focus your aura like that? Seriously?" Joshua said.

"How the hell did you do that?" I asked

"You saw that?" they both said.

"The thing you..." The elevator door opened and they both silenced me, and we walked out of the room into the café. "The thing you did pulling the colors into you and becoming, well, trust," I said.

"He really is fucking special," Jinau said, looking at Joshua. "We can discuss that when we are on the plane."

"Okay," I said and then I got a concern and reached out for Ursula. 'Do you know what his real plan is?' I thought. 'I have one piece of information that you do not have,' she projected into my head and I knew instantly. 'Is he really?' My thoughts went to my concern. 'Yes.' The new method of communicating was fascinating, as was the fact that she was surprised by the way I conveyed my concerns. "Joshua, he is going to recall The Shop agents back to the Mill for questioning. When he does, this is going to force their hand."

"How can you be so certain?" Jinau asked.

"Never mind that—we need to figure out if there are any others involved," Joshua said.

"How about the agent in Louisiana? Let's see about getting a secured room and secured line to talk to him," I said. 'Ursula, can you get word to...' I started to think... 'I have contacted him. Go to your room and I will establish a secured link.'

"Okay so let's..." Joshua started

"Go to my room. Everything will be set up," I said.

"You have a tone of trust in his computer system," Jinau said.

"The information is not available to him," I said simply, not really knowing for sure nor caring to have a long discussion. 'You are safe, Judas.' I looked at Jinau. 'I know,' I thought to Ursula and headed out of the café. I saw they were following me in my peripherals.

"I am not nervous about it either, Jinau. We need her to make this call," Joshua said.

"I don't mean to be such a bitch, I am just feeling this entire situation is going to fall down on us," Jinau said as we walked to my room. As we turn the corner before the room, we ran into Billings and Meglar.

"Judas!" Billings ran up and gave me a hug. Congratulations. Andelos told us you passed your Level Fours." When he backed off, Meglar took her turn and she congratulated me as well.

"Can you two do me a huge favor?" I asked.

"Of course," they both acknowledged.

"I need you to stand outside my room and not let anyone stand about and listen to our call. And if anyone is intent on standing about, get our attention," I stated.

"Sure, we can do that," Billings said, turning his back to the door opening. Meglar took the other side.

"Thanks," I said, stepping through the door and shutting it once Joshua and Jinau had stepped inside. 'Ursula, place the call. We are in my room,' I thought.

'You forget sometimes, Judas—I know everything, and I see everything,' Ursula conveyed.

'No—I treat you with respect and communicate with you from that respect,' I thought. The phone rang and I pushed the speaker button. "This is Judas," I said.

"Hello, this is Tolivest, local agent of Louisiana,"

"I also have Jinau and Joshua with me," I said.

"Are you secured?" Joshua asked.

"Yes," Tolivest said.

"Good. When we were there, you mentioned..." Joshua said.

"Visitors, yes, sir, we have had several governors over the last month, and when I accompanied the governor to Texas, I was surprised that the same group was there."

"So, Tolivest, which governors were there?" Jinau asked.

"The obvious ones, Louisiana and Texas, but there was also Alaska." Tolivest said.

"Thank you," I said. I shook my head, shaking the anger that I felt. We already knew this; there really was no other method, other than pulling in either the governors or the agents.

"Oh, I don't know if it is important or not, but we traveled to a conference on natural resources and while we were there, the governor spent the majority of his time with the governors of New Jersey, Virginia, Florida, and New York."

"That may be very important. Thanks. We may need to speak with you again," Joshua said.

"I will do whatever I can," Tolivest said.

"Oh and remember, this entire conversation is Article Eighty-Seven." Jinau said.

"Understood. Out." The line went dead.

"So what did we learn there?" Jinau asked

"Well, I don't know about you but I learned that I should be sleeping in a gas mask," I said.

"We don't need to worry about that; the air filtration in the Mill would never allow anything in that doesn't belong in here," Joshua said.

"Good to know the truth in it. I learned that the three highest users of our natural resources were at a meeting with the largest suppliers. Based upon that and the fact that Kincade was brought into the mix, I would suggest the other two governors were as well," I said.

"That is what I took away as well. They are going to be the governors who brought their shattered states back from the virus," Jinau said as well.

"Stronger than the virus? It does sound as good as the storm," I said.

"Okay okay, so how can we use this information?" Joshua asked.

'Call in the kids in the hallway,' Ursula projected to J-cubed—I could tell as they reacted.

"Go let them in," Joshua said, as I was already walking to the door.

"Step in here. Thanks for watching for us. Now we are going to bring you into the middle of some serious shit," I said.

"Are you sure?" Meglar asked. I answered by putting my fist out and then grabbing hers and Billings', pulling them into mine in turn, reforming the fist triangle. "Okay, I get it."

"You better," I said.

"All right you two. Judas says you are the real deal," Joshua said, and he watched both their faces and neither showed fear. "Good, we have a serious national security issue. This is strictly Article Eighty-Seven. Do you know what that means?" Neither said anything.

"It means if you open your mouth outside this room you will assume room temperature," I said. "I know there is nothing to worry about, but you needed to hear it."

"So do you want to be read in still?" Joshua asked.

"Yes," they answered.

"Okay, then." Joshua took a deep breath and blew it away, "We have a plot to release a virus within the United States. Worse, there are at least five governors who know it is going to happen."

"So what exactly are we looking to do?" Billings asked

"We need to figure the best method of figuring out how this plot is going to go down," Jinau said.

"Okay. What exactly do we know?" Meglar asked.

"The governors of Texas, Louisiana and Alaska had several meetings that we have it on good intel that they discussed the drain certain other states are putting on our country, taking in all the natural resources they need and giving nothing in return. With regard to the governors of Virginia, New Jersey and Florida, this meeting took a different tone, and families were threatened."

"So the largest producers told the largest consumers that shit was going to change whether they liked it or not so they had better get on board and protect their families," Billings summed up.

"That's how we see it," I said.

"Then start there, when will the families be away from their homes?" Billings said.

"Well, if the governors are all out of state at the time of the attack, that would be awfully suspicious, don't you think?"

"I said the families — we are in the summer break across the country. It wouldn't look odd at all," Billings said.

"Good point. We can get access to the governors' schedules without raising any suspicion, and we have to visit all of them after all," I said.

"So you are saying we should abuse our stations to save the country?" Joshua asked.

"Well, duh," Meglar said.

"Good answer. So I have to grab the records for all the governors and look for a group of similarities," Joshua said. "You guys stay here; I will pull the data and then come back."

"I have the data. Pull it up on Judas's tablet," Ursula projected. I actually laughed when Billings and Meglar jumped. *Not cool.* I walked across to my locker and pulled out my tablet. Connecting to the projector, the five governors in question had their schedules overlaid on top of each other. The only common dates fell four days hence: another conference for global resources.

"There!" Meglar was the first to say it, jumping up and pointing to the common meeting.

"Excellent. Boy, you two have earned some praise, I will say," Joshua said.

"So we have four days to put together a plan to stop this attack on our soil," Jinau said.

"Is it time for lunch?" I asked.

"I am surprised he waited that long—he didn't get to finish his breakfast," Joshua poked me.

"We have earned a bit of a treat I think," I said. "You think there are leftovers from last night?"

"Ha, not a chance," Joshua said.

"Not cool," I pouted.

"Deal with it, big boy; you are just never going to get that kind of celebration," Joshua said with a hint of smile.

"Oh well, let's go eat and maybe I can make it to the gym finally," I said as I tucked my tablet back into my locker. "I am kidding about the gym. I know we have a lot of discussions that need to take place." I never looked back—and when I did turn, I realized no one was there. I love talking to myself. At least I know the words are well-received. When I entered the lunch area it was full of people. I had never actually noticed but the room was almost always empty when I was there.

All of a sudden I was no longer hungry. I don't know if it was the people here, in my area, or perhaps the fact that Molly was talking to everybody else and I didn't feel special. My own selfishness, the continuing thought that I am special and that I was better. I walked out of the café. "Judas, where are you off to?" It was Jinau. "We have a lot to do."

"Yes, Jinau, I know, but I just got hit with a reality, and I don't want to be in this room," I said.

"That sucks for you. Get some food and get to the corner table so we can save the country." Jinau, with her gray eyes and white hair, so amazing that she fears nothing anywhere.

"You're right. Thanks," I said. As I walked past her, she smacked my butt.

"Get in there and give 'em what for, big guy," Jinau laughed as she said it.

"Thanks, coach," I said as I walked up to the counter. Molly smiled and asked what I wanted." I told her, "Give me a turkey sandwich with hot peppers, onions and cheese. Actually make that two sandwiches. Please."

"Hold up, you don't want a special left-over sandwich?" My eyes went wide and I nodded my head like a fool. "Well, tough—there isn't any." And she burst out laughing. I definitely did not feel special.

"Not cool!" I shook a finger at her.

"Ladies and gentlemen, for those of you who have not heard," Molly's voice carried like a true orator, "this big boy is Judas, and he just set a record for both completing the Level Four qualification and reaching Level Four the soonest after joining The Shop." The room at large applauded.

"Not to mention the most hospitalized days prior to becoming Level Four," Joshua added.

"Speech!" a bunch of people said.

"I am not big on words. Thank you to my Shadow Partner, and all the others who have helped me, and the instructors, and especially Molly," I said, and the group clapped.

"Aren't you sweet? Maybe I can scrounge up one special sandwich. You want horseradish on it?" Molly asked.

"Oh, hell yeah," I said as she shooed me away from the counter. I walked in the direction of the corner table. On the walk over, several people including Andelos stopped me and shook my hand.

"Okay, before Judas's head pops, let's get our thinking caps on," Joshua said. "What can we do to get an idea of who else may be involved in this?"

"I was bouncing around the idea of other people who attended the meetings the governors attended," I said.

"Are we going to be attracting attention?" Jinau asked.

"I think anything we do here on out is going to be causing some type of issues," I said.

"I would have to agree; I think we are past the easy stuff," Joshua said.

"Maybe we could have the agent in Louisiana ask for the list of attendees. As he and his governor were there, it may not set off a big flag," Billings said.

"I like that," Jinau said.

"What about comparing arriving and departing air travel?" Meglar asked.

"It would have to have a buffer like two hundred miles away and five days before and after," Joshua said.

"And what if they didn't even fly there—what if they flew into New York and drove cross country?" Jinau asked.

"Let's just pull all international arrivals for two weeks before, and then check the border crossings?" Joshua said.

"Isn't it easy to forge that?" Billings said.

"It isn't as easy as you would think. The database takes a lot of information. If you try to leave a state with certified health papers, if you don't show as arriving in the state, you will be detained. So if I fly to New York and check in through customs, I will be in New York location in the computer; however if a person arrives in New York illegally and then tries to leave, they will be caught. If I flew into Denver and drove to Texas, each checkpoint will see me and it will be in the database. If I try to fly out of a state that does not show me in, I will be detained. So unless the forger has access to a person who is in the system, and is within the state, it is a tough sell. Additionally, when you are arriving International, you have an optical reading and a thumb print in order to get a travel document. All in all, yes, you can beat the system, but it is not easy," Jinau finished.

As Jinau was talking, I started trying to talk to Ursula. 'Can you get a message to Tolivest, tell him we need him to request the names of all the people who either participated in, worked at or visited all the events he attended with the governor. Also the dates of the events.' She agreed.

"But if they have Shop people on the inside, can't they forge the documents?" I asked.

"The majority of Shop people a) don't know all this information and b) don't have access to this information. So if they tried to modify documents it would be flagged," Jinau said.

"Okay. that sounds better than I thought," Billings said.

"But if the person used a fake ID at the event?" Meglar asked.

"Same rules apply: if there are governors or Shop personnel at an event you need ID to enter—and that includes all staff; each time they walk out of the area they are scanned. If anything changes on the scan within a twenty-four-hour period, the person is detained. By the way, when I say detained, a cage closes on them at the scanner," Jinau said.

"That is so strange. How is it that this isn't broadcast everywhere to keep people from doing it?" Billings asked.

"Some people you just want to break the law," Joshua said.

"Okay, so we need a listing of the people who attended..." Jinau started.

"I have already started this—with who attended, worked and presented at all the events Tolivest attended with the governor," I said.

"Man, you better calm down a bit; this telepathy with Ursula is going to give you brain cancer—or get us all arrested. Or killed," Jinau poked at me.

"Yeah, yeah. We need to take some chances in order to get through this, as I see it," I said.

"I agree," Billings and Meglar said.

"Well, gee, the lollipop guild is singing together. What—no dancing?" Jinau started shuffling her feet and kicking randomly.

"Are you okay? You look like you're having a seizure," Meglar said.

"I think she was trying to dance," I said. "I think."

"Oh, you!" Jinau jumped up, mussing my hair. "And you too!" jumping over to put Meglar in a little headlock.

'If you are done goofing around, I have the dates you asked for. And Tolivest is contacting the event coordinator, saying to have the information by five p.m. tonight,' Ursula let us all know.

"Ursula, thank you. Can you do a cross-reference of the all international arrivals and departures, plus and minus five days? With travel into and out of the event city," Joshua jumped right in and requested.

'That will take about twenty minutes. I will send it to Judas's tablet,' Ursula projected.

"What are we missing? I feel like there is an obvious approach we should be looking into," Joshua said.

"What about restaurants? The governor has to have an itinerary with The Shop—right?" Jinau asked.

"That was the one. Ursula, can you cross-reference the meals during the conferences?" Joshua asked.

'Of course,' she let us know.

"I am not going to get used to that; even if I hear her every day for years, it simply is wrong," Billings said.

"Unless you're with Judas, she doesn't talk to you like this. Hell, in the last month I have heard more internal dialogue than the previous ten years combined," Joshua said.

"Well I will remember that when deciding who to spend time with here on base," Billings said with a mocking angry face at me.

"Well, let's grab some junk food and head back to my pad. We can have a grand time while we sit around and not use all the tools available to us," I said.

"Oh, zip it Mr. Grand Time... but yes, let's head over to the hospital wing," Joshua said. "At what point are you going to get worried that they are housing you in the hospital wing permanently?"

"I think if I make it back from a couple more trips out in the field and I have no need for the hospital, I will petition for a new room," I said, to a large response of laughter. They all got up to leave. "I ain't going anywhere — not until I get my lunch." I crossed my arms and stayed in my chair. A few seconds later Molly came up with our food. I looked at my sandwich, prime rib on a hoagie roll, and I wiped away a pretend tear. "It's beautiful."

"Bring it with you — we got work to do," Joshua said and we took our lunches with us.

Chapter 20

When we got to my room, I removed my tablet from my locker. "Have you changed your password to that thing?"

"No." I started walking to the bed, connecting to the Blue Tooth projector.

"You are messed up — you know that, right?" Joshua said.

"Oh, absolutely — but why change my password?" I asked. "No mail yet."

"So why do you know his password? I thought that was a super-secret thing that no one could guess, ooh hush hush," Meglar said.

"When dummy got hurt, he wanted to use his tablet and, well, he couldn't get in his locker," Jinau answered.

"You know too?" Billings said.

"It's 'for my children,'" I said to shocked faces. "What? If I can't trust them with my tablet and underwear, how can I trust them with my life?"

"True," Joshua said.

"Why is that f'd up?" Meglar asked.

"Do you know much about this massive man mountain?" Joshua asked.

"Apparently not," they said.

"Well, he was the most amazing quarterback who has ever played the game. And he got hurt in the National Championship game," Joshua said.

"You are Alec Tearson?" Meglar asked.

"Who?" Billings said.

"You got a helmet to the groin when a cheating bastard hit," she said.

"Who?" he said again.

"Last season he took a shitty school all the way to the National Championship, and the year before they should have gone — stupid point system," Meglar complained.

"So you see why his password is so wrong?" Jinau asked.

"Well, if the hit was really that bad, then yes. But they never said," she said.

"Yeah, it was that bad. I got two fake ones now," I said.

"Oh, *oh*… Dude, that is messed up." Billings said.

"Yup, but who would ever guess that password?" I said.

"True," all four said.

"Enough about my super testes — let's talk about…" I started.

"Super, what's super about them?" Meglar asked.

"Look at the shit you started," I said to Joshua.

"Hey, you are Mr. Full Disclosure, trust unlimited," Jinau shot back.

"They are truly high-tech. I can inject pain suppressant, a chemical that will allow focus and other stuff," I said.

"That is pretty sweet," Billings said. "Can they help you stay awake in class?"

"It could but I never had to use it," I said. "We've got mail. Holy crap, forty-seven gigs?"

"That's a huge file," Jinau said.

"And that is only the restaurant file and it's compressed," I said.

"Look, the airline file just came in too," Jinau commented, "Odd — that one is smaller." About then the first file finally opened, and we were all shocked: pictures of every person were off to the side of the spreadsheet.

"Well, that is interesting — pictures of everyone," I said.

'What did you expect? I would have done that for the airlines but it would have been just too big,' Ursula said. 'The last tab is the people who appear on both lists.' I clicked that tab. Fifty-four people had traveled into the city by either plane or car, and had eaten in cities with the events.

"How many of the people are in multiple cities with the governors?" Joshua asked.

"Try sorting by city, and then allow duplicate entry. Like that," Billings said as he helped me manipulate the spreadsheet. "Now add a new level of sorting. Good. There—alphabetical. Yes, now sort again; that will allow the duplicates to appear. Wait—take out the city. Okay. There, now sort." The names that were duplicated now showed more than once. I copied the names that did so, and made a new tab. "Twenty people were in multiple cities at the same time as our five governors."

"You are pretty good at that," Meglar said.

"Thanks, I had a little help," I said.

"Ass," Billings said. "Thanks, Meglar. I do have some talents." He smiled.

"Now, if we can get the list of people who were at the events," I said.

"Try sorting that list by countries of origin," Joshua said. I did, and this showed no correlations. "Try flight numbers into the country." This brought the list down to five groups: fifteen in one group, two in one and the others one in each of the last three. "Focus on those fifteen. Put up their pictures." I looked at Billings.

"Here, let me." He quickly made a new tab and the pictures of the fifteen were up on the projector in short order.

'Tolivest says he has four of the five events. He is sending them now.' Ursula said.

"Thank you, Ursula," Jinau said. I looked at her, "What?" I smiled and shook my head.

"When the sheet comes in, can you do a name and face recognition, Ursula?" Billings asked.

'Of course. Just the fifteen — correct?' Ursula asked

"To start, yes," he replied. I was rather impressed how well he was taking to this data steward role.

'I have the files and am doing correlations. Do you want a new spreadsheet or to add it to that one?' Ursula said.

"New one, please — smaller file that way." The file came in and Billings opened it. Twelve of the fifteen were at every event, sometimes listed as workers, sometimes presenters and sometimes as attendees, but their names were different depending on the role they were playing. Billings duplicated his effort from before and the twelve faces now populated the wall. "Here are our people — seven men and five women."

"I can't say how impressed I am with this," Joshua said.

"I have one more question: Ursula, do any of these names have current travel plans within the United States?" I asked. I already had that sinking feeling that I got when the opposition shifted into a blitz when I knew we had the wrong play called and there was one second left on the snap clock.

'One moment...' she said and then went silent. We all waited. "I found one person with that name traveling to New Jersey. I am performing a facial recognition on the rest of the passengers." Again we waited. 'It appears there are four of the people who have flown into New Jersey. They landed one hour ago," Ursula said.

"Can you do facial recognition of all flights into Florida and New York also?" Joshua asked.

'Yes, but that will take a couple hours. I will notify you when it is done,' Ursula projected to us all.

"Thank you again," Jinau said. "All right, we have the first group already mobilizing. Do you think they are on to us?"

"Ursula, do you have any change in itinerary for any of the five governors?" Meglar asked.

'Yes, just New Jersey,' she answered.

"New Jersey, here we come," Billings said.

"No, not you two—we don't have permission to bring you with us," Joshua said.

"Can you ask?" Billings asked.

"No—that would tell people where we are going. As it is, we can beg forgiveness; if we ask and get shot down, then we are screwed," Joshua said.

"I understand," they both said.

"Driving or flying? The governor, I mean. Ursula," I stammered.

'He is to leave by plane at six a.m. tomorrow,' she answered.

"Excellent. So we have until tomorrow morning. From four days to fourteen hours—no pressure," Jinau said in her special way.

"Okay, let's get mobile," Joshua said. I started to put my tablet away. "Take that with you this time." I agreed and then took my guns, ammo and other miscellaneous gear out of my locker. "My stuff is on the plane already—yours?" he said, looking for input from Jinau.

"On the plane," she said.

"I guess we are flying." We headed out.

Chapter 21

We arrived at the airport less than thirty minutes later. The plane was there, thank goodness. We had debated calling to check on the status of the plane but this mission had to continue under the radar. When we got on the plane Joshua said, "Get us to Atlantic City, New Jersey. Fly under the radar. Do whatever you need to do to get us in the air — now."

When the pilot saw who it was, and that he was pulling his guns and all his gear out of the lockup, he looked at Joshua. "Yes, sir," Cartner said simply.

"Thank you," Joshua said as we walked to the back of the plane without turning.

When we were seated, Jinau turned to Joshua and said, "I'm kind of glad you threw down on that last trip."

"Me too," I said.

"We have clearance. I told them it was Triple-A priority," The pilot yelled back through his open door.

"Perfect. We can get the signatures when we get back," Joshua said.

"Thank you. The follow-up would save me an ass-chewing," Cartner said.

"Will do," Joshua said.

"Why Atlantic City?" I asked.

"Mostly because I couldn't think of any other airport in Jersey off the top of my head." His coy smile came out.

"Probably the best bet for virus dispersal — I would have to guess it is going to be an aerosol agent," Jinau said.

"Do we have full HazMat suits?" I asked.

"Shit." As we were already in the air and pulling away from the airport, he walked up to the cockpit. "Gentlemen," I heard him say, "I need you to put on your containment gear prior to landing. Once we get off, you need to fly away."

"Full gear?" the copilot said.

"Yes. Level Three containment." He paused. "I also need you to have three cars, no drivers, at the ready for us."

"Okay." The pilot started telling the copilot to get suited up, as Joshua walked out of the room.

"Here," Joshua said, tossing a package to each of us. "Get dressed." He opened his own package and started removing the suit. I did notice his face was grim — only the second time I had seen that face.

"Why three cars?" I asked.

"One for each of us. Jinau, you have the highway operations. I will take the Port Authority and, Judas, you have the airport. Make certain this plane is airborne prior to the freeze. We are pretty certain they are going to wait until the governor is gone so fifteen minutes shouldn't hurt," Joshua said.

"I don't like the separating approach," I said.

"It is a divide-and-conquer approach and it is needed. Put your badge on the chain that is in your briefcase. It needs to be outside your suit across your chest," Joshua stated, leaving no room for argument.

"I agree it has to be done but when our areas are secured, where are we meeting?" Jinau asked.

"We will decide at that time. It depends if we have any new information from Ursula," he answered. We finished getting dressed in silence; Joshua clipped his badge as he had told me to. The chain that Joshua had told me to grab out of my briefcase had a hard cover to hold my badge and ID open, and a band to go around the waist, with a breakaway lanyard around the neck. As it was the first time I had seen his badge, I looked at the stones — diamonds, four diamonds. I looked at Jinau's — four diamonds also. They stones obviously had some meaning, it wasn't the time to ask. After we had the IDs secured, we helped each other with the headpiece. My heart started to really pick up now.

It was really happening. I sat back and waited for the plane to land so I could stop thinking and just do.

"We are cleared for landing. I have gotten clearance for immediate departure also, and we have five minutes in and out." This told me we had to get ready to jump up, open the door and get off the plane as soon as we were stopped. The plane seemed to land and taxi very quickly. Before I knew it, we were outside watching it leave.

"Okay, let's go." Joshua got in the first car and headed out, Jinau the second and I took the last one. I looked for the tower. That seemed logical. I started driving in that direction. People were coming from everywhere waving at me to stop. Finally a group of armed men came out of the base of the tower. I stopped and waited in the car, with my hands up of course.

"Who the hell are you and what are you driving on my airport runways for?" the one who had a red beret said loudly as if the head cover I had on was soundproofed.

"My name is Judas. I am here on a Level Three containment. I am one of The Six." He looked down at my chest and backed off, saluting. "At ease," I said, saluting. "Get your people to suit up. I need to stop air traffic."

"Take me with you — they won't let you in," he said.

"Can you grab your gear on the way?"

"It's right next to the stairs," he said as he ran around the car barking orders to his men. I started driving in the direction he indicated. "I am in charge here, and I am Level Four, Ridge. What exactly are we looking at here?"

"There is a terrorist threat to the entire state of New Jersey. As it is an airborne virus that our intelligence has alerted us to, we are starting with Atlantic City populous and many visitors," I said, hoping this was okay.

"Oh, my God," was all he said. When we parked where he indicated, he jumped out and ran. I followed, grabbing my briefcase. He suited up very quickly. I assisted with the last snap on his headpiece and we walked to the tower. This opened and admitted us both. I noticed then that his gun was out. "That would have told me if you were a fake, and I would have shot you, no questions."

"Nice," I said, thinking, *not cool.*

"Ladies and gentlemen," he said as we walked up the stairs and arrived at the tower level. "This is not a drill. Get all planes diverted, stop all take-offs, and then get suited up. *Now!*" I was glad he was here; everyone did as he said and then the group gathered around me in their suits.

"Until you have word, there are no planes allowed to take off or land in the entire state. Get word to all the other air traffic controllers; do not send any traffic here."

"Look here, agent, this is not protocol, and we are supposed to be contacted by..." the lead controller was starting to get on a roll.

"Do you know who The Six are?" Ridge asked.

"Yes," the controller answered.

"Look at his badge," he said with finality.

"Yes, sir. I just had to..."

"I understand this is not the proper nor is it normal channels, but I am here officially. Make the calls and shut down all air travel in and out of this state," I said.

"Yes, sir." He turned and gave his people the go ahead.

I got on my phone and called Joshua. "All air traffic frozen. Where do you want me next?"

"Start heading to the beach or the boardwalk area — maybe we can get as many people out of that area without a panic," he said.

"Okay. Any word from Jinau?" I asked.

"Not yet. She had farther to travel than you, but she should be reaching the first checkpoint anytime now. I will let you know." He hung up.

"Ridge, can you or one of your people help me get to the boardwalk?" I asked.

"I can," he said, and he turned to the lead controller. "You have my number. Call me if there are any issues."

"Shall do," the controller said to both of us.
"Okay, Judas, this way." We took a different way down which took us right out on the runway. We got to the car.

"Do you want to drive? It may be faster," I said. He nodded and took the driver's seat, and we headed out to the beach. "How busy is the beach at this time of night?"

"Beach may not be bad, but there are fireworks tonight on the boardwalk," he said.

"Can you get us there—seems like the perfect venue," I said, not really asking a question.

"You got it. Same direction."

My phone rang. "Judas," I said.

"This is Joshua and Jinau is conferenced in."

"Hello," she said.

"I told you I could do it." He had a slight chuckle in his voice.

"You got lucky," she said. "The highway department was actually quite helpful; I borrowed their chopper and their pilot and I am getting ready to head to the beach."

"Careful; there is a fireworks display that is setting up now. I am headed there to stop it and send the people home," I said.

"Perfect, both of you. I am still trying to get to the Port Authority. The roads are all messed up."

"Is there a good way of getting to the Port Authority?" I asked Ridge.

"Not really. But make sure you don't crash that gate like you did at the airport—they will shoot," he said.

"Joshua, did you hear that?" I asked.

"I got it, thanks. I am almost there; ask him if he knows the agent in charge there."

"It's Staloan," Ridge said.

"Tell him thanks," Joshua said. In the background I heard his car stopping and the helicopter starting up. I hung up the phone.

Chapter 22

"There is a shit-ton of traffic. Your friend may beat us there," Ridge said.

"I would walk but I would be afraid of starting a riot. Bad enough all the people are staring at us," I said. He nodded his head and we kept driving. When were close, he parked the car and we got out.

"Riot or not, traffic ain't moving. Grab your shit and let's scoot," Ridge said and we started walking down the road.

My phone rang. "Judas."

"We're blown. Do you have your containment suit on still?" Jinau was shouting over the helicopter.

"Yes," I said and heard Joshua say it as well.

"I am following a boat that has a rooster tail that is dissipating into a vapor that is moving onto the beach road. It looks like our group is starting their show early. I am going to try and get in closer to see if I can shut them down," Jinau said.

"Negative. Do not get close — these are..." Joshua's voice started to say but the line went dead.

"Ridge, does your phone have a signal?" He looked.

"No, it says 'no service.' Shit, they must have a jammer." Just then I started to hear the sound of a helicopter and a loud motor sound.

"There they are. You all fastened?"

"Yes I am — there who are?"

"Sorry, my partner said she is tailing our terrorists." As I said this, a group was walking past us already staring at our outfits.

"Terrorists?" a woman said. "There are terrorists at the beach!" she screamed and then started running, holding her child's hand. Other people echoed her scream and also started running. I could see this getting out of hand quickly. I ran across the street and we jumped down to the walk and kept running in the direction of the chopper. There were hundreds, maybe even thousands, here already getting seats. The mist that Jinau had described was coming off the back of the boat. The boat appeared to be throwing a rooster tail twenty feet in the air but there was a second pipe that was blowing a fog into the rooster tail. This fog was carrying far above the rooster tail and then followed the wind over the crowd. We were too late. I heard the sound of a gunshot as Jinau was trying to stop the boat. I heard screaming on the boardwalk ahead of me; the stampede of people who were coming toward us was quite intimidating. I pulled Ridge behind me and I felt the impact of the smaller people bouncing off my extra-large frame. I heard another gunshot. This time it was right next to me – Ridge had fired and the crowd stopped stampeding as I pushed forward.

At that moment there was an explosion and then all hell fell apart. I saw the boat Jinau was chasing crash into the barge that had the fireworks and explode, then all the fireworks exploded, apparently blinding the chopper pilot or damaging the rotor on the chopper. A moment later it nosedived into the barge, in a terrible explosion that shook the boardwalk. "Jinau!" I yelled and, forgetting myself, I started running over the people who were in front of me. I hadn't gotten but a few steps when I felt arms around my waist and heard Ridge screaming for me to stop, that jumping in the water or tearing my suit would only get me killed as well. I knew he was right. That even if the crash or explosion hadn't killed her, the fire would have ruined her suit and she would have the virus. I stopped dragging Ridge and bowed my head. I was only two feet from the end of the boardwalk. "We have to contain the people who have been exposed; we don't know what that boat was pumping," I said to both Ridge and myself, in a dreamlike state.

"Judas, get to that lifeguard stand and see if there is a megaphone – there should be." I jumped over the side rail.

It was a ten-foot drop. I ran over to the stand, climbing up to the seat, and found the bull horn there.

"Ladies and gentlemen, this is a member of Sensenmann's Six. I am fully authorized to take control of this situation. I want you to return to the beach. If you attempt to leave the area, I will authorize my men in the buildings surrounding us to shoot you and anyone in your party, as we just shot down that helicopter and boat." The crowd, fearing what I had said, started back to the beach area. The bluff was all I had. Some didn't listen and continued on. I made a motion and pointed. *Crack*. The person who was walking away with his family dropped dead on the street. "There will be a group here shortly to take your blood and to coordinate what is to happen next. If you attempt to leave, you will be killed." I stepped down from the lifeguard stand. I looked down at my phone. The signal was back. I called Joshua.

"Joshua." He answered on the first ring.

"Jinau is dead," I said. I heard the words but couldn't believe it was me saying it.

"I know. I saw the explosion. Now, pull yourself together. Where are you?" he asked.

"On the beach. There is a lifeguard stand right in front of where the barge is at," I answered.

"Well, get back up to the road. I am calling in a containment team and Strandtov. You are going to need to start getting blood samples as soon as he gets here," Joshua continued.

"The ports?"

"They are secured. This may seem hollow, but we did contain it. It isn't leaving New Jersey," Joshua said, but I could feel his bitter pill being choked down. "I have to make some calls. Meet me at your car." I walked through the crowd, realizing it must have been Joshua who had taken the shot.

By the time I returned to the car with Ridge, Joshua was no longer on the phone. He looked at me and gave a slight nod of recognition, "Here is where we stand: There are four terrorists on a plane right now to Florida, and the other four are flying from Colorado to New York in an hour. If we grab the four in Florida before the boarding of the plane in Colorado, I am afraid we will lose the last four. I have made it clear to follow the Florida team until the Colorado agent confirms the flight is boarded."

"Can we get the four in Colorado before the plane takes off, in case they hear something on the plane that makes them want to hijack it?" I asked

"That is the plan. The airlines have been told to delay the take-off until the Florida plane is landed so we can take both groups at about the same time. All in all it feels right," Joshua said.

"I agree; it sounds like a good plan," I said. Ridge said nothing, just looked on.

"As far as here goes, how many men do you have?" Joshua said to Ridge.

"The ten I have at the airport are suited up and within five minutes of here—well, less the one who is staying at the airport to control things there. My name is Ridge, by the way," he said, his voice surprisingly strong.

"I am Joshua. Let your man know that The Shop has a containment team and a Disease Management Specialist flying in—he should be there in ten minutes." Ridge walked off to make the call. "Strandtov will be on that plane. He is the best."

"I hope so," I said.

"This is going to get worse—you know that?" Joshua said, putting his hand on my shoulder.

"I, er, I mean, we will be fine. This is what we are here for," I said. I didn't even convince myself. *Not cool.*

"You were actually right." A short time later, Ridge told us The Shop's team had landed as we continued getting the people to the beach, attempting to keep them calm. Word came to Joshua that the remaining eight had been arrested; I could see a great weight lifted off his shoulders.

Chapter 23

The team arrived, a tent was built and Strandtov coordinated the taking of blood samples. After personally drawing blood from the first ten people, he took the vials to a makeshift lab. "Joshua, Judas, please come to the lab," I heard over the radio. It was Dr. Strandtov's voice. We walked into the lab to find him pacing anxiously. "This is impossible," he was saying as he paced.

"What is impossible?" Joshua asked.

"This virus — it's mine. We invented it specifically for close-quarter terminations. It has a strange cycle: it is extremely fast to become infectious, almost instantly, and then within twelve hours, it becomes dormant. Within forty-eight hours it starts forming micro-clots in the blood. These clots are a special formulation. They do two things: they over-oxygenate the blood, and then when the person is giddy, the clots break free and go to the lungs, heart and brain. The people will die. One hundred percent of infected people will die. I am so sorry." Strandtov broke down and started crying. "I have been working on a vaccination for this, which is the only reason I even still had the formula."

"So is there a vaccine?" I asked.

"Trial, yes. But it won't cure them. How well do you think this was contained?"

"Jinau said…" I started, but my voice broke.

"Jinau was chasing them down the beach, so I am guessing about a mile of release prior to the craft being destroyed," Joshua finished for me.

"There is no sense in vaccinating here. It *will* wipe out this city. But if we stop the travel of people out of the city, within seventy-two hours we will have a good idea. Best to vaccinate the surrounding cities, but I need to coordinate the duplication and production of the vaccine. Let me see if Kadodadeh can assist in this." He walked over and got on the phone.

"One hundred percent kill rate. Holy shit!" I said.

"Judas, stay in the game—too much at stake to dwell on the casualty rate, not yet." Joshua helped me again to pull it together. For a guy who can compartmentalize everything so well, I am failing horribly right now, I chastised myself.

"I am fine, thanks," I lied. "I don't understand one thing: how did the virus…" Joshua's phone rang.

"Joshua." He listened. "I understand." He hung up his phone and took out his gun, walking over to Dr. Strandtov. "Doctor, hang up the phone."

"I need to finish this. One second," he said and then looked up at Joshua. "What is the meaning of this?"

"You are under arrest for crimes against the United States and her people," Joshua said.

"I am trying to stop this outbreak—can we do this stupidity later?" Strandtov pleaded.

"I am afraid not," Joshua said coldly.

"I had nothing to do with this," he said. I believed him, with all my being I believed him.

"Joshua, let him finish the call," I heard myself saying. When Joshua turned, my gun was already on him. "He needs to; he is being set up and you know it." And yet another betrayal.

"Judas." He rarely called me that. "Don't back the wrong horse."

"It's a phone call and we can listen. Let him give Kadodadeh the information, then arrest him."

"What if they are in it together?" he said. But I could see he didn't believe his words. "Fine." He lowered his gun, walking out of the lab, and Strandtov finished the call. I thought I was going to throw up.

"Thank you," Dr. Strandtov said. When he hung up the phone, I arrested him.

"Could there be any residual effect like my suit or car? If we drove to the Mill would there be any risk?" I asked.

"Absolutely none. If it isn't breathed in, the virus dies within an hour," he said.

"Let's go, then. You have done all you can do." We walked outside. "Joshua, I am going to drive him back to the Mill." My words left no room for discussion. I knew Joshua was supposed to kill him, and there was no question about it.

"Go ahead; I am afraid you will not get there. And it may get you killed. But I will not be a threat to either of you," he said, shaking his head.

"Thank you, my friend," I said.

"Do you point a gun at all your friends?" Joshua poked.

"Only those I want to know they are my friends; the others I just shoot when I draw," I said. I got into the car and we drove away. There was nothing to say so nothing was said. We passed the border checkpoint after quite a lot of fancy driving. We crossed into Maryland and I turned on the radio, expecting to hear something about the issue in New Jersey.

"They won't discuss it; they will have put a media blackout on it," Strandtov said without an ounce of doubt.

"Why?" I asked

"They don't want people to know that The Shop is vulnerable. It is ridiculous, but controlling this type of thing is normal," he said.

"This has happened before?" I asked

"Not to this extent, but yes."

"Not cool," I said, and then a question came to me. "How could anyone get your virus?"

"I have no idea; my security protocol is higher than any person at the Mill, simply because of this," Strandtov said. We drove in silence again, listening to the stupid announcer making stupid conversation about how beautiful the night was.

"The day we were working on my inventions," I said, "you logged me into your file server."

"Yes, I did, but I am sure you didn't…" he faded off.

"My tablet is not secured, though. Could someone have hacked in through my tablet and gotten in?" I asked.

"Yes, but consider the odds of this. They had to know I did that. And as I had never done it before, why would anyone suspect?" Strandtov said.

"The Dobbers," I said after a couple more minutes of silence. My words came out so harsh that I startled him.

"What?" he said

"Not what — *who*. The Dobbers are the hackers who broke into Sensenmann's computer. I need to find them," I said.

"Find hackers? Good luck." Strandtov laughed.

"Get my tablet out of the briefcase in the backseat." He did and booted it up. "Try 'I am the traveler' dot gov." He shook his head no, "The traveler?" Still nothing, "Make it one word."

"Got it I think. It was 'wearethetraveler.'" He showed me the screen, the familiar black background with red letters that looked like drops of blood spelling 'We Are The Traveler — for we are many…'

"That's it. Find a nested porthole on that page, click every letter, and click every space between letters," I said frantically.

"The hyphen took me to a speech, I think," he said.

Chapter 24

"Read it to me," I said, looking down; I was driving a hundred miles an hour. I backed off, setting the cruise control so as not to let my emotions weigh down the gas pedal.

"Okay, let me make it bigger.

"'I am still the Traveler; I have been silent for many years listening instead to those who were speaking out, reading those who dare put their words into publication. I prefer to read those who travel the road with me, but these days it seems there are less and less of us. I have heard sinners and saints. I have read all types in between and still I stayed quiet, along with many others.

"'As we watched, the 'regulations' imposed by our government, churches, and press combined to establish our country's new internal warfare. Fought on the podiums, pulpits, and pages by each in turn, to empower themselves, again, while in the corner sat those who should not have stayed silent, did. As per Lord Tennyson's words, 'The quiet sense of something lost echoes to the canyon.'

"'I had taken my shots at everyone and gave my version of causality and the inherent solutions as I saw them, before. To what end? We continued on a path and I, a person born with no special gift or visions, could see where it was leading. But today of my own volition I am writing again. What a great word, volition, let me say it other ways: Volya, Vullnet, Pasya, Icchā, Wollen, Ishi, Voluntad, and the language it stemmed from, Volitio. It means the act of making a choice of free will. This is something that this country has forgotten… We chose to not pay taxes to a King in England – remember taxation without representation or don't tread on me. Perhaps that one you recall. We chose to not allow slavery, we chose to fly with the birds, we chose to create an assembly line; we chose many things, including the choice to allow our country to forget there was a better way.

"'Perhaps I bashed too many people in my last paper to be taken seriously by any specific group. I still see an independent mind is one that will not follow any one group blindly. Again, it is *my volition to accept what you say. Fear is the easiest method of crafting people's opinion; it is, however, not the right method, so I will try to stay away from that. And so with that in mind, I plunge into my second monologue.*

"'When the liberty of freedom has been modified from the power of ability and the choices of the fathers into a new ruling class that writes laws so that they may get rich. And then cast their actions as legal and earned.

"'When the country has turned into fifty-one percent Entitled Group, hereafter to be called the Hands-Out Class, and thereafter we have no chance for a future.

"'When the most important person in the country sets out to destroy everything those who came before him lived and died to do by making assertions such that democracy is a failed experiment.

"'When the people believe that the press gives you the truthful unbiased information.

"'When schools educate the children on planned parenthood and gay rights in the name of fairness but kids are suspended for wearing a crucifix and Merry Christmas shirts.

"'When the country does not even know enough to ask 'Who is J. G?'

"'When education falls so far that the nation's children no longer understand that we are a Representative Republic and not a Democracy.'"

"'When people are not required to work and they can once again simply hold out their hands.

"'When people are too ignorant to understand their own ideologies or dogma, telling their betters that they should spend their money in a certain way. When their own liberal doctrine says 'I will take your money and spend it as you should have.'

"'When the masses continue to prove that they no longer should have the right to decide.

"'When people are made famous by the boobtube, for no other reason than Reality.

"'When our government starts telling American companies that it would be better for them if they purchased components from overseas rather than make them here.

"'When a statement like 'What Difference Does It Make?'… doesn't make a difference.

"'Then it is time – time to reevaluate, time to close up our thirty-million-dollar-a-day dependency on this drug called Congress and figure out how to save this once great nation.'"

When he finished reading, I sat perfectly still and ran through the dialogue in my head. "Hell of a commentary on the times back then," I said.

"It is brutal and honest and I imagine no one read it—or cared. I wish I had a copy of the first monologue that he mentions," Strandtov said.

"Click on the word *Volitio*," I said.

"It took me to a chat page. I am waiting for an operator to reply. Or at least that is what the screen says. Okay, it now says, 'Hello, Ye ole seeker of brotherhood, how may I assist you?' What do you want me to type in?" he asked.

"How about, 'My name is Judas. I am in desperate need of your assistance,'" I said.

"He knows you are one of The Six. Wow," Strandtov said.

"Type, 'I know it is strange; however, we are under attack and I feel you could assist me. I know you are the hacker at the gate. I am impressed—and will you lend me your support?'" I had to restate a couple things as his typing was slower than my speaking.

"He says to ask and he will determine how he should proceed."

"Okay. Um, on June second, around eleven p.m., I was in the hospital wing. Can you produce either images of that day and/or see if any files were copied to a jump drive off my tablet?" I stumbled through the question. Strandtov read it back to me. "Send it—and let's see how deep they go." We crossed into Virginia while we waited for a reply.

"He says, 'Hold on to your butts.' The screen is now blank," Strandtov said. "Holy shit—it's us." A video of my room from a ceiling camera. "And, look, we are leaving. We left the screen up with your invention." Time passed as he watched the screen. I stole glances every now and then at the empty room. I noticed the car get much darker. "He wants to know if we want to see more. I typed in 'Please, until Judas walks back into the room and shuts off his tablet'," Strandtov said.

"*Come on...*" I said impatiently, just as the car brightened again and I knew the playback had continued.

"Okay, we are just leaving. Apparently he had to rewind." He waited and watched. Then he took a long intake of air. "*Suka!*" Strandtov blurts out.

"What?" I said, jumping.

"It was that suka, Khera," he said, turning the screen so I could see it. Dr. Khera was getting into the tablet and copying the files to a flash drive, and then she pocketed it and walked out.

"What is 'suka?'" I asked.

"It means 'bitch,'" Strandtov says.

"Okay, I can't argue there." I took my phone out of my pocket and dialed Joshua. When he picked up I said, "Joshua, it's Judas. The bad guy is Dr. Khera. She stole the files, it's on the surveillance video." Away from the phone to Strandtov, "Get a screen shot while he has that frozen."

"I already did. Do you want me to type a message to him when he comes back up?" he asked.

"Yes. Tell him thanks, and someday I will repay him," I said.

"Judas, who will you owe? What are you talking about?" Joshua was yelling into the phone. "How can you be certain that is what is happening on the video — can you see the screen?"

"No, but what else would she be taking off my computer and putting on a flash drive? Let's have her held just in case," I said.

"I understand — but *you* need to understand: only I can do that," he said very cryptically.

"Is she there?" I asked.

Joshua waited a bit and said, "Yes, absolutely."

"So she is right there and she is holding the vaccine or something, so if you tip her off we are fucked," I stated.

"Young *ma'un*, there is never a time for language like..." I could hear the phone hit the ground and then shuffling. "Listen, Khera, you need to come with me."

"It's *'Doctor'* Khera. I am a doctor. I deserve respect. Since that one-armed moron came into my lab, I have been playing the stooge. He doesn't understand the problem with natural resources. He doesn't understand that these leeches are going to end up killing us all."

"So you are doing this because of a one-armed man?" Joshua asked.

"No — he is nothing. He can't see how important this is..." Khera started.

"Then explain it to me; maybe I can help you and your cause," Joshua said, interrupting her, presumably to get her into a better position.

"This planet has a set amount of resources. The people can't simply take, take, take — they need to do their fair share, and they need to give and take." I could imagine her intertwining her fingers. "It is symbiotic, the give and the take." She paused.

"What would you have us do, doctor?" Joshua said using the word she wanted to hear.

"This state we are in has the highest number of people per square mile in the country. It uses the second largest amount of natural resources in the nation, but when asked to utilize a wind farm that could be constructed right off the shore of this very beach, you know what they said?" Khera paused again.

"No?" Joshua said.

"What, and ruin our beach?" she said in a great imitation of a surfer. I love surfer voices. "But he understands… he wants us to do this."

"Wait—*who* wants you to do this?" he asked her.

"I know he does because he told me about the virus on Strandtov's private server, and he told me that Judas left his computer on. Well, actually *she* told me that but I know it was him who told her to," Dr. Khera said, more to herself than anything else.

"The one-armed doctor?" Joshua asked.

"No, Joshua. I told you—he doesn't even understand our cause. It was…" *Bang! Bang! Bang!*

"Who fired those shots?" I heard Joshua yell.

"I did." I recognized the voice as Agent Ridge, the leader at the airport.

"Why did you shoot her?" Joshua was asking. I heard scraping and guessed he was picking up the phone.

"I got a call that said you were being held by the doctor who caused all this death. I was told she was attempting to destroy the vaccine, and that I needed to deal with her with extreme prejudice. When I looked through the opening, she was reaching for the vials, so I shot to kill," Ridge finished.

"Who called you? How did they identify themselves?" Joshua said emphatically.

"It was Ursula," Ridge said simply.

"Thank you, agent. You may go." Joshua sounded crushed. "Judas, you still there? Young *ma'un*?"

"Yes, we are here," I said.

"You did it. She was the bad guy. How did you get the surveillance tape?" he asked, blowing out a long breath. "I will call Sensenmann so they call off the hunt for Strandtov."

"I got the tape from the Dobbers. You didn't tell him that I stole Strandtov from you?" I asked and answered. I love knowing someone well enough to have two conversations at once.

"No, that li'l episode will stay between us girls. The hackers? You found the hackers?" He was smiling, I could hear it in his voice. "I worked for three weeks looking and you found them driving in a car..." And then he hung up the phone.

"It's over. She got three bullets in her forehead," I said to Strandtov.

"That reminds me of a band, Semi-Charmed," he grinned, "Oh, he sent you a message back." He held the screen for me to read. It said, 'Yes, you will...' in the blood letters from the Traveler page. Great. I owe this hacker — apparently in blood.

Chapter 25

We entered the Mill. Several agents were there to meet us. No guns were drawn, but it still felt like they were there to kill us. "You must go straight to Sensenmann, straight away," the leader of the group said when we reached them.

"Very well," I said and followed them into the Mill, marching straight to the elevator, the doors of which were open. Waiting for us were Sampar and Deces. I wondered if I was no longer a Level Four—a selfish thought, but there it was. I knew I would be upset—I was proud of the accomplishment: I was the top ten percent of the top five percent in the country. If the feeling that gave me was pride, then this must be the fall. "Sampar, Deces," I said in greeting as we got into the elevator.

"Judas," they both said as the elevator rode up and I half expected to see Jinau in the

Room

"Gentlemen, please come in." There he was sitting at his table. As Dr. Strandtov

and I walked across the room, he made no effort to make us feel welcome. When they reached the table we waited by chairs. "Please sit, sit." He sounded more agitated than I had heard him before. We both sat. "We are here to discuss a couple things. First, Strandtov, I gave an order for you to be killed. I am not certain how you are alive, but I am glad you are—without any apology that I don't mean and will never feel is required, I will give you that: I am glad that you are alive." He put an interesting accent on 'am.' "We need to work at clearing up the files that you have on that server of yours. What do you need to put those diseases to bed once and for all? Put together a proposal. Include whatever resources and timeframe you need. We will find a way to make it happen." He wiped his brow, and his expression changed. "You are excused."

When the doctor was just at the elevator, Sensenmann said, "Oh, and Doctor Strandtov, I want that proposal in forty-eight hours or my orders will be carried out this time. You have had years to understand these viruses and it's time to show me that I am keeping you alive for a reason." He waved his hand and Deces shut the elevator door. He said nothing until the elevator came back up. "I wish to have some quiet time with Judas. Tell Gypsy to clear out of her cave. When she is out, send for me. We will take the pole down. I do not wish anyone, including The Four, to join us in the cave—is that clear?" They all acknowledged and went to the elevator. Still he said nothing.

Finally Ursula said over the table speaker that the cave was empty. We went to the pole and slid down—it was certainly more fun with two hands but I was still glad I took the brake bar; it was a long drop, and I'm certain that, in sliding that far like a fireman, burned inner thighs would not have been the worst of my concerns. When we were alone in the cave, he said, "Ursula, I want you to shut down all your functions. I will hard-start you when I return upstairs." I guess I thought if Ursula shut down, the Mill would stop functioning. It didn't. He looked at his watch, and then started talking. "This isn't actually a watch; it tells me Ursula's biorhythms, as it were. No light pulse and she is truly offline." He pulled his sleeve down and sat on the rocks, his very expensive suit and all. "Judas, I want you to answer a question, and I think I know the answer to it already, but humor me."

"Okay," I said.

"Do you understand that every thought, every conversation, every request that you have between yourself and Ursula, I have recorded, and/or transcribed?"

"Yes," I said.

"But on several conversations you profess to others that Ursula does not share nor document these *interactions* – shall we call them that? Yes, I like that, *interactions*," Sensenmann continued.

"Yes." My voice sounded dead to me, lower than normal, but it was true; there was nothing in me that questioned that he was pulling every string.

"Then why? What possible reason could you have for allowing her to gain access to your deepest recesses?" he asked.

"First, I didn't care. It was actually fun talking to her and playing the game," I said.

"And second?"

"She was a tool, a means to an end," I said.

"Ah, a tool," Sensenmann moved his neck in an odd way and I heard a crack. "Robert Kennedy made a comment and although I am not a word man, I do remember he said, 'Too often we excuse those who are willing to build their own lives on the shattered dreams of other human beings.' While that is a great sentiment, if those dreams could be used as tools to improve what I hold important, then by not building upon them, should I not be unexcused? I am not shattering their dreams. I did not ask them to have a dream; they chose to, and they could not fulfill their dream. I don't see why I have to allow that failure to remain..." While he had been talking, he was looking off into the lake. When he stopped, his eyes focused on me very intently. "But what did you hope to accomplish using that tool?"

"I was learning – about you, about her, about here," I said.

"You were only learning what I let you learn, again you understand that right?" he asked, but then kept going. "I allowed her to tell you that you are no longer real in the outside world, and while I didn't care for the method she showed you, in the end it was I who allowed it. You see, I was a lot like you, and I like the similarities between us. Someday I will need a replacement — why not you?"

"You aren't looking at switching our heads are you?" I said, half-serious.

"Nothing like that. Although..." he paused. "Just kidding."

"Not so convincing there, chief," I said.

"You see, once Ursula got into your head, I knew there was no question: you were going to be perfect. But I needed you to see the big picture, to understand everything, so I had her test you. I needed to know the metal you were forged from. Even the Dobbers, I know who they are — I could crush them today — and I wanted to see what rabbit hole that may take you down. Once again, I could not have predicted the outcome, which was very effective."

"When did Ursula get into my head?" I asked.

"In the hospital, my boy. You don't think Ursula can travel up to that engineering school you went to, do you?" Sensenmann said, smiling. "You really should sit. These rocks are not too bad."

"I spent a little time there, and in there," I said, indicating the lake. "I'm good right here."

"Sure, sure. Fine. I have to say this: I didn't think I knew one person who could deal with so much and still have the cognitive function to solve the biggest plot in our history."

"I had help."

"True, true. You had help in some parts." I didn't like that he was repeating words; it felt a bit like he was coming unwrapped — or was he already there? "But the part about Dr. Khera — hell, you even drew a gun on Joshua, and I think you love him." I felt a cold shiver going down my spine.

"How did you find out about that?" I asked.

"Why, Strandtov, he is one of mine. That is why I am so glad I didn't have to kill him. You see, he has a chip in his eye—I think his left eye was lost during his defection. Now I can see anything and hear anything he does." I looked down at my crotch, inadvertently. "Now, I don't think I want to see what's in view there, and hearing your bodily functions, I will pass on that as well. You have no bug or video-capturing device. I swear. I will not lie to you. I want you to know everything—and maybe someday you will be here," he indicated to himself. As a fished jumped, he looked out across the water dreamily.

"Regarding Dr. Khera when she went on her rant, she said '*he*' knows; it sounded like she was saying you knew because Ursula gave her the information." I said, holding my breath.

"My boy, do you think I am the only one that has input on Ursula? Besides, forbidden love will make you do strange things." Sensenmann said, without malice that I had just tossed the blame at him albeit gently.

"Why did you shut Ursula down?" I asked.

"Having a record of my telling you that you are the heir apparent—not good," Sensenmann said, looking at me again. "You know, when I took this post it had been offered to another; he didn't want it because he didn't have the stomach to do what needed to be done: getting in and stopping wasted spending, getting us off the petrodollar standard and allowing our country to pay off our debts, simply by gutting the 'moral' imperative crowd out of Washington. That was the right thing to do. Everyone figured I was going to get killed when I fired the Federal Reserve—that entire subplot on the wars against the oil world, just to keep their pockets lined; controlling that petrodollar became the biggest waste of our money in the world. So now there is no reason that the world can't be on one currency. We're not, because it no longer matters; we don't need their backing of our dollar anymore."

"If I may ask — is this all stemming from my question about Ursula?" I asked.

"No. Just more stuff that no one knows." Sensenmann said, I vaguely heard fatigue in his voice, the unsung hero syndrome that has happened so often in history. Many great leaders did some good things and then they wanted to do more, and then more, and then when things didn't go right they turned into tyrants. And the tyrant then looks back and feels, *How can everyone hate me? Look at all I did for you.*

"Thank you for that interesting piece of information. Sir did my grandmother and Kat — did they die like I have been told or was The Shop involved in some way?"

Without looking from the lake, he said, "Your grandmother and fiancée died without The Shop's influence." He turned slowly and looked at me. "Let's go upstairs and see where the arrests of the governors are at. I am going to have them all killed. This will not go unpunished. You know, I think a hanging — I think so. Just line them all up and pull one lever. I liked Jinau. I had known her for over twenty years. I can't believe she is dead." I was starting to think like Joshua. Even a cracked pot can carry water for a bit. Sensenmann's water was about run out.

"I liked her too," I said, and he got up and we walked to the lift. "Do you mind if I go for a walk when we get upstairs? I am pretty spent."

"I imagine you are spent. We can talk another time. I think you've heard the majority of what I wanted to say. You know, I am proud of you; most people would have turned tail and run from a conversation like we just had. I look forward to working into the future with you," Sensenmann said.

"Sir, one more thing if I may," I said.

"Of course, please," he said.

"You had referred to Joshua and me as 'The Sword and the Truth.' What does that mean?" I asked.

"Simply this: I consider myself Justice, as each and every day I have to act in the best way I can to uphold and administer justice. In my dealings with other countries and internal situations, I, as the head of The Shop, I need to act accordingly, as Justice. When the scales of truth are contained, and not skewed by emotion or bias in any way, and that containment is defended by the sword, then justice does not have to be blind. Justice must act in accordance.

"So with you as my scales of truth, letting me know people are giving signs that they are not being truthful, and Joshua doling out the punishment of justice, sword in hand. You are the last two members of my Six." He patted my shoulder and stepped on the lift. "I will see you tomorrow." And Sensenmann lifted out of sight, leaving me alone to try to decipher what he had just said. *Justice is supposed to be blind.* I thought, while I waited, that I remembered there were some lady Justice statues around without the blindfold; the explanation of Justice being portrayed as a maiden, that already symbolizes impartiality — the blindfold is redundant. I know this Sensenmann is no maiden, that's a certainty.

I let one platform lift go by and stepped on the same one that he had rode up when it came around. I saw Gypsy pass by on her way back down. I walked off the lift and went straight outside. Walking around the grounds and seeing a big rock in the middle of an island in the river, I walked to where the river thinned out and then split into two smaller tributaries that went around the island. I took a running leap and made it pretty far but still ended up with a wet foot. After climbing to the top of the island hill, I looked down on the rock, feeling I would probably spend more time on this boulder in the future, as it was a great thinking spot. I stood on the island and just listened to the water babbling on the stones.

In the end, I sat down on the rock, looking back on both the Mill and the actions that led me to this point. I followed each series of actions like a movie in my head. I looked down at my hand and felt the scar, then reached up to my shoulder, feeling the scar that was there as well. I had worn them like badges of honor, but now, after all was said and done; I would see them as marks of guilt and shame.

I didn't want to dwell on it but I touched on the memory of the governor whom I'd killed, remembering for the first time that he was simply a man who had been pushed one step too far. A person who had worked hard for something he believed in—not standing on the shattered dreams of men he thought were lesser than himself. But he saw what he had worked so hard for destroy itself, adapted and decided to follow this new way. Watching what was left of what he had lived for being destroyed by an overlord whom he had started to believe in, and witnessing the spirit of men being broken, for no good reason. That was when Joshua started asking his six questions, and lording over him, and when Joshua told him to pack his stuff, I imagine he saw that his final liberties were being taken away. While his actions were completely inexcusable, desperate men do desperate things when the final straw has been broken. When his partner saw that we had taken his life's life, he reached out to reap revenge, to no avail. I ended two people's lives that day, simply because someone wanted to know what dreams were available to be shattered.

I bowed my head and cried. I cried for those I had killed, and those who had died; the one who had killed herself, and the one she had killed. And I cried for the ones who were left. I cried away the compartments that I had set up, and then I set them up again and blew away my tears, saying goodbye to Gram, to Kat, to the baby who never got to be, and then to Alec. I felt better and worse, but I knew I could go on. "We are the bad guys." I said to Joshua who had, at some point, shown up across the river.

"Young *ma'un*, there is and always will be a good guy and a bad guy. Which side we are on is yet to be determined." Joshua replied walking slowly across the river.

"This is nothing more than a communist state, America is a communist country! I thought we, The Shop, were making things better..." I trailed off.

"So, young *ma'un*, did I tell you I am scared to death of flying? How would you feel about a bus— maybe you can use that engineering melon of yours to work and customize me an office on wheels?" And then he sat down next to me on that rock and we listened to the water babbling on the stones.

Epilogue

"Well, Dot, that's about it." I put my hands behind my head, cracking my neck and relaxing into my desk chair. We sat in the building that had started off as a little personal cabin for Snow's retreat—which had now turned into a cabin of awesomeness. I looked around the room. There was no fire burning in the fireplace like when Snow had told Dot *his* story, but that fireplace and the pictures and letters that hung on the wall were the only things that were recognizable from that day a year ago.

"So you really can talk," Dot finally said. Her notebook and tape recorder were still in front of her. "In everything we have done in the Cabinet, you say very little.

"Man, I didn't even know most of that stuff—and I call you my big brother. I mean I can't believe you invented Un Sukiru. There are world championships in that." Snow said as he wrestled a cookie back from the baby, Alec Joshua Snow, his son, my AJ.

"Hey, he didn't cry as much as Dad did when he told his story," KJ, the little gem said, while drawing pictures on the huge fish tank that Snow had made for outlining stories, like a dry erase board. The fish were chasing her pen up and down while she drew.

"Now, we can't go giving your daddy a hard time; he cries when a butterfly gets caught in the bug zapper," a once again pregnant J was saying to KJ. "Dot, at least now I get why you were sorry about being involved with my sadness."

"I honestly didn't put two and two together. Like Sebastian had about you and your family history. Although I am still blown away about the throwing-up thing with Sebastian when he quit The Shop," Dot said.

"But why didn't either Dot or Sebastian recognize you?" Snow asked, looking at me.

"Mainly because I was ordered to stay away from the press, in Dot's case — but Sebastian did recognize me. He just couldn't say anything without coming out as a Shop lackey," I said.

"Give me some credit I did think something was up with you the one time I saw you." Dot said.

"So why weren't you in the story, Dad?" KJ asked when she'd finished her picture, which was really good.

"He was in the story. So was your mom," I said.

"Yeah, I almost wiped him out when he was getting off an elevator in the hospital," Snow said.

"And I was the little gem he talked about when he came to visit my mom and dad," J said.

"I remembered you, Mom, but I missed the part about Dad. I know you didn't say he was crying," KJ said, cracking herself up.

"That's it. AJ, sic her," Snow said, turning the baby around to look at KJ. He crawled across the floor toward her. "Sic her — get your tickle on." Snow was waddling behind him now, his fingers looking a bit jazz-handy to me. I stood up and walked over to the gym room. Like I said, totally different place. We'd even added a blacksmithing forge and inventing wing — yeah, it's that awesome.

"Where are you going?" I heard Dot asking as I headed out, taking off my shirt.

"Sauna. I'm really stiff from sitting there for so long," I said, turning to face her again.

"Hey, you ended up getting that tattoo," Dot said, pointing at the three fists bumping on my left pectoral. "Billings did a great job drawing it up."

"Are you sure you're sore from that or from getting your ass kicked by Gypsy and Jinau?" Snow poked at me from his position under two kids who'd decided he needed to be tickled. "You traitor, AJ," Snow was wining as AJ had gotten the teething cookie back and was mashing it into Snow's face.

"*Wait! What?*" Dot started bouncing around.

"Snow, that's Joshua's story to tell." I walked into the sauna, KJ tailing right on my heels. I laughed as I heard Dot still trying to get more out of me. *Not Cool.*

The End.

'Любовь есть жизнь. Все, все, что я понимаю, я понимаю только потому, что я люблю.

Все есть, все существует только потому, что я люблю.' - Лев Толстой

James W. Scott

Quotes:

Lord Tennyson - 'The quiet sense of something lost echoes to the canyon.

Robert Kennedy - 'Too often we excuse those who are willing to build their own lives on the shattered dreams of other human beings.'

Leo Tolstoy (From War and Peace (The Russian Messenger)) - "Love is life. All, everything that I understand, I understand only because I love.
Everything is, everything exists, only because I love"

Thanks:

To Twentieth Century Fox for permission to use the Doogie Howser.character.

Special Thanks:

To Army Sgt/E5 Marc B. Cox for his assistance with the scene that Judas first picking up a fire arm.

www.ingramcontent.com/pod-product-compliance
Lightning Source LLC
Chambersburg PA
CBHW051521260626
47170CB00003B/724